Courage and Other Demons

Jill Daugherty

D1738240

First Printing, 2013
ISBN 978-0-9887284-0-0 (Paperback)
ISBN 978-0-9887284-1-7 (ebook)
Open Mike Publishing, Denver, Colorado, USA
Cover design and formatting by Damonza
Visit www.jilldaugherty.com for more information
about this book and the author.

1 2 **3** 4 5 6 7 8 9

This book is dedicated
to the memory of my step-dad,
Ray Grable. I wish you could have
hung around to see how the whole
thing ended.

Come away, O human child!
To the waters and the wild
With a faery, hand in hand,
For the world's more full of weeping than you can
understand.
-W.B. Yeats

Prologue

I walked down the steps of the small plane, my fingers skimming the thin layer of moisture that clung to the rail. A light mist was still falling, dampening my hair and clothes, and the thick fog seeped into the pores of my skin, adding to the general creep factor that had been building inside of me for weeks. It didn't matter. Creepy fog or no, I couldn't turn back. I had to move forward and face my new reality, which was wrapped up in the ring and the prophecy and everything else— and by everything else, I mean Simon Brady.

"We're almost there," Simon assured me as he reached down and took my hand in his.

I pulled away and tucked my hand inside the pocket of my fleece jacket, not ready to be nice to him. The cold or the fog or the fear of the unknown made me shiver as we walked toward the waiting car. I noticed Simon's arm twitch, the compulsion to offer me his coat or wrap his arm around my shoulders an automatic response, but we both knew I would reject any offer of kindness he made. I wanted to punish him for being who he was—for not letting me be who I wanted to be—and rejection seemed like an appropriate punishment. He'd challenged the way I saw the world. He'd taken away my security and the view I'd had of myself and replaced it with one I couldn't come to terms with. He'd made everything around me seem cold and harsh and perilous—including him.

A man I didn't recognize opened one of the back doors of a black SUV (the apparent car of choice for Simon and the others). Simon acknowledged him with a brief hug before turning to me as I slid into the back seat.

"Sit in the front," Simon suggested with kindness. "It'll be warmer up there."

"I'm fine," I said.

"Maggie, you're shivering."

"I'm fine," I repeated, not even making an attempt to hide my hostility.

Simon sighed, a look of regret pushing down from his brow and into his eyes, which were clear and blue and reminded me of tropical waters. He nodded and walked to the back of the car where he helped our driver load the luggage into the back. When we were all inside, Simon introduced me to our driver, but I wasn't listening and missed his name.

"Nice to meet you," the man said to me in a thick Irish accent.

"You too," I told him, trying to pull every bit of politeness I had out of me and into those two words. It wasn't this guy's fault that I hated the world and everyone in it.

Simon turned around and looked at me. I wasn't fooling *him*. I looked away and rested my forehead on the cold glass of the window. It was dark outside, and the farther we drove from the small airport at the northern tip of Ireland, the darker it became. I could see the faint glow of the moon as it strained to be seen behind the thick cloud cover, and a few stars made brief appearances in the breaks in the clouds, but it wasn't enough light to show me what was waiting for me here.

I watched Simon for a few minutes as he stared out the front windshield. I knew the sweet and kind boy I'd first gotten to know was still there, but I also knew there was so much more to him. Whose fault was it that I hadn't seen the rest before? Had he deliberately hidden the prophecy and everything I'd have to do and everything that he was? Or was it my fault for turning a blind eye so I could focus only on what I wanted to see? There had been signs, I know that now, but had those signs been enough for me to figure things out sooner? It occurred to me as I stared into the darkness that it was probably a good thing it had taken so long for me to see Simon for who he truly was. If I hadn't fallen in love with that sweet and kind boy, I wouldn't have gotten on a plane; I wouldn't have trusted him enough to do what he was asking me to do. And as angry as I was, as much as I hated what my life had become, I knew I had to do what Simon and the others were asking me to do. It all came down to one inescapable belief. I would have to kill or be killed. There were certainly other pieces of the puzzle that were more complex and harder to understand, but that one piece was very clear and unrelenting and it drove me forward, even in those moments when giving up seemed like the most sensible choice I could make.

I didn't want to think about any of that or sort through all the incongruous information that was constantly shifting inside my brain, so instead I leaned back against the seat and willed myself to fall asleep.

Chapter One

I sat in our school's cafeteria with my best friend, Lexie Hyun, my eyes drifting to Simon Brady on the other side of the cafeteria where he was talking with three girls. He was smiling, and I really loved it when he smiled. While I was staring at Simon and wishing it were me making him smile, I felt a wadded napkin hit the side of my head and instinctively moved my hand to the spot where it had made contact with my temple.

"Hey!" I protested.

"What's going on with you?" Lexie asked. "You've been out of it for two days now."

Two days. That's how long it had been since I'd had The Dream—a wonderful, but confusing dream about Simon.

In The Dream, I was sitting on the front porch steps of my house kissing Simon Brady, which should have been my first clue that I was dreaming, but I was lost in the kiss and chose to ignore anything that would distract me from Simon's lips. So I was kissing Simon, and he was actually kissing me back, and I was thinking I never wanted the moment to end. Then a really obnoxious giant pounded down the street, shouting death threats at me as he got closer, and it totally ruined the moment. Simon stopped kissing me and while I was looking right at him, he disappeared. That's when the old lady showed up. As long as I could remember, the same old lady had popped into my nightmares and calmed me down. I didn't know who this woman was, or why I saw her in my dreams, but she was there, and just looking at her familiar face made everything feel okay. I moved on to a more pleasant dream and forgot about the ugly monster, but I couldn't forget about kissing Simon Brady.

I'd had a pretty normal life before The Dream. I'd grown up in the southern suburbs of Denver and my parents were still married, so no messy divorce or custody battles to worry about. I had a little brother who was definitely a pain in the neck, but he was a pretty normal kid and I loved him. I had a well-adjusted and supportive best friend. I got good grades and was on-track to being accepted to a decent college. I held my own on the school's tennis team. I went to parties and to the mall and to the movies like any other sixteen-year-old. Nobody bullied me, and I didn't feel left out or unfulfilled. I was happy.

I met Simon during my third period Western Civ class on the first day of school my junior year. He was new to Castlewood High School, a transfer student from Ireland, and he was definitely not someone you could miss. I'm sure I wasn't the only girl in the room who felt her heart race at the sight of Simon folding himself into one of the desks toward the back of the room. He was undeniably cute—like Abercrombie model cute—tall with lean muscles and light brown hair and seriously beautiful blue eyes. When he smiled, his whole face lit up, and the skin around his eyes crinkled, and I found myself wanting to say funny things to him just to see it happen.

None of this would have been a problem if it weren't for one small thing. Well, actually one not-so-small, five-foot-eleven, 170-pound boyfriend. *My* boyfriend. Luke Hunter. Flirting with Simon seemed harmless enough, and kissing him in The Dream hadn't really felt like cheating, but liking it did.

I hadn't told Lexie about The Dream, which was weird because I told Lexie absolutely everything. I started to a couple of times, but stopped myself and couldn't figure out why. Lexie knew I'd thrown up on the school bus when we were in second grade. She knew I'd walked out of the girls' bathroom with my skirt tucked into my underwear in seventh grade. She knew about every crush and heartache and triumph, and she never judged me. So why couldn't I tell her about The Dream?

I chased away the lingering memories of The Dream and Simon's fictitious kiss and turned to talk to Lexie.

"Do you ever wonder if there's more out there than Max?" I asked. "Someone who could make you even happier?"

Max Levy and Lexie had been dating for over a year, and it was hard to imagine anyone being happier than the two of them, but maybe she had doubts and hadn't told me.

"No." She hadn't needed to consider my question for a single nanosecond. "Why? Are you having doubts about Luke?"

I shrugged. She took that as an affirmation.

"About time," she said. "I was beginning to seriously question your intelligence. When're you breaking up with him?" Lexie didn't put much effort into disguising her true feelings about Luke.

"I'm not planning to break up with him, just trying to decide what I want."

"If you need help with that decision let me know."

"Very helpful," I said sarcastically.

"Seriously. Why date him if he doesn't make you totally happy?"

"It's not that he doesn't make me happy. I was just sort of wondering if there's something better."

"If you're having doubts, you should break up with him. You're sixteen. You're supposed to date a lot of guys so you can figure out what you want."

"You don't date a lot of guys," I pointed out.

"Yes, but I'm not having doubts. You are."

"I'm not having doubts. I'm just wondering what my options are."

"Well, Simon Brady's an option," she said with a playful smile.

I could feel the heat of the blood rushing to my face and knew I was turning a very bright shade of red.

"He's staring at you again," she said, looking in his direction. "And I think he'd make a great Plan B if things with Luke don't work out." She picked up her tray and stood up, walking toward a trashcan, and I walked beside her with my own tray.

"It would be so much fun to double date," she added as she dumped her trash. Max and Simon were best friends already, and a double date that included Simon in the mix would definitely make her happier than one that included Luke.

"There are a lot of variables that would need to fall into place for that to happen," I said.

"Like?"

"Like—I would need to break up with Luke. And Simon would have to actually be interested in me."

"Of course he'd be interested. Why wouldn't he be interested?"

The idea that a guy wouldn't be interested in a girl was a foreign concept to Lexie. She wasn't one of those girls who was gorgeous but didn't know it. She was one of those girls who was gorgeous and knew it and just assumed that every guy tripped over himself to get to me, just like they tripped over themselves to get to her. Her dad's family was from Korea, and her mom's family was from Brazil. Lexie was the youngest of three beautiful daughters, all with long, thick, curly black hair, brown eyes, and long legs. The Hyun girls were über-smart overachievers who attracted members of the opposite sex like magnets. Case in point, a sophomore whose name I didn't know, and whose name I was pretty sure Lexie didn't know, was practically running across the cafeteria to pick up a pencil that had just fallen out of Lexie's bag. She smiled at him sweetly as he bent over and picked up the pencil that was lying beside the black stiletto heels she wore with her skinny jeans and shimmery black top. He handed it to her with a goofy smile, and she thanked him before walking away. I knew there were probably several guys in the general vicinity who were kicking themselves because they'd missed an opportunity to kneel at Lexie's feet.

"It doesn't even matter," I told her as we headed toward the doors of the cafeteria. "I'm still dating Luke."

"For now," Lexie said glibly as she walked through

one of the open doors.

I glanced back one more time to find Simon before we left the cafeteria. My heart gave a lurch when I saw him and I realized that I felt a connection with Simon Brady I had no right to feel.

෨෬

"That is the stupidest idea you've come up with so far," Cameron Montoya said with exasperation. "And you've come up with some really stupid ones, so that's saying a lot."

I was in our high school library with Cameron, his twin brother, Connor, Katie Hill, and Simon Brady. We'd been assigned to work together on a long-term project for our Western Civilization class and were meeting to brainstorm ideas. Each group in the class had been assigned a different time period from our textbook, and we had to develop some sort of presentation to show the rest of the class. Our group had gotten the Middle Ages, and Katie suggested we put together a fashion magazine, using Marie Antoinette and Queen Victoria as models. I had to agree with Cameron. It did sound like a stupid idea, but it didn't seem worth the effort to argue about it.

"It's not stupid," Katie protested. "What do you think, Simon?"

Simon had been sitting at the table with a slightly amused expression plastered on his face. "I think it's a fabulous idea," he told Katie. Simon had the most wonderful Irish accent when he spoke. It made everything he said seem somehow more important and intelligent. Word on the street (and by street I mean

the halls of Castlewood High School) was that Simon
had moved from Ireland to Denver over the summer.

Katie beamed and shot Cameron an I-told-you-so
look, and Cameron rolled his eyes in response.

"There's just one minor little hiccough," Simon
said. "So tiny it's almost not worth mentioning, but if
we're going for accuracy, Marie Antoinette and Queen
Victoria didn't actually live in the Middle Ages."

"See," Cameron said, "it *is* a stupid idea."

"We can still do a fashion magazine, but just use
people from the Middle Ages," Katie protested.

"I don't want to do a fashion magazine," Cameron
insisted. "It's lame."

"You have a better idea?" Katie asked.

"Let's just do a Power Point."

"That's *boring.*"

"It'll get us the grade," Cameron said. "That's all I
care about."

I drifted off and started to develop a pros and cons
list in my head for being assigned group work for class.
The only thing on my pro side was Simon.

"Earth to Maggie."

I looked up and saw Luke standing beside me. He
was wearing a faded Castlewood T-shirt and jeans, his
blonde, shaggy hair was wet from the shower I'm sure
he took when he'd finished football practice, and his
feet were bare. Only Luke could get away with going
barefoot in school. Teachers seemed to turn a blind
eye to a lot of rule breaking on Luke's part, but I'm
not sure if they were sucked in by Luke's natural
charm or by his ability to help our football team win
games.

"Sorry. I was just thinking about some ideas for our

project," I lied.

Katie and Cameron had stopped their debate, and everyone at the table looked at Luke expectantly.

"I can't give you a ride home today," Luke said, ignoring everyone else. "We have a team meeting so I have to stay late."

"We can give her a ride," Connor volunteered, gesturing toward his brother.

Luke gave him a dark look, and leaned down to kiss me. I got the feeling it wasn't a goodbye-I'm-going-to-miss-you kiss, but a let-me-remind-you-guys-that-she-has-a-boyfriend kiss.

"I'm sure my dad can come pick me up," I assured him.

Luke walked away, and Katie watched as he left the room, her eyes boring into my boyfriend's ass. I wished I could say I was jealous, but I wasn't. I certainly admired Luke's good looks, but I didn't feel possessive about him or anything.

"Maybe we could do a virtual museum," Simon offered after Luke had left the room, kick-starting the group back into gear.

"Like a website?" Connor asked.

"Yeah," Simon told him. "A lot of museums do that now. They take pictures of their exhibits and put them online with information. I think it would be a nice mix of Cameron and Katie's ideas. We'd still integrate technology, and we could include a page on fashion from that time. Everybody wins."

He was quite the diplomat. To my overwhelming relief, everyone agreed to do a virtual museum, thus putting an end to Cameron and Katie's argument.

"Well, let's pull our socks up and get to it then,"

Simon told everyone.

Katie giggled. "Is that something they say in Ireland?" she asked.

He looked a little bemused. "You don't have that saying here?"

Katie shook her head and smiled in Simon's direction while twisting a strand of her dark brown hair. I resisted the urge to roll my eyes—or vomit—and pretended to be fascinated with the pencil in my hand so I wouldn't have to look at the train wreck Katie was causing with her shameless flirting.

Simon cleared his throat and Katie widened her smile and Cameron took out a piece of paper so we could start divvying up the work that would need to be done to get us started. My dad worked as a freelance web designer, so my job was to start by asking for his help.

After leaving the library, I walked outside and sat on a metal bench in front of the school, calling my dad to see if he was available to give me a ride. He worked out of an office in our home so his schedule was pretty flexible, but sometimes he was on the phone with clients or in meetings and wouldn't answer. This was one of those times. I could easily walk home in a half an hour, but I had a heavy load of books and decided to give my dad five more minutes in case he was on a quick call.

It was a warm day for late October in Denver, and I sat back against the bench and closed my eyes, letting the sun soak into my ghostly pale skin for a few minutes. I registered a shadow, and when I looked up, Simon was standing in front of me, the warm colors of the evening sun backlighting him, filtering around the edges of his body, creating a celestial effect that highlighted the subtle orange and red hues in his light brown hair.

"Are you waiting for your dad?"

"He isn't answering his phone," I told him.

"I can give you a ride," he offered.

My heart lurched forward a few beats. Simon Brady was offering me a ride home. I was going to be in his car. Alone. With Simon Brady. Just the two of us. Alone. Before I could decide if the seven minute drive was too long to be alone with Simon (because I had a boyfriend), or too short to be alone with Simon (because, well, it was Simon), I grabbed my bag and walked with him to his black SUV.

"Thanks for coming up with a compromise for the group today," I said when we were driving toward my house, wanting to fill our seven minutes with something other than me staring at him shamelessly.

"Trust me when I say it was my pleasure," he said with a bright smile. "Those two were driving me batty with their bickering."

I chuckled. "They were driving me batty, too." I didn't tell him that Katie's flirting drove me even battier.

We pulled onto my street, far too soon for my liking.

Our house was in the middle of a quiet neighborhood where the trees on either side of the street reached toward each other and formed a canopy with their orange and yellow leaves, giving the street a cozy, protected feel. My dad told me that our house was a "Craftsman" style, which, he explained, meant that it was made to look simple but elegant. There was a large wooden porch in the front with a swing and some rocking chairs. Waist-high shrubs lined the stone walkway between the sidewalk and our house, and four wide steps led up to the porch.

When Simon pulled to the curb, he turned the car off and started to open the door.

"You don't need to walk me," I said, surprised that he was even considering it.

"Yes," he said with a mix of amusement and chagrin, "I do."

He took my bag from my shoulder as we walked away from his car, and gave it back when we were standing at my front door.

"Thanks for the ride," I said before turning the knob.

"Any time," he said with a smile before turning to leave.

∞⸎

Brandon, my thirteen-year-old brother, was sitting in the living room playing video games when I walked through the front door, but I didn't see either of my parents. My dad was probably in his office at the back of the house and Mom was at an office somewhere in the Denver Tech Center doing something vaguely office-like that I never really understood. I knew she had employees and she had bosses, and they all did something that was loosely tied to telecommunications, but any time she tried to describe her job to me, she started to sound like the teacher on old Charlie Brown cartoons—"Wa-wa-wa-wa."

I said hello to Brandon before heading up the stairs, and he ignored me, too focused on the game he was playing. When I was in my room, I threw my bags on the floor, grabbed my laptop and sat on my bed, balancing the computer on my knees. I logged on to Facebook and tentatively typed "Simon Brady" into the search bar at the top of the page, knowing I shouldn't want to know more about him, but finding myself unwilling to stop. There were one-hundred-and-seven Simon Bradys on Facebook, so I typed in the name of our high school to refine the search. No Simon Brady. I entered "Ireland" as the location, thinking that maybe he hadn't updated his profile since moving. Two Simon Bradys popped up, but I didn't have to look at the pictures long to know that neither of them was my Simon. Not that he was *my* Simon. Oh, you know what I mean.

I set aside my computer and lay back on the pillows on the bed, my mind floating back to the kiss in my dream—soft and tender and loving, unlike the lustful slobbering that was Luke's trademark. Sometimes, when Luke kissed me, I couldn't help picturing a hormone-driven puppy humping my leg. I wanted a much different mental image to form after kissing my boyfriend, but maybe sweet, wonderful kisses happen only in dreams.

෨෬

I sat down in Western Civ later that week, eager, as always, to see Simon. I had inexplicably developed a love for history when Simon had walked through the door on the first day of class that semester. Okay, so maybe it wasn't all that inexplicable.

"Don't forget you have a paper due," Mr. Warner

reminded us before class. "While you're all sitting there gossiping about who's dating whom this week, you might want to go ahead and turn it in."

I had, in fact, forgotten the paper, and opened up my bag to look for it. It wasn't in my history folder, and I started to wonder if I'd even remembered to take it out of the printer tray the night before. The idea of not turning in a paper when it was due made me a little itchy, but I didn't want to waste the time before class searching for the paper when I could be talking to Simon, instead. I was in the middle of working myself into a panic over the lost paper when I noticed the long, lean, 501-wearing legs of Simon Brady walking toward me.

"Hi, Maggie," he said as he slid gracefully into the desk next to mine. He was smiling at me in a way that gave me goose bumps and fogged my brain.

"Hi," I mumbled, my eyes unable to move away from his.

"Is anything wrong?" He looked pointedly at the array of notebooks and folders scattered across my desk.

"I can't find the paper that's due." I said as I tore my eyes away from him and went back to tearing through the contents of my backpack.

"Can I look?" he asked, picking up the blue folder I used for English Lit.

"Yeah," I said as I continued my search, certain it wasn't in the folder he held in his hand.

After about two seconds of shuffling the papers, Simon pulled out the one I'd written for the assignment and held it up to me, a brilliant smile on his face.

"Thank you." I was so grateful I could have kissed him. Well, to be honest, my desire to kiss him had nothing to do with my gratitude. If I didn't already have a boyfriend, I'd happily kiss Simon for no other reason than because it was Wednesday.

Simon took my paper and his to Mr. Warner's desk and came back to sit beside me. Before either of us could say anything, Mr. Warner started a riveting lecture about the decline and fall of the Roman Empire, and I worked really hard not to think about Simon and the fictitious kiss and the way he made my heart skip a few beats every time he talked to me.

Chapter Two

I sat in front of the school after another mind-numbing work session with my Western Civ group and waited for Luke to finish football practice.

"Do you need a ride?" Simon asked as he walked toward me from the front doors of the school.

I shook my head. "I'm just waiting for Luke."

He sat down next to me and dropped his leather book bag to the ground.

"Group was as fun as ever today," he said sarcastically.

"Those two just don't let up," I agreed, thinking back to Katie and Cameron and the many arguments they'd had during our work session—the background color of our web page, the order of our sub-pages, the equitable distribution of work, the timeline for finishing work, and on and on and on. Their constant arguing made me want to drive a white-hot poker through my ears just so I wouldn't have to listen to them anymore.

"I'm going to make a prediction right now," Simon said. I thought he was going to predict which one would kill the other first, but instead he said, "Those two will be married within ten years."

I laughed out loud and was really embarrassed when I heard a snort come out of my nose.

"Did you just snort?" Simon asked with a chuckle.

"No," I responded, and then a sound worse than a snort came out of me—a giggle. A really girly giggle.

"Yes you did," Simon insisted. "I heard it. You snorted."

I shook my head, but my laughter betrayed my denial.

"Don't worry," he told me with a smile. "It'll be our little secret." Then he leaned over and bumped his shoulder against mine, and it felt almost intimate—not a boyfriend-girlfriend kind of intimacy, but more of a best-friends-for-life kind of a thing.

"You ready to go?" I looked up and saw Luke standing over us.

I nodded and gathered my things, trying to stifle a smile as I said goodbye to Simon.

"You and Simon Brady seemed to be having a good laugh," Luke pointed out as we drove to my house.

"He told me he thinks Cameron and Katie will be married in ten years, but they're always fighting," I explained.

"If they're always fighting, why would he think they'd get married?"

"That's the funny part."

"I don't get how that's funny."

"I guess you'd just have to see how they are together."

"Yeah, I guess," he said, sounding a little grumpy. We finished the ride in uncomfortable silence, and I got out of his car quickly when we got to my house, not exactly sure what I was trying to avoid with my hasty exit.

"Hey, Maggie, come look at this," Brandon called out from the living room when I walked into the house. He and my dad were sitting in front of the television, and my first thought was that he wanted me to see a new high score he'd achieved on a video game, but then I saw that the two of them were watching a news program. "It's a flood," Brandon explained as I sat down on the sofa between him and my dad. "In China."

The station was cutting between different reporters and anchors and chaotic video clips of rushing water. On the bottom of the screen, scrolling information explained that a dam had broken, flooding several small towns and killing at least 150,000 people in the area. The number of missing was at least twice that number. I cuddled closer to my dad for reassurance, wanting him to shelter me from the sadness of the disaster, and he put his arm around my shoulder, pulling me close.

"How'd the dam break?" I asked.

"I don't know," Dad said. "I'm sure they'll do an investigation, though."

I nodded my head absently.

"Nothing like this can happen in Denver, Mags," he assured me. "You're safe."

"Well, we're safe from a dam breaking, but all kinds of cool stuff could happen here," Brandon said enthusiastically. "We could have an earthquake or a tornado or a tsunami."

"Given that we live like a thousand miles from the nearest ocean, don't you think a tsunami is slightly beyond the realm of possibility?" I reasoned.

"A tsunami in Denver may not be *probable,* but it is *possible*," he argued, his expression taking on that excited look he got when he was trying to suck me into a debate.

"If there is ever a tsunami big enough to reach Denver, it would mean that something so catastrophic had happened on the planet that it would be the end of all life as we know it."

"The tsunami wouldn't necessarily have to come from the ocean," Brandon explained. I could see this argument was taking a turn toward the ridiculous. *Any* debate with my little brother tended to take a turn toward the ridiculous at some point.

"I don't think we could get a wave big enough out of the Cherry Creek Reservoir to be classified as a tsunami."

Brandon lifted his finger and opened his mouth to begin his rebuttal, but my dad interrupted him. "As riveting as this conversation is, I have work to do and I want to be finished before your mom gets home so we can all have dinner together." He stood up and headed to his office.

"And I have homework," I told Brandon.

"This isn't over," Brandon said as I stood. I had to stifle a laugh—his face looked so sincere, but the rest of him was a disheveled mess. He was wearing a pair of blue sweats that had paint stains and holes in the knees and were about three inches too short. It was his favorite pair of sweats and any time my mom tried to throw them away, he dug them out of the trash and took them back to his room. He was also wearing one of my dad's old T-shirts that was many sizes too big, and his black hair was standing on end and making him look like a demented troll doll. "I have some very strong points I still want to make," he said with passion.

"My toes are tingling with anticipation, Brandon," I called over my shoulder as I headed up the stairs.

߷

Luke and I drove to Lexie's house the following Saturday night to hang out with her and Max. Her house was similar to mine—different color, different floor plan, but basically the same style. She only lived a few blocks away from me, and when we were growing up, we would ride our bikes back and forth between our two houses all the time. I'd known Lexie since the first day of kindergarten, and her house—and the space in between—was as familiar to me as my own.

I was a little surprised that Lexie would invite Luke to her house given how she felt about him. I'd never been able to figure out why Lexie didn't like Luke, and any time I asked her about it she'd shrug and say it was just a feeling she had. I sometimes wondered if the reason she didn't like Luke was because Max was such a good boyfriend. He was attentive and sweet and always opened her doors and pulled out her chair and asked her if she needed anything. Most guys our age would have a difficult time living up to Max's example, but Luke had his own redeeming qualities. He could be sweet and attentive when he wanted to be.

It was his tenderness that actually drew me to him to begin with. We'd first started dating because he was comforting me after a horrible tennis match. It was late spring my sophomore year, and my opponent had humiliated me on the court that day, and after the match, our coach chewed me out. She'd been right about everything she'd said, but she said it all publicly, in front of our team, the opposing team and all the spectators. It felt like everyone was staring at me after she'd finished, and I decided to pretend I had to go to the bathroom to get away from their pitying gazes.

I focused my energy on not crying as I walked toward the school and the sanctuary of the girls' locker room. Unfortunately, I was so focused on staying calm that I didn't pay attention when I came to the concrete steps at the back of the school. I tripped on the first step and fell to the ground, the palm of my left hand breaking my fall. Luke was walking in from baseball practice and helped me up before going with me to the training room and wrapping an ice pack around my hand. He was sweet and gentle and kind in a way that pulled me toward him. I knew who he was—everyone at Castlewood knew who he was—but I'd never talked to him. He won my heart that day when he sat with me for over an hour in the trainer's room, comforting me and telling me how wonderful I was.

He called the next day and asked me out, and I was so impressed that he knew my number that I wouldn't have dreamed of turning him down. In the beginning, it was magical. He was the first boy I'd gone out with more than three times, and he was a year older than me, and I felt so grown up when I was with him. Since we'd started dating, I'd found that he wasn't always as attentive as he had been on that spring day, but I thought back to that time in the training room when he had been so kind, and knew that side of him was still there.

But sometimes I would look at Lexie and Max and the way they were together and I'd wonder if I was missing out. The way he held her hand and brushed the hair from her face and whispered something in her ear that was meant for only her—all of that seemed to be missing with Luke. Should I be able to expect more from my boyfriend, or was Lexie just lucky because she was dating the sweetest, most attentive guy in the school?

"You suck!" Max told Lexie playfully after she'd beaten him at a game of virtual tennis.

"You have to expect to lose when you play with the master," she said as she ruffled his curly black hair.

"Archery next," Max suggested.

He got up from his place on the sofa to get the adapters needed for virtual archery.

"So, what are we doing for your birthday?" Lexie asked me while she waited for him. "It's only a week away."

I shrugged, not really certain how I wanted to celebrate. Since we were dating, I'd just assumed Luke would want to spend at least part of my birthday with me, but he hadn't brought it up, and I'd been too timid to bring it up myself.

"Do you guys already have plans?" Lexie asked Luke.

"When is it?" Luke asked, obviously clueless.

"Next Saturday," Lexie answered for me.

"Oh. I'm going to be hanging out with the football team that night," he said.

"On Maggie's birthday?" Lexie asked, incredulous. It was the first I'd heard of Luke's plans, and I was a little surprised myself.

"It's the end-of-season get together. We have it every year," Luke said.

"So instead of taking Maggie out somewhere fun for her birthday, you expect her to hang out with a bunch of football players?" Lexie asked.

"It's a no-girls night. Just the guys."

"You're not even going to see her on her birthday?"

"We could do something in the afternoon," Luke offered, looking at me. "Or there's a Halloween party the night before. We could go to that and celebrate your birthday together at midnight."

I thought it was a really crappy suggestion. I was disappointed that Luke had made plans without me on my birthday. A little voice inside my head told me I should stand up for myself instead of letting Lexie do it. I wanted to tell Luke that he was being a big jerk, but that little voice was the silent minority of my brain and I said nothing.

಄಄಄

"So, what do you think?" Luke asked when we were alone together in his car later that evening. "About the party on Halloween?"

I shrugged.

"It might be fun," he said. "A bunch of people're going up to Red Rocks to hang out."

Red Rocks was an amphitheater literally carved into the foothills west of Denver, about twenty miles north of my house. In the summer there was a concert there almost every night, but it was pretty dead in the colder months. Some of the kids at school liked to go and sit in the empty stands during the off season and hang out, watching the lights of Denver flicker in the distance beyond the stage. Going to concerts at Red Rocks was great because it was so scenic, but I really didn't see the appeal in the colder months. It seemed like more fun to go and hang out in someone's warm house than to sit in the stands and freeze your butt off.

"Yeah," I said. "That's fine."

"I'm sorry about your birthday." We'd pulled to the curb in front of my house by this point, and he was reaching over, running his fingers through my hair. "The team does this every year, and since it's my senior year, it'll be my last time. You understand, right?"

I nodded, and I really meant it. I did understand. Of course he would want to go since it would be his last time.

"We'll have fun at Red Rocks, though," he promised before leaning in to kiss me. I knew what was coming. We'd kiss for a few minutes, then he'd move his hand under my shirt, inching his fingers toward my bra. I would stop him, telling him I should go in. He'd sigh heavily as I opened the door to leave before he started the car again and pulled away. I wasn't really in the mood for our well-rehearsed end-of-the-night routine, so I pulled away after a short kiss and pointed out that it was six minutes past my curfew, the dashboard clock acting as confirmation. He kissed me one more time before I got out of the car and he drove away.

Chapter Three

The giant was back and he was mad. Simon threw himself between me and the massive menace making his way toward us, but the giant flicked him away as if he were a dead fly on a windowsill. I tried to run, but I was paralyzed with fear. Then the old lady was there, as she always was, and I felt safe and protected again. It was the second dream I'd had about Simon and the giant, and this one felt just as creepy as the first.

❧❦❧

"Maggie, do you have a minute?" Simon was standing next to me as I was gathering my things at the end of our Western Civ class the Friday before my birthday.

I nodded, curious.

He opened his leather book bag and pulled out a small package wrapped in brightly colored paper with pictures of balloons and party hats. "I know your birthday isn't until tomorrow, but since I won't see you then, I wanted to give this to you now."

I was surprised Simon knew when my birthday was but figured Max had probably told him. Lexie, Max and I were driving to the condo Max's parents owned in Breckenridge for my birthday, and since Max and Simon were friends, he would naturally tell him about our plans.

"You didn't have to get me anything, Simon," I said, feeling a little awkward.

"I wanted to. Besides, it's not something I bought. It's something I already had. It's a bit manky, really."

"Manky?"

"Yeah, um, old and worn out. It might even be a bit smelly. I'm not making any promises."

I raised my eyebrows with interest and took the gift from him, trying very hard not to let my eyes linger on the way his T-shirt hugged his shoulders. I tore at the paper and saw that it was a very old book with a faded green cover and a tattered binding. Definitely manky. "Irish Folklore" was printed on the front cover in faded gold ink and when I opened it, I noticed that the pages were yellowed and crumbling at the edges.

"I thought since you're Irish, you might enjoy reading some Irish stories."

"I'm not really Irish," I said. Sure, my last name is O'Neill, and that's definitely Irish, but I also knew having the name didn't necessarily make me Irish. I had read once that there were more people in the United States who claimed Irish ancestry than there were in Ireland, but since my parents and grandparents were all born in the United States, I considered myself American more than anything else.

"I bet you're more Irish than you think," he said. "You're last name is Irish, and you have red hair and freckles and blue eyes. If we stick a Guinness in your hand and stand you in front of a stone cottage, we could take a picture and sell postcards." His eyes were twinkling, and I could see that he was having fun teasing me.

"Thank you, Simon—for the book."

"You're welcome. I hope you enjoy your weekend." He started to walk away, but stopped before he got to the door, and turned around. "There's a story called 'Margaret and Simon' in the book." He smiled, looking slightly nervous, and left the room without giving me any details about the story, but that little piece of information suddenly made the book seem a lot more interesting. My full name was Margaret, and the idea that there was a story with both of our names was weirdly exciting. I had a penetrating urge to sit down right there and read it but I was already late for my next class, so I stuffed the book in my bag and walked quickly out the door.

೮ೲ

"Simon gave me a birthday present," I told Lexie at lunch. I tried my best to sound casual as I said it but knew Lexie would see through my forced nonchalance.

She turned quickly to look at me, her eyes wide with curiosity. "What did he give you?"

"A book."

"What kind of book?"

"A really old book. Irish Folklore."

"Let me see," she said, holding out her hand.

"Not here. I don't want anyone to know." And by anyone, I meant Luke. "It's just an old book of Irish folklore. He thought I'd like it because I'm Irish."

"Are you Irish?" she asked.

"My name's Irish and Simon said I look Irish."

"You actually do look Irish," she agreed. "You have the whole red hair and freckles thing going on."

"Do you really think the red is all that noticeable?" I asked as I pulled a long piece of my hair up to look at it. "I always thought of it as more blonde than red."

Lexie laughed out loud. "Trust me. The red is definitely noticeable."

I looked at the strand more closely and knew she was right. There were blonde strands running through my hair, but there was no question that the red outnumbered the blonde by at least fifty-to-one.

"Do you still want to sit there and tell me Simon doesn't like you?"

"It doesn't matter," I reasoned. "I have a boyfriend."

"A boyfriend that isn't even spending your birthday with you," she reminded me once again. "I really don't understand why you stay with him."

"You don't see the good side." I picked up the unused straw on my tray and folded it nervously. I didn't want to talk about Luke, and Lexie caught on and changed the subject.

∞Ω

I didn't get a chance to look at the book until later that evening. Lexie came home with me from school, and we went to my room before I pulled the book out of my bag. We flopped down beside each other on the pink and brown quilt that covered my wrought iron double bed and opened the book to the story about Margaret and Simon, each of us reading silently as we held the book between us. It was a long story, and the way it was written was super old fashioned. Here's the shortened, Cliffs Notes version (you're welcome):

Simon was a prince of a far off land and he met Margaret when he sailed near her home in Ireland to get supplies for his ship. They fell in love with each other, and Margaret went with him when he sailed away from Ireland. Before they had gotten far, a giant came out of the sea and demanded that the crew throw Margaret overboard. Simon refused, and the giant said he would destroy the entire ship if they didn't do as he asked. Margaret knew that if she didn't throw herself off the ship everyone would die, so she jumped into the sea.

She managed to make it to shore, where she found a stone cottage. She asked the old woman who lived there if she could have shelter for the night, and the old woman agreed. Margaret ended up staying there a long time, and in that time many people came to the cottage and asked to try on an old ring that the woman kept in a box in her cupboard. One day Margaret asked her about the ring. The old woman said a giant had killed her mother and she had fled to this cottage to escape him. People came to the cottage to try on the ring, and whomever the ring fit would be the rightful heir of a golden sword that would kill the giant, but the ring had fit no one.

After living with the woman for many years, Simon came to the door of the old cottage. He had heard about the ring and had come to try it on. He was surprised to see Margaret. He thought she had been killed by the sea swell when she'd thrown herself overboard. He tried on the ring, but it didn't fit him.

"It'll fit me," Margaret told Simon and the old woman. She tried it on, and it did fit her.

She and Simon took the sword and went to slay the giant. When they got to the giant's castle, Simon fell into a deep sleep. Margaret tried to wake him up, telling him that the giant would kill him if he didn't wake, but he continued to sleep, and Margaret suspected he might be under a spell cast by the giant. She went in search of the giant, but couldn't find him. When she went back to Simon, she saw the giant standing over him with a dagger in his hands. Margaret used the sword to cut off the giant's head and killed him. Simon woke up and was so grateful that she had saved him that he asked her to marry him, and they lived happily every after. When the people of the far off land heard that she had saved their prince, they asked her to stand beside Simon and lead them.

"Oh my god," Lexie said when we'd finished reading, looking up at me with wide eyes. "He doesn't just like you. He's in love with you."

"Come on, Lexie," I protested. "Don't be ridiculous. He hardly knows me. He can't possibly be in love with me."

"Then why would he give you a book with a love story that just happens to have two characters named Simon and Margaret?"

I shrugged. "Coincidence?"

"Wake up and smell the pheromones, Maggie. There's nothing coincidental about this."

I knew she was right. There was definitely something going on with Simon that went beyond friendship, but I wasn't ready to admit that to myself, or anyone else—including Lexie.

"Luke's coming over in a little while," I reminded her. "I should get ready."

"Are you trying to change the subject?" she demanded playfully.

"No." I stood to go to my closet. "It's all the same subject. It doesn't matter what I think about Simon or what Simon thinks about me because I have a boyfriend and he's going to be here soon to pick me up so I need to get dressed." I grabbed a pair of jeans and a long sleeved T-shirt from my closet and leaned down to get some shoes. Since we were going to be outside all night, I was tempted to put on my Sorels, but decided on a fashion compromise and pulled out an old pair of Adidas tennis shoes.

"Are you interested in Simon?"

"It doesn't matter," I reiterated. She looked at me with laser-eyes, willing me to tell her everything. "I have a boyfriend," I reminded her.

"You're not married to him. A quick five-minute conversation could end that problem. You won't even need to have a lawyer present."

I flopped onto the bed beside Lexie, wanting to give in to what she was saying—wanting to believe that discarding Luke would be as easy as she insisted it would be—but also knowing I owed Luke more than that. He was my boyfriend, and I couldn't just dump him because a cute guy was showing some interest in me. Simon was just a phase, I tried to convince myself, and this phase would pass. Luke was something more enduring, and I needed to give our relationship the respect it deserved.

"I've got to get dressed," I reminded Lexie.

"Don't go tonight," she pleaded. "I heard someone's taking a keg to Red Rocks, and if there's drinking, there's going to be trouble of some sort or another."

"I'll call if there's any trouble," I assured her. "Luke's not going to let anything happen to me."

She looked at me with skepticism and hugged me before she left.

I knew I needed to get in the shower so I'd be ready when Luke picked me up, but I couldn't resist the urge to look at the book again. I turned to the inside cover and saw that Simon had written an inscription. "To Maggie. Happy Birthday. Simon." I flipped to the title page, looking for the copyright date, but there wasn't one. There were twenty-one stories, and a foreword written by the author said he had traveled around Ireland, gathering the stories that had been passed down generation after generation. I didn't have time to read the others but wondered if they would all make my spine prickle the way it had as I read the story about Margaret and Simon.

ॐ

Luke did something very uncharacteristic that night. He actually walked to the door to get me instead of sending a text and waiting in his car. I soon saw that the reason for his change in habit was the small fish bowl he was holding in his hands. The red bow around the middle told me that this was my birthday gift.

"It's a fish," he said, seriously underestimating my powers of observation. It was hard to miss the orange lump swimming around in the bowl of water. "I thought since your last one died and all."

My last *three* goldfish had died, actually. Over the summer Luke had won the first Bubbles at a fair and given it to me. That one died in three days. Luke said he felt bad that it had died and got me Bubbles II. That one died within three weeks. Bubbles III lasted five days. I wasn't optimistic about Bubbles IV's chances of survival.

My dad wasn't too happy about the succession of live fish coming into the house. He had a very strict no-pet policy, and evidently that policy extended to small, harmless fish, in addition to the puppies and kittens Brandon and I always begged our parents to get us. He'd put up a pretty big fuss when I'd brought the first Bubbles home, but finally gave in to allowing it in the house if I agreed to keep it in my bathroom with the door closed.

I thanked Luke before taking the fish up to my bathroom.

On our drive to Red Rocks, Luke told me that the Castlewood football team had made it to the playoffs, which meant that their season hadn't yet ended.

"Does that mean your party's been postponed?" I asked, hoping he'd be able to spend my birthday with me after all.

"No, we're still having it tomorrow. We already made the plans and everything."

I was disappointed, but it made sense to go ahead with the party as planned. Everything had already been arranged, and rearranging it would be a hassle.

"Well, I'm glad you made it to the playoffs." I didn't want him to see how disappointed I was.

There were already several cars in the parking lot at Red Rocks when we pulled in. People were standing around talking, and someone had the stereo in their car turned loud enough that we could all hear it.

"Hey, Luke, you made it." Zach Peterson, one of Luke's friends from the football team, came over to us when we got out of the car. He had fake blood on his face and a white bandage wrapped around his forehead, but I wasn't sure if he was supposed to be a crash victim or a zombie. Luke and I had both skipped the whole costume thing. Too much work. "What's your poison?" Zach asked. "I've got beer, vodka, gin, whiskey."

"Beer's good," Luke said. I gave him a disapproving look as Zach walked away to get the beer. "What?" he asked. "One beer."

"I don't think this is a good idea," I said quietly. "If the park rangers come by and start carding people, we could get in a lot of trouble."

"You worry too much, Maggie," he replied. "Have a drink and relax a little."

I shook my head. If I were Lexie, I would have insisted he take me home, but I wasn't Lexie and I didn't say anything.

"Why don't I get a beer and we can go for a walk," Luke suggested. "If the park rangers come, we won't be here and we won't get busted."

"It's too dark," I pointed out.

"We can go on some of the trails," he said. "I have a flashlight in the car."

I nodded, but was definitely less than thrilled with the whole situation. Separating myself from the group seemed like a good idea, but I really just wanted to go home.

Luke grabbed his flashlight and went to get a beer from Zach before we walked behind the amphitheater to the trails that ran along the foothills. We walked far enough back that we were hidden from the rest of the group, and the music was becoming distant. We sat down on the path and looked out at the city lights glowing in the distance, the stars shining up above. Luke twisted the cap off his beer bottle and flicked it into the darkness before taking a long swig.

It was a chilly night, and despite my heavy parka, hat and gloves, I found myself shivering. I should have worn the Sorels.

"Come here," Luke said gently. He pulled me to him and wrapped his arms around me. "Better?"

I nodded. "Thanks."

He leaned down and kissed me, tenderly at first, but, as it always did, his kiss became more heated. He put his arm around my back and eased me down until I was flat on the ground underneath him. All of the confusion I'd been feeling about Luke over the past couple of weeks came rushing into my head. Since I had a body that was just a few hours short of a seventeen year old, my hormones were out of control and pushing for my brain to shut up and let Luke have his way with me. My brain was putting up a good fight, however, screaming out all of the reasons I should stop Luke before he went any further. Before I could think too much about it, Luke started rubbing my breast.

"Luke," I protested gently. He didn't stop or respond in any way. "Luke," I repeated. "Luke, I want you to stop."

"It's okay, Maggie," he said in a seductive voice, his beer-laden breath filling my nostrils. "I won't hurt you."

He slipped his hand under my shirt, and I quickly moved my arm in a defensive move meant to keep his hand away from my breast, but he grabbed my wrist and pulled my arm over my head. My other arm was pinned under his side, so I had no way to stop him when he reached his hand under my shirt and lifted my bra. When I tried to free my hand from his, he tightened his grip painfully around my wrist, his fingers digging into my flesh and twisting around the bones in my hand.

"Luke, stop!" I said loudly. He continued to ignore me, pressing his lips against mine and making it difficult for me to continue talking. Even breathing in and out was becoming more challenging as I felt my panic rising. I couldn't get the words out of my mouth that would make Luke stop what he was doing. I tried to twist my body out of his grip, but that just made him pin me down harder. When he shoved his hand between my legs, I tried to scream, but couldn't produce any sound through the panic. I worked to calm myself down, knowing I needed to figure out a way to get Luke to stop. I realized he didn't have one of my legs pinned as tight as the other and used it to kick him as hard as I could. He pushed my leg beneath his body with his own leg, his body lifting slightly as he did, giving me just enough room to knee him in the groin. He let out a loud groan and rolled away from me.

"Are you insane?" he asked through gritted teeth.

"I was trying to get you off me!" I said, sitting up

quickly, pulling my shirt down as I did.

"We've been dating for five months," he said with a strained voice. "We should have done this a long time ago."

"So you thought *forcing* me would be a good idea?"

"We're *dating*. I shouldn't have to force you."

"I want to go home," I told him firmly as I stood up. The fact that my voice was shaking probably diminished my authority.

Luke was still lying on the ground, curled into a loose fetal position and making little panting noises.

"I need a few minutes," he said angrily. "Start walking. I'll meet you at the car."

"I'd rather wait for you." I really didn't want to spend another minute with him, but the idea of walking back to the parking lot alone was worse than the idea of walking back to the parking lot with Luke.

"Go," he said, his voice still strained.

I hesitated, everything about the situation making me uncomfortable. "I can't see without the flashlight."

"Take it," he grimaced. "I know my way back."

I picked up the flashlight and waited a beat before I started walking toward the parking lot, hoping Luke would decide to show me one small flicker of decency and walk back with me. He didn't, so I gave up and headed off on my own. Even with the light, it was hard to see what was trail and what was field, so I used the music playing in the parking lot to help guide me. It didn't seem to be getting any louder, however, and I started to worry.

"Luke!" I yelled into the night. "Luke!"

No response.

I tried not to think about the rattle snakes and

mountain lions and bears that sometimes wandered into populated areas, but the more I tried not to think about them, the more I thought about them. Every time I heard a rustle in the tall grass I was convinced it was a wild animal ready to propel me into the lead story on the evening news.

I knew it was taking me a lot longer to get back than it had to walk out, and at some point I realized I could no longer hear music. Was I that far from the parking lot, or had someone just turned the music off? Despite the flashlight, I still tripped several times on the rough rocks that dotted the fields and the trail, my hands sore and scraped from repeatedly catching my fall. I was ready to kill Luke. All of this was his fault. I was out in the middle of nowhere because of him. I was lost and cold and scared, and it was all Luke's fault.

After stumbling around in the dark for at least an hour, I found my way to one of the roads leading to the top of the amphitheater. I started walking up, knowing I would eventually hit the parking lot. Several cars passed me as they drove out of the park, and when I got close to the top, I saw flashing lights and park rangers. Some of the partygoers were in handcuffs or sitting in the back of the police cars. I hid behind a large boulder at the side of the road and peeked around the side to look for Luke. His car was gone, but I didn't panic. He wouldn't leave me. He would come back for me after the police had gone. I started to grab my phone out of my pocket to call him when I realized that my purse, with my phone in it, was in Luke's car. *Okay. Maybe I could panic now.*

The last of the partygoers drove down the

mountain, and the police and park rangers weren't far behind. I looked at my watch and saw that it was almost midnight. The park closed at eleven, and I figured the park rangers would close the gates at all of the entrances on their way out of the park, which meant that Luke wouldn't be able to drive back up to get me. My only option for finding him was to walk the mile or so down to the highway and wait for him by one of the entrances. It was twelve-thirty by the time I got to the bottom, but Luke wasn't there. I decided to stay close to the park entrance, knowing he was probably driving around looking for me.

I didn't like standing alone by the two-lane highway that late at night and every time a car drove by I was certain it was an ax murderer ready to grab me and chop me into little pieces, making me the "Irish" in someone's Irish stew. I was in the middle of calculating the distance to Morrison, the nearest town, and the probability of finding a convenience store open with a phone I could use to call home, when a black SUV pulled to a stop along the side of the highway. It looked like Simon's SUV, but I knew there would be no reason for Simon to be out on that highway in the middle of the night. Like all of the sane people from school, Simon would have stayed away from this particular party. Besides, thousands of people in the Denver area owned that same model of car, and I didn't want to think about which of them owned the one stopped before me. When a tall man got out of the driver's side, the panic I'd been fighting to keep in check took ahold of me, and I crouched, screaming, to the ground.

Chapter Four

"**M**aggie! It's me. Simon."

I opened my eyes to see Simon Brady kneeling in front of me, his hands on my shoulders. I took a few deep breaths in an attempt to steady myself, but couldn't stop the waves of shivering that had started to cascade through my body. Simon must have assumed my shivering was a result of the cold and quickly took off his coat and wrapped it around me. He sat down beside me and put his arm around my shoulder, rubbing it briskly in what was most likely an attempt to warm me up.

"What happened?" he asked with compassion and concern. I started sobbing, the anxiety of everything that had happened pouring out of me. Now that Simon was with me, I felt safe, and since I was no longer in survival mode, my brain was now thinking about everything I'd been through in just a few short hours. Luke had tried to force himself on me. I'd gotten lost in the foothills, wandering alone in the cold and dark. I'd been abandoned and scared.

I tried to calm myself down so I could talk to Simon and tell him I was okay, but the harder I worked to calm myself down, the harder I cried.

Simon sat next to me, rubbing my shoulder, waiting for me to regain control of my emotions.

After several minutes, the sobs started to subside. "Come sit in my car with me," Simon suggested. "I can turn on the heat and warm you up." I nodded, feeling a little numb and exhausted. He stood and offered me his hand, pulling me to a standing position.

When we were both sitting in his SUV, he adjusted the heat to full blast and turned the vents toward me before reaching into the center console and retrieving a small box of tissues. I gratefully took them and wiped the tears from my face. I was a hundred miles south of embarrassed and I had no idea what to say to this gorgeous boy who kissed me in my dream and caused me to go all mushy inside when I was awake.

"Simon?"

"Yes, Maggie?" His voice was soothing and warm and wrapped around me in a way that the heat from the vents in his car couldn't.

"Why are you here?" I asked, not wanting to look a gift horse in the mouth, but curious as to why he would be at Red Rocks that late at night.

He hesitated a moment before answering. "I heard the party got out of control and I knew a friend of mine was there. I wanted to make sure they got out okay after the police showed up."

"Is your friend okay?"

He smiled. "Yes. My friend's okay. Now to you. I assume you need a ride home."

I nodded. "Can I borrow your phone to call my parents?"

He pulled his phone out of his jeans pocket and handed it to me, then put the car in drive and pulled away from the shoulder of the highway while I called my mom and told her I'd gotten separated from Luke, but was getting a ride home with Simon. When I handed the phone back to him, his fingers brushed against my hand and my breath caught in my throat. I turned and looked out the window at the passing landscape and concentrated on steadying my breathing and my heart rate before turning back to him.

"I read the story in the book you gave me," I said when we were on C-470 and heading in the direction of my house.

"The one about Simon and Margaret?" he asked.

"Yes. It was interesting."

He smiled. "'Interesting' is a nice, non-committal way to describe something you don't really like."

"I liked it," I assured him.

"What did you like about it?"

What I was thinking: *I liked that it was a story about you and me and how we fall in love and live happily every after.*

What I said: "I like that Margaret saved Simon from the giant. Guys usually rescue the girl in old stories, so I liked that the girl did the rescuing in that story. And I liked that Margaret was so fearless. She didn't even think twice before going after the giant. She was so brave."

"Do you think *you're* brave?"

I laughed. "No. I'm actually the opposite of brave."

"Why do you say that?" he asked with genuine interest.

I shrugged, not because I didn't know how to answer his question, but because I didn't want to tell him and make him think less of me. I wasn't proud of whatever personality trait prevented me from standing up for myself with anyone except Brandon and I didn't want him to know that I was still tempted to run to my parents' bedroom on stormy nights.

When we got to my house, Simon walked me to the door. My purse was hanging on the doorknob. I pulled it off and checked my phone. No messages from Luke.

"Thanks for the ride, Simon," I said. "I better get inside."

He nodded and started to walk away but turned around before he got to the steps of the porch.

"Happy birthday, Maggie," he said with a smile. I smiled back and turned to go into the house. My mom and dad were both waiting for me in the living room when I walked in.

My mom greeted me with, "What happened?"

I flopped into a chair and took a deep breath.

"Luke and I went for a walk behind the amphitheater and we got separated. He left with my purse in his car and my phone was in my purse. Simon Brady, that kid who transferred from Ireland, found me before Luke did and gave me a ride home."

"Isn't that your purse you're holding?" my mom asked.

"I guess Luke dropped it off before he went home," I explained.

My mom gave my dad a look that I'm sure conveyed an entire conversation to him, but meant nothing to me.

"Your dad and I have been talking about you and Luke," she finally said. "We're not going to tell you who you can date or be friends with, but we do have some concerns about Luke that we'd like you to think about. It was incredibly irresponsible of him to leave

without you tonight, but this isn't the first time we've
seen red flags, and we're a little concerned."

"Don't worry, Mom," I assured her. "I'm breaking
up with Luke. He smacked me in the face with about a
thousand red flags tonight, and I'm absolutely certain
that Luke isn't trustworthy."

My parents looked at a loss for words, and I was
pretty sure they had spent a lot of time preparing for a
long and drawn out argument. I hated to disappoint
them, but I was exhausted—both physically and
mentally.

"What happened to your hands?" my dad asked
before I could stand to go to my room. I looked down
and for the first time saw the scrapes and flecks of
dried blood on the palms of my hands from where I'd
fallen as I'd tried to find my way back to the parking
lot at Red Rocks.

"I tripped," I told him.

Both of my parents looked at me in a way that said
they knew there was more to the story and I better
start talking. I resisted sharing all the gory details, but
ended up telling them what Luke had done. When I
was finished, my mom came and hugged me and my
dad started pacing the room.

"Do you want me to kill him?" my dad asked,
trying, I'm sure, to sound calm. "Because I will gladly
kill him. Or maybe I could just break a few of his
fingers." It was a very uncharacteristic thing for my
dad to say. He was generally quite the pacifist.

"Let's let him live this time," I suggested, trying to
suppress a smile.

My dad looked me in the eye and said very
seriously, "If there is ever a 'next time,' I *will* kill him,

with or without your permission."

My mom and I both chuckled, and I loved that my dad could make me feel better about something so horrible.

ഔ൪

I woke up shaking from a nightmare. In my dream, I'd heard someone in my room and reached over to turn on the lamp beside my bed. When I turned on the light, however, the room grew darker. I switched on the overhead light, but it again caused the room to get darker. I turned on my desk lamp, but it got darker still, and I started to panic because I couldn't see anything. Then I saw the old woman. This time she was standing near my window, and the light from the moon illuminated her as she stood calmly, silently watching me. A current of relief passed through me, and I said, "You're here." She simply smiled—the warm, calming smile I'd come to know through my dreams over the years. Then the dream ended.

The old woman had visited my dreams since I could remember dreaming. She had gray hair that was always pulled back into a long braid and she wore black pants and a white blouse with the sleeves rolled up, and she looked like she was ready to go for a hike or cut some wood. No matter how horrible the nightmare, I always felt calm when I saw the old woman in my dreams. Lexie said it was my stress dream. Some people dreamed about being naked in public when they were under a lot of stress. Lexie dreamed about missing too many classes and failing tests. I dreamed of the old woman. I thought it was great that my mind had invented a protector in my dreams. The old woman kept the bad dreams from becoming truly horrible, and I was always grateful when she showed up. If she weren't a figment of my own imagination, I would definitely send her a thank you card.

I got out of bed and started packing for my trip to the mountains with Lexie and Max. The three of us had done different variations of the snow dance all week, but it didn't work. The ski resort wouldn't be opened in time for my birthday weekend, but we decided to go anyway, hoping for a miracle and knowing we'd have a good time whether we skied or not.

I had brunch with my parents and Brandon at a restaurant downtown first, and I hoped my parents were still planning on letting me make the trip, considering I'd broken curfew—by a long shot—the night before. I planned to use my sound and mature decision to break up with Luke as leverage but I didn't need to bring it up. My parents let me go, asking only that I call to let them know we'd made it safely and again before I went to bed for the night.

On the drive to Breckenridge, Luke sent me a text wishing me a happy birthday. I ignored it. A few minutes later I got one apologizing for the night before. I wondered which part he was apologizing for—the part where he forced himself on me, the part where he left an ugly ring of bruises on my left wrist when he held me down, or the part where he abandoned me in the middle of nowhere, which ended up causing the scrapes on both of my palms. A few minutes later, I got another text asking me to please let him know that I was okay because he was worried about me. I let out an involuntary snort of derision, and Lexie turned in her seat next to Max to look at me. I'd already told her everything that had happened while we drove to the mountains, and she had been ready to go knock some sense into Luke, but I told her I didn't want to waste any more of my birthday on him.

"Luke's worried about me," I explained wryly.

"Better late than never?" she offered.

I shook my head and rolled my eyes in disgust. "Given what he did last night, do you think it would be wrong of me to break up with him in a text?" I asked.

"I actually think it's more than he deserves," she said.

"What about you, Max?" I asked him. "What's the guy's perspective on this?" He'd been silent while I'd told Lexie everything that had happened, and I wasn't sure if he'd been listening or not.

"Personally," he began, "I think carving your desire to break up with him into his chest with a twelve inch dagger would be too good for him."

Lexie and I both started laughing. Like my dad, Max was generally a pretty easygoing guy, so it definitely wasn't the advice I was expecting from him. When I had calmed down enough that tears weren't rolling down my cheeks from laughing so hard, I sent Luke a text telling him that I didn't want to date him anymore. I felt a twinge of empowerment.

Lexie and Max cooked pasta for my birthday dinner, and we walked into town afterward to get some hot chocolate. Max led us to a restaurant that had a large fire pit outside and told us to sit down and warm up while he went in to get the drinks.

"You have him trained well," I teased Lexie when we were alone.

"He *is* good to me," she agreed.

"And you're good to him." I sat down on one of the wooden benches surrounding the fire pit. Lexie sat down next to me and took off her mittens, stuffing them into the pockets of her white parka.

"It's easy to be good to someone when they're good to you. I know he'd do anything for me, which just makes it easier for me to do anything for him."

"You're very lucky. You know that, don't you?"

"I do know, but you're going to find someone as good as Max. As a matter of fact, I bet you find someone who is so like Max that they could be best friends."

It didn't take a rocket scientist to know she was talking about Simon. "You're relentless."

"I think it's one of my more endearing qualities," she said proudly.

Max came back with a full tray. "I got hot chocolate and the stuff to make birthday S'mores."

"*Birthday* S'mores? Are they any different than regular S'mores?" I asked.

"These come with seventeen birthday candles." He placed the tray on the table in front of our bench. He took the candles from the tray and handed them to me, smiling. "I suggest you stick them in your marshmallow *after* you take it out of the fire, though."

Lexie stood and fingered the curly, brown hair that was sticking out below Max's black fleece hat. "You're a really nice guy, Max Levy."

Max put both of his arms around Lexie's waist and

nuzzled her nose with his. "And here I thought you already knew that."

"You just keep finding ways to remind me."

They kissed, and I felt jealous of what the two of them had.

We all took a metal stick and loaded them up, tapping our marshmallows together to toast my birthday before putting them in the fire. Max insisted that I put one candle in my marshmallow at a time and make a wish for each one. The first candle caused the gooey and burnt marshmallow to fall off the stick and to the ground. Max toasted another and we tried again with the same results. After a few more attempts, we were all laughing. There were bits of marshmallow everywhere, and we still hadn't gotten a single candle to stick long enough to light it. We tried sticking the candles in the chocolate, but even with the melted marshmallow, the chocolate was still too hard from the cold mountain air to push a candle through, and we all started on another laughing fit. Finally, Max and Lexie took turns holding a candle so I could make seventeen wishes and blow out seventeen candles.

Not surprisingly, my first wish involved Simon. The second wish was that we would get a blizzard overnight and the ski resort would open after all. I just kept recycling those two wishes on each candle I blew out, and since we didn't get a blizzard, I thought it was only fair that the wish about Simon should come true.

§○Ⅷ

I knew my decision to break up with Luke was a good one, but I was nervous about running into him at school on Monday. He hadn't replied to my break-up text, but I knew Luke wasn't the type of guy to slink away quietly, and I was bracing myself for possible retaliation. I avoided the hallways I knew he would be in during the various passing periods and left the lunchroom early so I could make sure I didn't see him when he came in with the other seniors for lunch. I was ready to take a deep breath of relief at the end of the day when I saw him walking toward me with Zach Peterson. Luke was wearing a crimson T-shirt that said "Single and Disease Free" in big letters across his chest—yeah, I definitely made the right decision.

I ducked behind a trophy case and waited for him to pass.

"What are we hiding from?"

I turned around to see Simon standing behind me and I couldn't stop the smile that sprung to my lips.

"The cruelty of adolescence?" I offered.

"We're going to be hiding for a long time then," he said, returning my smile.

I looked around to see the back of Luke's red T-shirt and started to walk to my locker to get my things before going out to catch the bus home.

"Would you like a ride?" Simon asked.

I smiled and nodded, not needing to give his offer a moment's consideration. A ride with Simon was much better than the bus.

After we pulled to the curb in front of my house, I reached behind me to get my bag from the back seat at the same time Simon did and our hands collided. He instantly froze, but I soon realized it wasn't because he was experiencing the same electric feeling his touch sent through me. The sleeve of my jacket had ridden up when I'd reached toward the back seat, and Simon was staring at the purple bruises forming a macabre bracelet around my wrist. He wore a horrified expression, and I quickly turned around and pulled my sleeve down to cover the marks. He reached over and gently pulled the sleeve back up to reveal the bruises. His expression turned unmistakably to anger.

Chapter Five

"Did Luke do this to you?" he asked, his calm voice not doing a very good job of hiding his fury.

I didn't know how to respond to him. I didn't want to lie, but I also didn't want to talk about what Luke had done.

"Max told me what happened," he said. "I know he shouldn't have without asking your permission first, and I'm sorry if it upsets you that he did."

"It's okay." It actually saved me the trouble of telling him myself.

"Did he hold you down by your wrists?"

I nodded. "Just the one."

I saw another flicker of his anger flair up before he dropped my hand and reached across the center console to put his arms around me. "I'm so sorry, Maggie," he said softly. "I'm so very sorry you had to go through that." He pulled away and looked at me carefully, seriously. "I would *never* do anything like that to you. I want you to know that you can trust me."

"I know," I said sincerely.

He held both of my hands in his, lightly brushing the scrapes and bruises from my night with Luke.

"Do you want me to hurt Luke for you?" he asked, a glint of humor pushing away some of the anger in his eyes.

"There's already a line forming behind my parents." I smiled back.

"I'm glad you're not dating him anymore. For a wide variety of reasons." My heart skipped a beat, and I tried really hard not to read too much into that comment.

We were silent for a few moments and I opened my door to leave before the silence became too awkward.

"Maggie," Simon said as he walked me to the front door, "I'd be happy to give you a ride to school if you want. I imagine it would be better than taking the bus."

Luke had been taking me to and from school since the start of the year, and after breaking up with him, I'd resigned myself to taking the bus, but Simon was a good alternative if I could keep my heart from racing any time he touched me or smiled in my direction. I knew that wasn't going to be easy, but maybe if I were alone with him twice a day I'd develop a resistance to his charisma. *Not likely,* a little voice in the back of my head told me.

"Okay," I said. "I mean, if you're sure it won't be a problem."

"I'm sure," he said with a dazzling smile, and my heart started racing. *Damn! This might be harder than I thought.*

ଛଦଙ

As promised, Simon pulled up to my house early the next morning. I'd been watching from a window at the front of the house and saw his black SUV as it stopped next to the curb. I grabbed my bag and started toward the door just as my dad was walking in from the direction of the kitchen.

"I have time to take you to school today, if don't want to take the bus," he offered.

"Oh, uh, I have a ride, Dad."

"You do?"

The doorbell chimed before I could respond. *Crud!* I had really hoped to avoid this moment, but my dad opened the front door, and we both saw Simon standing there, looking more adorable than anyone had a right to look.

"Good morning," he said politely with his lyrical accent. "I'm here to drive Maggie to school."

"Oh," my dad said. "Oh, of course."

"Dad, this is Simon. The guy who gave me a ride home after Luke—" I let the statement hang in the air between us. "Simon, this is my dad, Andrew O'Neill."

"Nice to meet you, Mr. O'Neill." Simon offered my dad his hand.

"So, Simon, you're a safe driver?" my dad asked as he shook Simon's hand.

Ugh! The "safe driver" talk! I hated when my dad had the "safe driver" talk with my friends, but having it with Simon felt one hundred times more humiliating.

"I think so, sir. No tickets. No accidents."

"Well, Maggie's mother and I expect anyone driving while Maggie's in the car not to text or use a cell phone."

"Of course, Mr. O'Neill. I understand how difficult it must be to hand over your daughter's safety to someone you barely know, but I'll do everything in my power to keep Maggie safe when she's with me."

Wow! Luke's response to that same lecture from my dad had been a shoulder shrug and a mumbled, "Whatever." When I looked at my dad, I could see that he was very pleased. A little too pleased, maybe. He had a look that suggested he might even walk over and kiss Simon in gratitude for taking his daughter's safety so seriously.

"We'd better go," I said quickly before my dad could do anything that would leave permanent emotional scars on either Simon or me. "We don't want to be late." I grabbed my coat and wasted no time in getting out the door.

"Thank you for being so tolerant about my dad's lecture," I said as we drove away from the house.

"I wasn't being tolerant, Maggie. I was being sincere." My heart started racing again, and I grudgingly acknowledged that it might be a permanent thing around Simon.

Luke had driven me to and from school for over two months, and I'd gotten so used to sitting beside him every day, but the thing that struck me as Simon and I drove to school wasn't the weirdness of sitting next to someone else. It was the weirdness that came from a lack of weirdness. Being with Simon felt easy and right, and I realized that I never felt completely comfortable beside Luke. I'd switched gears pretty easily between Simon and Luke. I felt a twinge of guilt for being so fickle, but then I realized that what Luke and I had wasn't right. I was forcing something that wasn't there. With Simon, it felt natural.

I think it was easier for me to break up with Luke because I'd already started to have feelings for Simon, and it was easier to transfer my affection to Simon because Luke had acted like a complete ass. Had Simon not been—well, Simon—and had Luke not treated me like he had, it probably would have taken a lot longer to move from one guy to another, but things are what they are, and Luke was my yesterday, and I *so* wanted Simon to be my today *and* my tomorrow. No sense dwelling on the past. It's always better to focus on the future—especially when the future had the potential for a hot guy with a sexy Irish accent who made my heart race when he smiled in my direction.

ၛၩ

I looked for Simon at lunch and found him sitting with Max at his usual table. I never understood why Max and Lexie didn't eat lunch together. She told me she didn't want to get too much of a good thing, but they only had two classes together, so it wasn't like they spent the entire day glued at the hip.

"Why don't you just kiss him and get it over with?" Lexie asked.

"What?" I looked at her, shocked.

"It's obvious you two like each other, and I think you should just kiss him and get it over with. You'll both be happier."

"Did Max and Simon know each other before Simon moved here?" I asked, ignoring her comment and hoping Lexie had more information about Simon than I did.

"Max said they met after Simon moved here. I guess Simon's family has some sort of business connection with Max's family, or something like that. Anyway, Simon and his family had dinner with Max's family a few times before school started in August, and they became friends."

"Did you ever go to dinner at Max's when Simon was there?"

"No. I didn't meet him until Max introduced him to me at school." She poked at the ravioli on her tray, and the look on her face said that she wasn't sure eating it was worth the risk. "Max thinks a lot of him though," she continued as she put down her fork, evidently deciding against the ravioli, "and I trust Max's opinion."

"Me too."

"He told me once that Simon has a lot of responsibility because of his family."

"What does that mean?"

"I'm not sure," she said. "I told Max that Simon sometimes looked really intense, and Max said it was because of all the responsibilities he had. Maybe he helps out with a family business or sick relative or something."

I nodded. I'd seen the intense look Lexie was talking about, but I'd never given much thought to the source of it.

"I need to go to the library," Lexie said as she picked up her tray. "You want to go?"

I nodded and picked up my own tray, dumping it in the trash before heading to the library with Lexie.

෫෬

When I was alone with Simon in his car after school that day, I started to get really nervous. He looked so fantastic, and now that Lexie had planted the idea, I couldn't get the thought of kissing him out my head. Well, to be fair, the idea had actually been there a long time before Lexie had suggested it at lunch.

"Are you okay?" he asked after a prolonged silence.

"Yes. Fine," I answered, feeling a little uncomfortable.

"You're just a lot quieter than usual. I thought maybe you were upset about something."

"No. Not at all." I tried to think of something to say to assure him that I was capable of social interaction, but was coming up with a blank. I racked my brain, trying to remember something I knew about him that might give me a conversation starter. "I bet you guys have a huge party on St. Patrick's Day in Ireland," I blurted out. *Stupid. Stupid. Stupid.* Of course they celebrated St. Patrick's Day. It was Ireland.

He smiled at me, clearly amused with my lack of conversational skills.

"Sorry. Stupid thing to say," I covered quickly.

His smile softened. "Actually, St. Patrick's Day is more of an American holiday."

"Really? I thought it started in Ireland."

"It did," he explained, "but until very recently, it was a quiet celebration that happened in church. Americans made it a big party. We have parades and parties in Ireland now, but it's mostly for the tourists. They expect it."

"Oh." Yep. I was a master conversationalist.

We were both quiet again.

"I was thinking we could go to the art museum this weekend," he said, breaking the silence. When I looked at him, I noticed that his cheeks were a little flushed. "We could do some research for our Western Civ project. Look at the different exhibits and how they set them up and stuff."

I was suddenly very nervous. I wondered if Simon was asking me out on a date. *No*, I told myself. *It's not a date. It's just Simon asking a fellow student to go to the art museum with him to do research.* Still, it would mean that we'd spend several uninterrupted hours together, and that thought started a warm glow that spread through every cell in my body.

"Yes. I'd like that." And I knew I really would. I wanted to spend time with Simon. I wanted to get to know him better and I wanted him to know me.

He smiled again.

We were at my house. Simon pulled to the curb as he always did and moved the gearshift to park.

"So," he said as we sat in front of my house. "Saturday. Ten o'clock?"

I nodded. He grabbed my bag from the backseat, and we walked to the front door together.

I called Lexie on her cell phone when I got to my room.

"We're going to the art museum on Saturday," I told her in lieu of a hello, unable to contain the excitement in my voice. I knew she would know I was talking about Simon.

"Like on a date?"

"No, I don't think so. He just wants to go for our Western Civ project."

"I don't know, Maggie. I think it's a date."

"It's just for school."

"Maggie, you're being stupid again. The guy obviously likes you. If you ever paid attention to the way he looks at you, you'd see it too."

I hoped she was right. I really, really hoped she was right.

‟)CAB

My stomach flipped over repeatedly when I heard the doorbell ring at ten o'clock on Saturday morning. My entire family was on hand to meet Simon, and I braced myself for whatever humiliation might result from Brandon spending even thirty seconds with Simon. My parents might inadvertently say something that would embarrass me, but Brandon would *definitely* put a tremendous amount of effort into saying or doing something that would make me want to crawl under a rock for eternity. When I walked down the stairs, I was relieved to see Simon in the entryway talking to my mom, my dad standing next to her. Brandon wasn't far away, however, and he had a look on his face that suggested he was waiting for an opportunity to do something really obnoxious.

"Please, call me Amy," my mom was saying as I walked toward them.

Simon smiled, but shook his head. "I'm afraid my brother would be very unhappy with me if I were to call you anything but Mrs. O'Neill. He's very old fashioned about manners."

"Nothing wrong with that," my mom said. "I think the world would be a better place if we were all more polite and well-mannered."

Simon caught my eye and his smile widened.

"Hi," I said. "Ready to go?" I wanted to get out of there before Brandon could follow through on any hideous plans he might be forming.

"So you're taking my sister to see some DAM art?" Brandon asked. I knew he was rude, but using a swear word in front of someone he didn't know was a new low—even for him.

"Brandon," Dad admonished.

"What?" he asked innocently. "It's the Denver Art Museum. D.A.M."

I rolled my eyes and my parents gave Brandon looks that implied he was treading on thin ice. Simon, however, was trying to stifle a laugh.

"Is there somewhere to eat at the DAM museum?" he asked Brandon. "We might get hungry after looking at all the DAM art."

"Oh please don't encourage him," I pleaded.

"I hope you wore your walking shoes," Brandon said. "There are a lot of DAM stairs at the DAM museum."

"Okay, that's enough." I opened the front door to leave.

"I'm going to drive your sister to see the DAM art now," Simon called over his shoulder as we walked down our front steps.

"Be sure to take a lot of DAM pictures," Brandon said as we walked away. "And bring me a DAM souvenir."

෨෬

Simon and I spent several hours looking at the various exhibits at the museum, taking pictures and making notes to help with our project. I was surprised at how much Simon knew about the art and the various artists—both contemporary and traditional. He showed me lines and colors and brush strokes that all had some sort of significance, but that I never would have paid attention to had he not pointed them out.

Simon was everything. Absolutely everything. He was tall and handsome and polite and smart. He'd rescued me during my damsel-in-distress moment. He joked around with my little brother. He had an amazing smile and beautiful eyes and an accent that sometimes made me go weak in the knees. And he knew about art.

He looked up from a placard he was reading and our eyes met and I heard a symphony playing in my head and I wanted Simon to take me in his arms and dance with me right there in the middle of the DAM museum. Not the swaying back and forth that everyone did at school dances when slow songs played. I wanted to waltz. I wanted him to twirl me around and dip me dramatically and lean down and kiss me. I wanted him to rub his hand along my jaw and whisper secrets in my ear. I wanted—

"Do you want to get something to eat?" he asked, pulling me abruptly from my fantasy.

"Uh, yeah."

He smiled and took my hand in his as we walked out of the exhibit, the symphony playing again in my head, slow and soft and sweet.

ℬℭ

"Are things going okay with you and Luke now that you've broken up?" Simon asked as we finished our lunch.

"Yeah," I admitted. "We never talk to each other,

so that's good."

He smiled and I smiled and our conversation stopped.

"Have you lived in the Denver area your whole life?" he asked after a few awkward moments of silence.

"Actually, I've lived in the same *house* my whole life. What about you? You're from Ireland?"

He nodded. "My family still has a home there."

"Why did you move to Denver?"

"My brother and sister-in-law made the decision to move. I live with them."

"You don't live with your parents?"

"No. My parents have really chaotic lives and haven't been able to provide a stable home for me." He looked intently at the napkin in front him. "It's really complicated," he continued after a short pause, returning his eyes to look at mine. "Finn, my brother, is quite a bit older than me and he's looked after me since I was born. He and Erin—his wife—have raised me most of my life. I can't imagine a better set of parents and I know they love me as if I were their own son."

"Do Finn and Erin have children of their own?"

"No. Just me. I guess I'm enough of a handful to keep them busy." His eyes were twinkling with amusement, and it was hard to look away. They were the brightest blue I had ever seen. Simon held my gaze for a moment, neither of us talking.

"Maggie," he said, breaking my trance, "you have the most beautiful eyes."

I laughed out loud.

"What?" he asked, obviously very confused at my

response to his compliment.

"I was thinking the exact same thing at the exact same moment—about *your* eyes."

He smiled, and when he did he looked so beautiful that I thought I heard angels singing in the background.

We went back to eating our lunch, and when I looked out the window a few moments later, I noticed light flurries swirling from the sky to the pavement, and seeing the snow made me realize that I had somehow lost track of my coat.

"I'll go and look for it," Simon offered when I told him.

"It's okay. I'll go."

"No, stay here and enjoy your tea. I'll just be a minute."

He left before I could argue. I had serious doubts about his ability to find my coat without a lengthy search. I had no idea where I had left it. We had gone to every floor in the museum, and it was a massive building. My coat could be any number of places in this DAM place.

Before I could give it much thought, however, Simon was back with my coat in his hands.

"How did you find it?" I asked, completely incredulous.

He shrugged and held it up to help me put it on. He pulled my hair from beneath my collar after slipping the coat into place on my shoulders, and that simple act felt so intimate and right.

He took my hand in his once again as we walked to the parking garage, the snowflakes falling around us becoming thicker once we were outside.

"I love the snow," he said. "We don't get much snow in Ireland, so it's sort of a new thing for me."

"If you like snow, you've definitely come to the right place."

"It's not just the snow that makes Denver the right place for me," he said with an enigmatic smile.

Oh yeah. He was everything all right.

ॐ

When we got to my house, he hesitated before opening his door to get out.

"I enjoyed spending time with you, Maggie."

"Me too."

He leaned over the center console and put his hand gently on the side of my face, his fingers tenderly caressing my jaw. Predictably, his touch made my heart beat faster. We stared into each other's eyes, his hand still on my face, and far sooner than I wanted, he took his hand away and opened his door.

We stood facing each other on the porch, and Simon took one of my hands in his. Then, hesitantly—almost as if he were moving in slow motion—Simon leaned his face toward mine. My heart sped up significantly as I anticipated the kiss, his lips coming to within an inch of my own before he altered his trajectory and kissed me on the cheek. As his soft lips touched my skin, the now-familiar warmth spread through my body. It was a feeling that was so uniquely Simon.

"Goodbye, Maggie," he whispered, his fingers gently stroking my jaw.

"Goodbye, Simon," I said, a little unsteady and

breathless. I turned quickly and went into the house before he could see how rattled I really was.

I called Lexie as soon as I got to my room.

"Tell me everything," she insisted.

"We looked around at the exhibits, then we had lunch, then he brought me home."

"*And,*" she prodded.

"*And*....he walked me to the door and kissed me on the cheek."

"The cheek? Really? Who does that?"

"Simon, evidently." I knew she'd be able to hear the disappointment in my voice. "I really like him, Lex. I felt like one big cliché all day. I couldn't stop staring at his eyes, and my heart skipped a few beats anytime he touched me. Ugh! I'm turning into *that* girl!"

"What girl?" Lexie asked, laughing at my distress.

"The girl who goes all doe-eyed for some guy. The girl who can't think straight because she's staring at his face. The girl who worries about whether or not he'll call. *Ugh!* I hate that girl."

"It happens to the best of us."

"When did it ever happen to you, Lex?"

"Are you serious? You just described how I feel about Max. And it happens to guys, too. I bet Simon's at home right now basking in the afterglow of your afternoon together," she said, dramatizing her last sentence.

"Not likely," I grumbled.

"So, what's next?"

"I don't know. I guess I'll see him Monday morning when he picks me up for school."

"No plans for another date?" She sounded almost as disappointed as I felt.

"No. No plans for another date. I really do wonder if he's just not interested in me that way."

"Not likely," she said, echoing my own words.

"Well, maybe that's why he just kissed me on the cheek," I reasoned.

"Or, he's just old fashioned. He's from Ireland. I've heard people are more polite over there."

"Whatever," I said, laughing. "I do actually think he just wants to be friends. I mean all he did was kiss me on the cheek. If he really liked me he would have done more by now."

"I'm sure he likes you and I'm sure he'd jump at the chance to spend more time with you and I bet he's dying to kiss you, but he's just too shy or polite or something."

"Thanks, Lex."

"No problem. I live to make your life less complicated," she said with a hint of sarcasm.

"Talk to you later?"

"Yeah."

A few minutes after I'd ended my call with Lexie, my phone beeped to tell me I had a text, and when I saw it was from Simon, the warmth returned.

Thank you for being the bright spot in my day—everyday.

My heart leapt from my chest momentarily, then started beating furiously once it was back in place.

Chapter Six

I don't think it would be an understatement to say that every student, and most of the faculty, went to watch the Castlewood Football Team compete in the state finals that year. We'd been warned in the morning announcements all week to take the "Spirit Buses" the school was providing because parking would be limited. I actually thought it sounded like a fun idea—I mean, they were called *Spirit* Buses—but Simon, Max and Lexie weren't so enthusiastic. Lexie said she'd rather walk to the city without shoes in a snowstorm than spend even one minute on a bus full of screaming students, but also had the excuse of a cello lesson. She wouldn't be finished with her lesson until after the buses had already gone, so we were forced to fend for ourselves when it came to getting to the game. In the end, Simon picked me up from my house and we made the trip alone in his car (*insert contented sigh here*). Max picked Lexie up from her lesson, and the two of them met us at the game.

I loved going to football games, especially later in the season when the weather was turning chillier. I liked the drums in the marching band, their beat reverberating in my chest, making me feel and hear the sound simultaneously while the cheerleaders worked the students into a frenzy, uniting us against a common enemy—in this case a team from one of the schools in the city with guys large enough to pound some NFL players into the ground. I found myself hoping that Luke would get a few tough hits during the game, and felt a little guilty for being so vindictive—but only a little.

"I have to go to the bathroom so bad, but I don't want to miss anything," I complained quietly to Lexie at some point during the first quarter.

"Go now. It's first and ten, and we're still almost sixty yards from the goal. With any luck, it'll be a long drive and you can make it back before anyone scores." There evidently were no bounds to Lexie's wealth of knowledge on all subjects, great and small.

After telling Simon that I'd be right back, I took her advice and ran as fast as I could toward the bathrooms. I realized I wasn't the only one needing immediate relief when I saw the line snaking out the door and along the building. I took my place at the end and hoped it moved quickly.

A man I didn't recognize approached me as I waited.

"Are you Maggie O'Neill?" he asked.

"Yes," I said, confused.

"Your brother, Brandon, was in a fight. They're detaining him in the security office. If you can come and claim him, we won't have to call your parents."

"Brandon's here?" I asked, a little stunned. He'd been sitting on our sofa at home when I left, watching a movie with his best friend, Sam. How would he have gotten to the game?

"Afraid so. If you'll just come with me."

"Okay. Yeah."

I was going to have to inflict some serious harm on Brandon for making me lose my spot in the bathroom line.

I followed the man to a set of stairs and walked down with him to a tunnel underneath the bleachers, my spine tingling in a way that told me something was wrong. The florescent lights scattered along the cinderblock walls didn't provide much light and, with the exception of two people standing at the opposite end, it was completely deserted.

I walked slower, letting some distance accumulate between me and the stranger leading me through the tunnel. "I think I better call my parents."

"You can call from the security office."

"No, I'll just call from here."

As I reached for the cell phone in my pocket, the man grabbed my wrist and started pulling me deeper into the tunnel. The two people I'd noticed before started walking toward us, and I knew I was in trouble. I screamed and kicked, trying to get away from the man holding my wrist, but he just tightened his grip and pulled me to him.

Very abruptly, my assailant let go. At first I wondered if my screaming had done the trick but then I noticed that Simon had appeared out of nowhere and was standing next to me, looking murderous. The man was lying on the ground, moaning faintly. Simon was shaking his hand as if it stung, and I realized he must have punched the man.

"Listen to me carefully," Simon said. He turned to me and placed both of his hands on my shoulders, bending down so that we were eye to eye. His voice was strained, and he was shaking. "I need you to run as fast as you can and get Max. Tell him where I am. Don't let anyone else know what happened and don't come back with Max. Stay in the stands with Lexie. Do you understand?"

I nodded mutely, a little afraid of the look in Simon's eyes. The man on the ground at our feet started to regain his wits and was slowly trying to stand. Simon pushed me away and turned to the man.

"Go!" Simon shouted at me over his shoulder. "Run!"

I turned toward the stairs and ran as fast as I could. When I got to the top, I saw Max running toward me from the direction of our seats.

"Max, Simon's in trouble. He's down under the bleachers." I spit it all out very quickly, and before I could finish the last sentence Max had nodded his head and was running toward the tunnel.

"Feel better?" Lexie asked when I sat down next to her.

"Yeah," I lied. *Note to self: Never put yourself in a potentially life threatening situation when you're desperate to use the bathroom.* I was absolutely miserable, but I was afraid to leave Lexie's side.

"There must be something in the water," she said distractedly. "Simon and Max both went up to the bathroom after you left."

I didn't tell her where Simon and Max really were. I didn't want to worry her, but I also didn't want to give words to the terror still running through me.

Five bladder-stretching minutes later, Simon was next to me. He cocked his head toward the top of the stands and held out his hand, indicating he wanted me to go with him. Max sat down next to Lexie, and she was too involved with kissing him to notice when I slipped away a second time.

"Are you okay?" he asked as we walked to the top of the stands.

"I really, really have to go to the bathroom," I said. I hated admitting that to Simon but figured the admission would be less embarrassing than peeing my pants.

"I think I know where there's one with less traffic." He took my hand and guided me toward a bathroom at the far end of the stadium.

"I'll wait right here," Simon assured me, standing beside the door to the ladies room. There were only a few women in the room, so I was able to finish quickly and head back out to Simon.

He smiled brightly when he saw me. "Better?"

"Immensely."

"Come sit down with me for a minute," he said, putting his hand on the small of my back and leading me to a section at the top of the stands that was fairly deserted. Once we were sitting, he looked at me carefully, his face turning serious, the remnants of his anger still boiling behind his eyes. "Are you sure you're okay?"

I nodded. I really did feel better sitting beside Simon. Safe. Protected.

"Can you tell me everything that happened?" he asked gently.

I took a deep breath and tried to organize the events in my head. I told him everything, and when I'd finished, I noticed that the dark look was back on

Simon's face. He stood abruptly and turned away from me, standing to face the field below. He rested his hands on top of his head, his fingers intertwined.

"Maggie, you really shouldn't go anywhere with someone you don't know," he said when he turned back around.

I gave him a withering look. I hated that he was lecturing me about all of this. He was one-hundred-percent right, but it still felt awful.

"I'm sorry," he said. "It's just that this could have ended so badly."

"Yes, I know. But it didn't. I'll be more careful."

"Thank you," he said, breathing a sigh of relief.

"I don't get how that man knew my name. Or Brandon's name. And why was he taking me to that tunnel? And Max was already running toward the tunnel before I told him. How did he know where you were?" I started to shake, and Simon came to me and pulled me to my feet, wrapping his arms around me tight. Is it wrong that I was really happy in that moment? A strange man had lured me to a dark and deserted tunnel to do god-knows-what to me, but the only emotion I experienced as Simon held me to him was complete happiness.

"I should call Brandon," I said when we pulled away from each other. "Just to be sure he's okay." Simon nodded in agreement, and I pulled out my phone to call Brandon on his cellphone.

"'Sup?" he asked in the goofy way he typically answered when his friends were around. He sounded normal and unharmed, and that made me smile.

"Where are you?" I asked, wanting to be on the safe side—or, more precisely, wanting to make sure

Brandon was on the safe side.

"Home. Why?"

"I thought I saw you at the game."

"Maggie, I was sitting on the sofa when you left."

"I know. I just thought I saw you. I'll see you when I get home."

"Okay, Crazy," he teased.

"He's okay?" Simon asked when I ended the call. I nodded and noticed that the sigh of relief Simon expelled was greater than my own.

Simon insisted that he drive me home right away. I told Lexie I had a headache and wanted to go home early, but I knew the reason wouldn't matter to Lexie. She would just be glad I was spending time with Simon.

As we drove home, I thought about what had happened to the creepy dude that had lured me into the tunnel. Had Simon called the police? Had he reported him to campus security? Had he threatened him to within an inch of his life, thus ensuring he would be too frightened to return? How had Simon known I was in the tunnel and needed help? Why was Max running toward the tunnel before I'd told him what had happened? I wanted to ask Simon so many questions, but being dragged into a deserted tunnel by a stranger hadn't helped me develop a spine, and I was too afraid to ask him. Too afraid of what the answers might be.

I had a tough time falling asleep that night. When I finally did fall asleep, I dreamed of the man in the tunnel, my panic rising as he approached me. Before long, the old woman came and calmed me.

ഇᏟᎩ

When I got into Simon's car on Monday morning, he smiled brightly, and any concerns I had about the football game and Creepy Dude and Simon's role in the whole incident flitted away like dry leaves across the pavement in a strong wind, and as my heart fluttered in my chest, I knew I would never get used to his smile. He reached for my hand and gave it an annoyingly friendly squeeze, but the thoughts I had of him caressing my hair and brushing his fingers against my cheek were anything *but* friendly.

"We have a short week," he said, breaking the spell I fell under every time I saw him. "Thanksgiving."

"Oh, right," I said, disappointed. That's when I knew how bad the situation with Simon really was. I had three extra days off from school, but I was saddened because that meant I wouldn't get to see him.

"Are you and your family traveling anywhere over the long weekend?" he asked.

"No," I answered. "We're staying home."

"Well, in that case, do you want to come to my house to watch a movie Friday night?"

I could feel the relief spread throughout my body, smoothing out all of the tension. I wouldn't have to go five days without seeing him after all.

"How about if I pick you up at six, and you can have dinner with us? I'd like you to meet Finn and Erin."

I nodded and tried to hide my excitement. I didn't want to look like a big dork in front of Simon but wondered if that ship hadn't already sailed.

We pulled into the parking lot at school, and Simon took my hand in his after he put the car in park.

"Your bruises had just healed, and now they're back." He was running his fingers over my wrist, tracing the new set of bruises that had bloomed there since the incident at the football game.

"Simon, what happened to that man the other night?" The gentle prodding in my brain that said something wasn't quite right wouldn't go away, and I rallied all of my courage to ask him about the football game.

"What do you mean?"

"I mean after I left. What happened to him?"

He took a deep breath and looked out the window. Finally, he turned back to me. "I called the authorities, and they took him away."

"Didn't they want to talk to me?"

"I told them everything that happened."

"Oh," I responded. "I thought the police would need to talk to me for their report."

"Not always," he said evasively before he went back to tracing the bruises on my wrist.

ഇരുൻ

Thanksgiving week that year was the longest week I'd ever experienced in my entire life. I was too excited about the idea of spending several uninterrupted hours with Simon again and, because I was looking forward to it, time seemed to drag so slowly. When Friday evening finally rolled around, I felt an overwhelming happiness when I saw him pull up to the curb in front of our house. Even the prospect of Brandon humiliating me couldn't dampen my mood.

"Have a seat Simon," my mom said when he walked into the living room, her tone friendly.

I tried to use my powers of invisibility as Brandon sat on the sofa looking, as always, like he was thinking of something extremely rude to say or do. Unfortunately, I wasn't a character in a Harry Potter book, so I remained stubbornly visible and vulnerable to any indignity Brandon might want to sling in my direction.

"Thank you, Mrs. O'Neill," Simon said as he sat on the opposite end of the sofa from Brandon.

"Did you have a nice Thanksgiving?" my dad asked him.

"Yes, sir," he said. "It's not a holiday we celebrate in Ireland, but we did our best to have all the traditional foods since we're here. There's this green bean casserole that Max's mom told us about that was really amazing."

"The one with the crispy onions on top?" my dad asked, evidently excited about the memory of the dish we'd also had the day before.

"Yeah, that's the one," Simon confirmed.

"Have you kissed my sister yet?" Brandon asked before anyone could say anything else.

"Brandon!" my mom, my dad and I all admonished at the same moment.

"What? It's just a question," he defended himself, not quite pulling off the innocent look he was trying to project. I knew his comment was a calculated move to embarrass me. "He comes over all the time, and I was just wondering if he was kissing her or not."

"I think now would be a really good time to leave,"

I said, standing up. I was afraid to look at Simon, afraid of what his expression might be, but when I did steal a glance at him, I saw that he was trying really hard to fight a smile.

℘℘℘

When we walked into the house, Simon took my hand, and the summersaults hit my stomach with intensity as his warm fingers weaved themselves into mine.

Their house looked like a Pottery Barn catalog. It was beautifully decorated, but it looked new, not like it had been lived in for a long time. There was artwork on the walls, but no photos, no books, nothing to say that Simon and his family lived there. It appeared that they had left all of their things at their home in Ireland and bought new stuff when they moved to Denver. It suggested a lack of permanence that made me uneasy.

Simon introduced me to Finn and Erin when we walked into the kitchen. It was hard to miss the resemblance between Finn and Simon. They both had the same light brown hair, blue eyes and tall build, but Finn was closer to my parents' age than to ours. Erin had beautiful brown hair that fell in soft curls, and she was several inches taller than me.

"Maggie," Finn said enthusiastically, wiping his hands on a towel before coming over and shaking mine. He spoke with the same lyrical accent Simon had. "It is so very nice to meet you. Simon speaks of you often." I turned to look at Simon and was surprised that his face was a little pink and he looked self-conscious.

"She really does look like the poster child for

Ireland, Simon," Erin added, her voice soft and quiet. "You have the most beautiful red hair, Maggie."

"She's the only one in her family with red hair. The rest of them have black hair," Simon said. The three of them all paused simultaneously for a split second.

Erin broke the silent pause. "Does anyone in your extended family have red hair?"

"Not that we know of. My dad says I just picked up on a recessive gene from way back in the family tree. My brother would like to pretend I was adopted and that's why I'm the only one with red hair."

They exchanged a brief glance with each other that made me feel slightly paranoid.

"We're having Chicken Florentine," Finn announced before their silence could become too uncomfortable. "I hope you like it. It's actually the first time I'm making it."

I helped Simon set the table, and Erin and Finn brought out the food. We talked about school, Ireland and my family while we ate, and I found that I was completely at ease with Simon's family. It felt like I'd known them all for a long time.

I helped Erin clear the table after dinner while Simon and Finn loaded the dishwasher.

"I'll take these last two in," I told Erin as I picked up two glasses from the table. She smiled and left to start the movie in the living room.

When I walked toward the kitchen, I saw that Simon was leaning against the counter, his head hung slightly while Finn talked to him. I moved behind the wall separating the dining room from the kitchen so I could listen for a moment. Shameless, I know, but I convinced myself that they wouldn't choose the kitchen to talk about anything *too* private.

"I know a lot of women don't want a man to open the door for them," Finn was telling Simon, "but you should always assume she does until she tells you not to."

Simon nodded, looking a bit contrite. "I know," he said. "I normally do open the door for her, but she doesn't wait in the car for me to come around when we're getting out."

Finn thought about that for a moment before responding. "I think you should just continue to be persistent when opening doors at other times. Let her know it's a habit you intend to continue, and let her decide if she wants you to open the car door when she's getting out."

Simon nodded. He stood upright and walked toward the sink.

"And don't forget to take her hand when you're helping her out of the car," Finn reminded him.

Simon smiled indulgently as he rinsed a plate and put it in the dishwasher.

"Yes, brother. I'll take her hand."

I smiled. It was such a tender moment between the two brothers—discussing dating etiquette. I wondered if my dad and Brandon ever had talks like that, knowing Brandon would need remedial etiquette lessons that started with why it was a bad idea to burp in a girl's face after lunch.

❧⚬☙

Simon sat next to me during the movie and held my hand in his, alternating between rubbing my palm and the back of my hand with his fingers. I honestly couldn't say what the movie was about. Simon, Finn and Erin laughed a few times, and I would laugh along with them so I didn't look like a complete idiot, but I was too busy thinking about Simon and his fingers touching my hand, and the feel of his shoulder against mine, and the fact that we were sitting so close to each other. Sometimes he would look down at me, and I could feel his breath brush lightly along my neck as he did. It was all driving me absolutely insane, and it took every bit of my concentration to keep myself from pulling him to me and kissing him in front of his brother and sister-in-law.

"Well, I think it's time for me to hit the sack," Finn said, the movie evidently over. I quickly removed my hand from Simon's, butterflies flooding my stomach at the thought of being alone with him.

"I'll come up with you," Erin said. "Goodnight, Maggie. It was very nice to meet you. Goodnight, Simon." She hugged her brother-in-law and kissed him on the cheek before stepping aside to let Finn hug Simon and tell him goodnight. I think most kids our age would be totally embarrassed to have someone in their family hug and kiss them goodnight, but Simon didn't seem to care at all and I liked him a little more for it.

After they left, I tried to figure out why I was so nervous about being alone with Simon. I was fine sitting next to him and holding his hand while Finn and Erin were in the room with us and I'd certainly spent a fair amount of time in the last few weeks fantasizing about doing a lot of touching and kissing with Simon, but now that we were alone, I was decisively anxious. I knew Simon would never force himself on me the way Luke had, so I couldn't quite put my finger on the source of my nervousness. Then I realized that I wasn't nervous because I was afraid we might do something I didn't want to do. I was nervous because we might do something I *did* want to do.

When I looked up at Simon, I saw that he had a very pensive look on his face. "I'm not Luke," he said gently after several long minutes. He pulled my hand from my lap and held it tenderly in his own. "I will *never* ask you to do something you don't want to do."

I knew I could trust him. He wasn't Luke. He wouldn't hurt me. The situation was similar, but it wasn't the same, and the main difference was that Luke wasn't here and Simon was. I *wanted* to do more with Simon. I wanted him to kiss me and I wanted him to touch me in a way I hadn't been touched before.

"I know," I said. "I trust you."

He put his arm around me, pulling me closer to him, and I leaned into his shoulder, feeling complete and total elation. We were alone in his living room, and it would have been the perfect time for him to kiss me, but he didn't. He just held me close and we talked about school and our families and our friends and everything and nothing. I wanted him to kiss me, and I should have been disappointed that he didn't, but I liked talking with him so much that I almost forgot about the physical ache—the longing to be kissed and to kiss him back—that I always felt when we were together.

☙❧

Simon was unusually quiet on the ride from his house later that night, and I wondered if he was upset about something.

"I was thinking about Luke," he said after he'd turned off the ignition. When we sat in his car alone together, it felt oddly intimate. Anyone could look in and see us, but it was as if the windows and doors created a buffer between the rest of the world and us, and for a few minutes, it was just me and Simon.

"On purpose?" I teased in response.

Simon smiled before he continued. "Were you surprised to find out that he wasn't a very nice guy?"

"I don't know." I sighed. "I guess there were clues along the way, but I didn't want to see them."

He was quiet for a moment, and I could see his chest rise and fall as he breathed in and out and I wanted desperately to know what he was thinking about.

"What if you really cared about someone but you found out he wasn't who you thought he was? Would you still want to date him? To be friends with him?"

"Are you asking about someone in particular or is this a hypothetical question?"

He hesitated. "It was just something I was thinking about."

I wondered what was rattling around in his brain. Did he think I wouldn't want to date him? Is that why he was asking these questions? He reached across the console and took my hand in his, and it felt so comforting, and I couldn't imagine Simon as anything but good and wonderful and kind.

"Simon," I began. He seemed to need reassurance, but I wasn't sure what to say to him. What would put his mind at ease? "*You're* not bad for me."

"You should probably go in," he whispered. "It's two minutes past your curfew."

"Okay," I said reluctantly, opening my door. He took my hand as we walked up the steps to the porch and hugged me briefly before kissing my cheek.

"Goodnight, Maggie," he said.

"Goodnight, Simon."

I went inside and Simon left and I wondered what had triggered his sudden shift in moods from kind and understanding to morose. Then I wondered why the heck he still insisted on kissing me on the cheek.

Chapter Seven

"Let's walk to the park," Simon said abruptly. We'd gone to my room after school the following week, and Simon had been anxious and jittery since the moment I'd closed my bedroom door. There was a smoldering intensity behind his eyes (*yeah, I know, super corny line, but it really did describe the look in his eyes at that moment*), and he looked like he was fighting a tremendous internal battle.

"Did you not notice the weather when we walked into the house?" I pointed out. It had started to snow before we left school for the day, and by the time we pulled in front of my house, there were at least three inches of snow obscuring the ground.

"You have ski gear," he suggested.

I gave in to his request fairly easily. I actually liked to go outside when it was snowing—mainly because other people didn't and that pretty much guaranteed some alone time for me in the great outdoors—but I was worried Simon might not be as enthusiastic about the snow and cold once we were out in it. He'd worn only the outer shell of his ski jacket and he didn't have gloves or a hat, but he politely refused the offer of some of my dad's ski gear as we headed out the door.

"Did you ever make snow angels when you were a kid?" Simon asked when we were in the park.

I chuckled. "Lexie and I made snow angels in my back yard after the storm *last week*," I confessed. "You?"

"Never," he admitted.

"Really?"

"Really."

"Well, I guess we don't have any choice then." I lay on my back and moved my arms and legs up and down in the snow. He smiled and lay beside me, making his own angel. We kneeled in the snow when we were done to admire our work.

"One more," I suggested, moving to an unmarred section of snow. Simon followed, and we made another set of snow angels, but didn't bother getting up to look at the finished product.

"Are you cold?" Simon asked.

"No," I answered. "I'm pretty bundled up." I'd made sure to put on plenty of layers and was wearing a fleece jacket with a thick parka over it, waterproof pants and two pairs of fleece socks under my Sorels. We were lying under a tree that had been stripped of most of its leaves, watching as particularly large and fluffy snowflakes fell between the branches. "It's so beautiful and peaceful," I remarked.

"Yes," he agreed, "but you have to be perishing."

"Perishing?"

He smiled. "Really cold. Maybe we should head back to the house."

"You're wearing less than I am," I reasoned. "If you're not cold, then I'm certainly not going to be. He squeezed my mittened hand with his own.

Watching the thick flakes fall toward me had a mesmerizing effect, and I felt like I was in a dream—a very wonderful dream since Simon was with me and he was holding my hand. I sensed him rolling onto his side and turned my head to look at him. Our eyes met, and I could see the intensity in his again, the quiet smoldering that he tried to keep below the surface. It wasn't hard to see the battle taking place inside of his head. The emotions that had been taking turns inside of him while we were in my room were now all present simultaneously in his expression—anxiety, passion, fear, anger, need.

"Simon?" I began, wanting to ask him what was bothering him. He didn't answer me, though. Instead, he started to move his face toward mine, and I tried to open myself up to him—to convey to him that I wanted him in my life and I wanted him to want me in *his* life. His lips moved closer to mine, and my heart sped up and I waited for his kiss, wanting desperately for him to not kiss my cheek. When his lips were within an inch of my own, he paused, and I thought my heart was going to pound a hole through my chest. I could feel the heat from him reaching out to me even before his skin touched mine, and when his lips did brush against my own, I believed that I might literally explode with happiness. The joy of kissing Simon—of *really* kissing Simon—sent a flush through my body that turned into an ache that reached into the joints of my fingers and toes.

When he moved his lips away from mine I wanted to protest, but I was having trouble catching my breath. He didn't move away from me, however, and after looking briefly into my eyes, he moved his lips to my jaw, then down to my neck, pushing aside the thick black scarf I was wearing so he could kiss below my ear. I wanted to rip the scarf off. I wanted to pull off my coat and his coat and all the layers underneath. I wanted to feel Simon—every bit of Simon—and I wanted him to feel me. He moved his lips back to mine, and the intensity increased and we both started to breathe faster and I heard a soft moan from deep inside of him. The heat of his lips touching my skin and the cold of the snowflakes biting at our cheeks and noses made it feel so magical and surreal.

After several minutes of heavenly kissing, Simon rolled onto his back and pulled me to him to rest my head on his chest. He rubbed his hand gently against the hair that was sticking out below the wool hat I was wearing. It was such a big moment for us—our first kiss—and I felt that I should say something, to thank him for being so wonderful, but I didn't want to break the spell we'd fallen under. I didn't want to ever move away from Simon's arms, but after a while, I could see that the snow was starting to pile up on both of us and the light was starting to fade and reluctantly I let him pull me to a standing position so we could walk back to my house. He took my hand in his as we walked, and I quickly pulled it away to remove my mitten before taking his hand again. I wanted to feel his skin touching mine. I wanted his lips to reach out to me again.

When we got to my house we sat next to each other on my front steps. The wind was blowing in such a way that the roof of the porch sheltered the steps from the falling snow, but it swirled around us and closed us off from the rest of the world. Neither of us had said anything the entire walk home, and we both remained silent as we sat next to each other. I started to worry that Simon regretted kissing me, but then he leaned in and kissed me again—a soft, sweet, wonderful kiss. His hand reached up and caressed the side of my face, and I felt like I was falling back into heaven.

"Maggie," he whispered softly as he rested his forehead against mine, "I want so much for this to be the right thing."

I pulled back and looked into his eyes, confused by his comment. "Kissing you *is* the right thing," I said adamantly. "I have no doubt about that."

"I want it to be the right thing," he repeated, but it felt like he was slipping through my fingers.

"Hey! Lover boy!" Simon and I both turned to see Brandon standing at the front door. "My parents want me to ask you if you want to stay for dinner. If you're done sucking my sister's face, that is."

Simon smiled, but it was another smile that didn't reach up to touch his eyes.

"You don't have to stay," I said.

"I'm not sending you in there to deal with Brandon on your own. I think he'll have plenty to say after seeing us kiss."

I chuckled. "I think I could actually use the support."

We walked into the house and I took off my snow gear before going to sit down with my family and Simon at the wooden table in the dining room.

"Just so you know, Simon and Maggie were kissing," Brandon told my mom before I could put my napkin on my lap.

My mom, who was already sitting, gaped at

Brandon. My dad paused mid-step with a bowl of stew in his hands, a confused look on his face, his eyes pointed toward Simon. I heard Simon clear his throat uncomfortably.

"Dad," I prompted, trying to jumpstart him back into action. It worked. He finished the short walk to the table and set the bowl down before taking a seat.

"Well, aren't you going to say anything?" Brandon asked my parents, incredulous.

My mom ladled some stew into her bowl before passing it to Simon.

"Maggie's seventeen, Brandon," she said calmly. "She's old enough to kiss a boy." I noticed the warning look she shot my dad.

"But they were kissing on the front porch," Brandon argued. "The whole world could see."

"Yeah, well, I'd much rather they kiss in public than in private," my dad mumbled wryly. My mom gave him an impatient look.

I wanted to crawl under a rock, and I got the feeling Simon probably did too. Talking with your own parents about kissing someone was bad enough, but poor Simon had to talk with someone else's parents about kissing their daughter. I didn't think there was a judge in the country that would consider it anything but justifiable homicide if I were to kill Brandon at that moment.

Simon cleared his throat again. "I'm sorry if my kissing Maggie has upset any of you," he said. "I wouldn't have kissed her if I didn't think very highly of her, and I will never treat her with anything but respect. You have my word on that."

(Insert the sound of crickets here.) My parents, Brandon

and I stared at Simon, our mouths slightly agape, all of us completely still and silent. For once, I was grateful when Brandon spoke.

"Dude, you're making it really hard for me to do my job as a little brother," he said.

Simon smirked. "I hate to take that away from you, but I feel I have a responsibility toward your sister that requires I do whatever I can to protect her from your teasing." He reached over and took my hand in his under the table. "Feel free to take your best shot at me, though. Fire away with any insults you have. I wouldn't want you to hold them in and give yourself a brain aneurism or anything."

"Nah," Brandon said, taking a piece of bread from the middle of the table. "The moment's passed."

"Well, if I got to pick a boyfriend for my daughter, Simon, it would be you," my mom said. "From what I've seen, you treat Maggie with respect, but you treat her family with respect, as well."

"Thank you, Mrs. O'Neill," Simon replied.

"Okay, we need to change the subject," my dad announced. "I don't think I can handle any more talk about my little girl kissing boys and having boyfriends—respectful as that boyfriend might be."

I grudgingly pulled my hand from Simons and started to eat my stew, grateful my dad had insisted on a subject change. Brandon asked Simon about his favorite sports, and I breathed a sigh of relief, knowing that would probably be a safe topic—even for Brandon.

ℰꞰ

We sat together in Simon's car in front of my house the following day after school, and he held my hand in his, a particularly pensive look on his face.

"Maggie," he asked without looking at me, "do you wish I hadn't kissed you yesterday?"

My heart sent a painful burning through my chest. "No," I said emphatically, "but it seems like *you* regret it."

"No." He shook his head. "I don't regret it. It was—perfect."

"Yes," I breathed.

He leaned across the console and kissed me, and if I thought it might be less intense the second time, I was definitely mistaken. The familiar heat rushed through me, and I felt like I was fading into something that was pure and magnificent. I was wearing far fewer layers than I had been the day before and I could feel the heat radiating from Simon, and the connection I felt with him made me want to be even closer to him. When his tongue reached out to mine, I shuddered and felt the gasp rising from my throat. His hand was at the back of my neck, kneading the skin he touched, and I reached up and put both of my hands on either side of his face.

He pulled away and smiled at me, and I could see the joy in his eyes, but it was mixed with regret or sadness or trepidation, and I wondered what it was about kissing me that caused his eyes to reflect those particular emotions.

"Tell me what's bothering you," I urged gently.

He pulled back and took my hands in his.

"I like you," he said softly, "and I want everything to be perfect for you. I don't want you to do anything you'll regret later."

"You think I'll regret kissing you?"

He took a deep breath. "I just want everything to be perfect."

I reached up and kissed him. "It *is* perfect," I said. "So perfect."

Perfect. *Everything* was perfect that December. I had never realized how unhappy I'd been with Luke until I started dating Simon. It was sort of like eating a candy bar and thinking that it was the best thing ever, but then someone gives you a piece of Godiva chocolate and you suddenly see everything you've been missing. Simon made everything better—even work with the Western Civ group.

We spent a lot of time with Max and Lexie that December. We went Christmas shopping on the 16th Street Mall and ice-skating in Skyline Park. We bundled up and took thermoses of hot chocolate to watch the Parade of Lights, an annual Christmas parade downtown—a procession of floats that lit up the night mixed with marching bands playing Christmas music. And sometimes we just hung out doing nothing, and that was just as good as doing something.

"You seem lost in thought," Simon said as we sat alone on the sofa in his living room a few days before Christmas. I was absently fingering the ring he always wore on his right index finger. I'd seen it many times before—he didn't seem to ever take it off—but I'd never looked at it closely. The silver band of the ring formed two hands that came together and held a heart with a crown on top of it. It seemed unusual for a guy to wear a ring with a heart.

"I was looking at your ring," I said.

"It's a Claddagh ring," he explained. "It's an Irish thing."

"What do you mean?"

"A lot of people from Ireland wear them." He slipped the ring off his finger so that he could hold it up and point out the details. "Legend says that the right hand symbolizes the god Dagda, a very powerful, but very kind god. The left hand symbolizes Danu, a goddess. Together they're holding the heart, which represents all of humanity, and the crown represents life." He handed the ring to me so I could look at it more closely. It was heavier than I'd expected it to be, and it looked really old.

"Some people think the ring is a symbol of love, friendship and loyalty," he continued. "Finn has one identical to mine, and Erin has one that Finn gave her when they were first dating."

I'd seen both of their rings. They wore them, as Simon did, on the index finger of their right hands.

I handed the ring back to him and he slid it in place on his finger. "So, people give them to each other when they're dating?" I asked.

"Sometimes," he answered, smiling. "Usually a person's given one by someone who loves them—a parent or a spouse or a friend."

"Maybe I should buy one to help me get in touch with my Irish roots," I said playfully.

Simon laughed loudly, but I didn't see the humor reach his eyes. "I'm almost certain someone will give you one someday," he said, his words dripping with an inside joke.

"Where did you get yours?" I asked, hoping

fervently he hadn't gotten it from an ex-girlfriend.

"Our mother gave Finn and me our rings," he answered, and I breathed a sigh of relief. "Most people in my family wear them as reminder of who we are and where we've come from."

He pulled me against him, my back to his chest and his arms encircling me. "This is the last time you're going to see me for a week." I was leaving the next morning to go to my grandparents' in St. Louis with my family. It had been almost a month since our first kiss, and in that time we hadn't gone a full day without seeing each other.

"We're going skiing with Max and Lexie when I get back," I reminded him. I hated the idea of leaving Simon for a whole week, but I was excited about the three days we'd spend together on the ski trip.

He kissed the top of my head. "Yes," he said quietly. "At least that gives me something to look forward to."

"You can wear your scarf when we go skiing." I pulled gently on the charcoal gray wool scarf I'd given him for Christmas. He never seemed to be dressed appropriately for Colorado weather, so a scarf seemed like a good gift.

"And you can take your picture with you to St. Louis so you don't forget us," he said playfully. His gift to me had been a framed picture of Lexie, Max, Simon and me that had been taken on our ice skating trip in Skyline Park.

"It would take a lot longer than a week apart to make me forget you," I said.

"Would you forget me after a month?" he teased.

"It would take one hundred lifetimes," I said

sincerely.

He traced his fingers down my jaw. "I'm going to miss this. I'm going to miss *you*."

"I'm going to miss you, too. But at least you have a ton of presents to open. That should keep you busy while I'm gone." The tree in the Brady living room was overflowing with presents, and when I'd taken the time to peek at them, I'd seen that most were for Simon. The gift tags revealed that they were all from people I'd never met.

"That's true," he said, wrapping me in his arms. "But I already have the only gift I really want." He moved his lips to kiss under my jaw, sending shivers up and down my body. "I have you."

Chapter Eight

I woke up the next morning in a mad rush. I hadn't finished packing, and we had to leave for the airport early. I flew around my room trying to throw anything I thought I might need into a suitcase, while at the same time pulling on some clothes and brushing my teeth. I grabbed Bubbles IV's food container and picked up a pinch to put in his bowl, but noticed that Bubbles IV was floating, belly up—a sure sign that he'd met with the same fate as all of the Bubbles that had preceded him. I gave him a nudge, and when there was no movement, I knew it was time to flush him down to the big fish bowl in the sky. I made a mental note to text Lexie to let her know that she didn't need to bother to feed it when she took in our mail for us each day, and went back to throwing my things into a suitcase.

My dad came in to hurry me along.

"If it's not in there now," he said, "you don't need it. We gotta go."

He zipped my bag for me while I quickly grabbed a pair of socks and started pulling them on. He put my suitcase on the floor and was on his way out of my room when he stopped and picked up the book of

Irish folklore Simon had given me.

"Where did you get this?" he asked.

"Simon gave it to me for my birthday." I hopped on one foot toward the door while trying to put a shoe on the other foot.

"My great-grandmother had this same book," he said, mesmerized. "She said one of the stories in it is about our family."

"Gotta go, Dad, remember?" I urged him, getting the second shoe on my foot.

He shook himself out of his momentary daze and wheeled my bag to the car.

"Another Bubbles bit the dust," he told me unnecessarily as we walked out of the house.

"Yeah, looks like it."

"I told you he wasn't happy in that bowl. He needed a tank."

"Dad, fish don't have feelings," I told him with a withering eye roll.

He didn't respond but instead tilted his head to one side and raised his eyebrows in a way that implied he didn't agree.

෨෬

My cellphone rang late Christmas day, and when I picked it up, I saw that it was Simon.

"Hi," I said when I answered. "I miss you!"

I could almost hear the smile stretching across his face. "I miss you, too. How was your Christmas?"

"Fine. Yours?"

"We had a nice day, but you weren't here. How was your Christmas with your grandparents?"

"We just opened presents and ate all day. I think I ate more today than I normally do in an entire week."

He chuckled lightly.

"Simon, before we left for the airport, my dad saw the book you gave me for my birthday." I'd thought about the book as we flew to St. Louis and about how much of a coincidence it was that my dad had recognized it.

"Is that a problem?"

"No. It's just that my dad said my great-great-grandmother had the exact same book. He said she thought one of the stories in the book was about our family."

Simon was silent for so long that I actually looked at the screen of my phone to see if I'd lost the call.

"Simon?" I asked.

"I'm here. Sorry. I just got distracted for a moment."

"Do you think it's weird that my great-great-grandmother had the same book?"

"No, I don't think it's weird," he said, an odd catch in his voice. He sounded almost somber. "Did your dad tell you anything about her?"

"No."

"Maybe you should ask him," he suggested. "I've always thought it was interesting to hear stories about my ancestors."

"*Your* ancestors might have been interesting, but I doubt mine were."

He chuckled again, and I pictured his smile and his eyes and the way the skin crinkled at the edges when he laughed. "Miss you," he reminded me.

"Miss you, too," I said.

"Talk to you tomorrow?"
"Talk to you tomorrow."

ⓈⓄⒸⓇ

"Hi, Grandpa," I said, walking into the den the following day. He was reading the newspaper, and I hoped he wouldn't be upset with me for interrupting. Brandon was playing a video game in the living room and was completely engrossed, and my parents had gone shopping with my grandmother.

"Hey, Maggie Girl," he said cheerfully, folding the newspaper and putting it on the coffee table. "What're you up to?"

"Nothing."

"Are you missing that boyfriend of yours?" he asked. I was grateful he'd brought up the subject of Simon. I'd wanted to ask my grandfather about the book, but was nervous about how to bring it up.

I nodded. "He gave me a book of Irish folklore for my birthday," I said, trying to segue into a conversation about the book. Since my grandmother's family was from Germany, I used my strong deductive reasoning abilities to figure out that my dad had been talking about my grandfather's grandmother when he'd seen the book.

"Well, that's a nice gift."

"My dad saw it before we left to come here and said his great-grandmother had the exact same book. He said she told him one of the stories was about our family."

"That's right," my grandfather said, seemingly taking a brief trip down memory lane. When his short journey had ended, he looked at me, confused. "Isn't your young man's name Simon?"

I nodded.

"Well isn't that a coincidence. That's the story my grandmother said was about our family. The story of Margaret and Simon." His look turned reflective. "You're named after her, you know?"

"Really?" I asked, genuinely surprised.

"Oh, yes. Well, not your middle name. Breslin was your mom's maiden name. That part came from her. But my grandmother's name was Margaret O'Neill. She used to say that Margaret O'Neill was destined to be a strong figure in history, but only a child who was *born* Margaret O'Neill. She was an O'Neill by marriage, of course, but according to Grandma Margaret, there was a prophecy about a Margaret O'Neill, and she said that the story in that book was the story of the prophecy."

"A prophecy? What kind of prophecy?" It felt weird to have my grandfather use that word. It was the kind of word you read in bizarre science fiction novels.

"I don't remember exactly," he said. "Something about a child named Margaret O'Neill and how that child would change the course of the world. None of us put much stock in the story, of course, but I guess your parents thought it was a nice story and they named you Margaret."

"What other stories did she tell?"

"She told a lot of stories from Irish folklore. Most of them involved faeries and the antics they got up to. She honestly believed that faeries were real and thought they should be treated with respect. We all thought they were fun stories, but Grandma Margaret, she took 'em dead serious. She was born in Ireland, and maybe that's why."

I nodded.

"Quite a coincidence—about the story and your boyfriend's name."

"Yeah," I said distractedly. Something didn't feel right.

✺

I went to the room I shared with Brandon, grateful that he was still engrossed with his video game in the living room, and picked up my phone to call Simon. I wanted to ask him about the prophecy and the book and the story.

"Hi," he said when he answered the phone. "How was your day?"

"Good. I talked to my grandfather. He said that his grandmother's name was Margaret O'Neill, too."

Simon was silent for a moment. "Were you named after her?"

"Evidently. I never knew that. My parents never told me. I thought they'd just named me Margaret as a way to make sure I never had any boyfriends."

"I think Margaret's a nice name," he said. "Besides, if that was their plan, they didn't succeed. You've already had two boyfriends."

"I always wished I'd been named Ashley or Kaitlin or some other fun name. Margaret is such an old fashioned name."

"I love your name and I'm really glad you're not an Ashley or a Kaitlin. Old fashioned is good. What else did your grandpa say?"

"He said his grandma told him the story about Margaret and Simon that's in the book you gave me and that she believed it was some sort of prophecy. She said there was going to be a girl born with the name Margaret O'Neill who'd change the world."

He was silent again.

"Simon, what's going on? This is all a little spooky."

"I think you're underestimating the frequency of coincidence, Maggie. Don't worry about it." But his voice seemed strained. And I didn't like hearing that word again—coincidence.

"Three more days until you're home," he reminded me firmly.

"Three more days," I confirmed.

"I can't wait to see you."

"I miss you."

"Miss you too. Sleep well."

ഇ൪ര

When we pulled into the driveway after our trip to St. Louis, I saw Simon sitting on our porch swing, a bunch of flowers in his hand.

"Oh man," Brandon groaned. "I was just starting to like the guy and he has to go and do something sappy."

"Well, I think it's sweet," my mom said. "But it's freezing out. He should've waited in his car."

I flung open the car door before my dad had even come to a complete stop and propelled myself toward Simon, throwing my arms around him. He kissed the top of my head and squeezed me to him tightly. I felt my body melt into his as we embraced.

"Get a room," Brandon grumbled as he walked by with a suitcase.

Simon chuckled and let his arms fall away from me. "These are for you," he said, handing me the flowers. "Welcome home." He kissed me briefly before going to help my dad with the luggage. I followed him into the house and went to the kitchen to get a vase for the flowers. When I walked into the living room, he was already settled on the sofa, playing a video game with Brandon. I sat down next to him and took his hand in mine when it was Brandon's turn to play the game. It was good to be home.

"Can you stay for dinner, Simon?" my dad asked, coming into the living room. "We're just ordering pizza, but you're welcome to stay."

"Thank you, yes," Simon said.

My dad soon took over playing the video game with Brandon, and I took their distraction as a good time to invite Simon up to my room so we could spend some time alone. As soon as my door was closed, I went to Simon and pushed him playfully backwards until the backs of his knees hit the bed. He fell back and pulled me with him, and I found his lips with my own. He responded to my kisses, moving his lips against mine, then up my jaw line and to my neck, his hand resting gently at the back of my head. I noticed that I was breathing rapidly, and Simon was breathing just as fast. I could feel his heart pounding through his shirt, and his hands started moving against me with eagerness. With his arms wrapped tight around me, and his lips moving gently along my jaw, he rolled me over onto my back and moved on top of me.

"I'm glad you're home," he whispered, his lips to

my ear. He moved his mouth back to mine and started kissing me again, his lips parting my own. I could feel the warm feeling start just under the skin of my arms and spreading throughout my body, and I found myself wanting to touch more of him. I pulled his shirt up slightly and moved my hands across his bare back. He responded by moving his own hand under my shirt and rubbing my side, gently at first, but then his touch became more intense. I moved one of my legs to wrap around his just as there was a knock on the door.

"If you're undressed, put your clothes back on." It was Brandon. "I'm opening the door in five seconds."

Simon shook his head and smiled before he rolled off me and we both sat up.

"Pizza's here," Brandon said, opening the door wide. "Uh, Maggie, your hair's all messed up. And Simon, your shirt's buttoned crooked. You might want to straighten that out before you come downstairs."

Simon looked down hastily at the buttons on his shirt, all of which were lined up perfectly. With a very ornery smile, Brandon said, "Made you look," before walking out of the room and shutting the door behind him.

Simon took a deep breath and kissed me lightly. "That was fun," he said in a strained voice.

"Good thing we were interrupted by a knock on the door?" I'd meant to say it as a statement, but it came out as a question.

"Good thing?" Simon agreed, also in the form of a question.

I nodded. "I hope to do more of that in the near future." I walked into my bathroom to brush my hair.

ഈ

"If the weather's at all questionable, pull over and stay overnight in a hotel," my dad cautioned Simon. "Maggie has a credit card for emergencies that you can use. And there's plenty on there for *two* rooms."

"Yes, sir," Simon responded.

"And remember that 4-wheel-drive doesn't make you impervious to the ice. You can still slide."

"Yes, sir," Simon said again, never losing a respectable level of politeness. "I checked the weather report before I came over. It looks like we'll have sunny skies and dry roads from here to Breckenridge."

"Do you keep any sort of emergency kit in your car?" My dad continued as if he hadn't heard Simon. "The weather in the mountains can be really unpredictable."

"Yes, sir. It's right here if you'd like to take a look. I have blankets, water, flares, jumper cables, a first aid kit, energy bars—" he took the lid off of the plastic box in the back of his SUV and let my dad rummage inside to inspect it for himself.

"Call us when you get there," my mom told me while my dad inspected Simon's emergency kit.

"I will, Mom," I told her. "And please help Dad calm down. It's just Breckenridge, and it's just three days."

"It's more than that," she said with a smile, and I knew she was right.

ഈ

As Simon had told my dad, I-70 was completely dry and the sun was shining brightly. Once we were out of the traffic of the city, Simon took my hand in his and smiled.

"Don't tell your dad that I took one of my hands off the wheel," he said, never taking his eyes from the road. "I'm sure he'd have something to say about the fact that they didn't stay in the ten and two position for the entire trip."

I chuckled and gave his hand a little squeeze.

"I don't know why he gets all preachy like that. You're like the most responsible guy in our entire school. He should be grateful I'm dating you and not Luke."

"I think he sees me as a bigger threat than Luke."

"What do you mean?"

He was quiet for a moment as we passed the Evergreen exit.

"You play tennis, right?"

I nodded.

"Do you ever play doubles?"

"Sometimes. With Lexie."

"Well, suppose Lexie came to you and said she might want to get a new doubles partner."

"I don't think that's likely."

He smiled again. "No, me either, but just hear me out." He took his hand from mine while he turned down the radio, and promptly put it back, twisting his fingers around mine again. "So Lexie wants a new partner and she's holding tryouts."

"Okay," I said, wondering where he was going with this scenario.

"And two people show up. One of them is really

awful. You can see how frustrated Lexie is while they're playing. But the other is really good. Lexie looks happy because the other person is doing everything Lexie wants them to do. Not that they're trying to do what Lexie wants. It just comes naturally to them. Which one do you see as a bigger threat?"

"The really good one," I said without thinking.

"Why?"

"Because if her only choice is the really awful one, she'd probably just stay with me."

"Exactly."

"So you think my dad is more upset about me dating you because he thinks you'll take me away from him?"

"Yes."

I thought about that for a minute and could see his point. Sure, Simon was a million times more responsible than Luke and should have been every parent's dream boyfriend, but I was happier with Simon and I didn't have any plans to break up with him. I wasn't wondering if there was anything better, like I had with Luke, because with Simon, I couldn't imagine that anyone could be more perfect.

"You're pretty wise for a seventeen year old kid."

He blushed—a deep red that started on his cheeks and spread to his forehead and down to his neck.

"But it's sort of ridiculous. I'm never going to leave my dad. I mean, I'll go to college and live on my own and stuff, but he'll always be my dad."

"But it'll be different."

"How do you mean?"

"I think you're dad is worried that I'm going to take away your childhood. With Luke, I don't think he could see it ever getting serious enough between you two to be a threat."

"But he thinks things could be serious with you and me?"

"I think so, yes."

"Do *you* think things could get that serious between us?"

"Yes."

That one word caused goose bumps to spread across both of my arms and a shiver went up my spine. Simon thought things could get serious with us and that was absolutely wonderful.

"Are you cold?" he asked when he noticed me shiver. He moved his hand away from mine again and started to turn up the heat.

"No, I'm not cold," I said, unable to stop the stupid grin on my face. "I'm perfect, actually."

He smiled and glanced in my direction.

"Yes, you are."

સ૭ભ

Lexie and Max were at the condo when we got there. They made the trip up with Max's family the day after Christmas and had spent the morning skiing, but said they wanted to get back to the condo so they could wait for us.

"My parents and brother and sister are still skiing, but they'll be back in a couple of hours. There's a hot tub out by the pool if you guys want to get your suits on, or we can go into town and walk around. Whatever you want to do."

We decided to hang out in the hot tub until Max's

family got back from the slopes. It was cold outside, but the water in the hot tub created a steam that kept our faces warm, even though they were exposed to the cold air. Simon held my hand under the water as we sat next to each other, his fingers occasionally brushing against the exposed skin on my thigh.

"You're not too cold?" he asked me after we had been in the hot tub for about twenty minutes.

"You're always worried that I'm cold," I teased. "If *you're* not cold, then I'm probably not either. Relax." I pulled his hand to rest on my thigh and saw the breath catch in his chest when I did. There was something about sitting in the hot tub with Simon that seemed forbidden. Max and Lexie were sitting together across from us, but the steam and bubbles prevented anyone from being able to see anything below the surface of the water. That, combined with the near-nakedness that was courtesy of our swimsuits, made sitting next to Simon a visceral experience. The urge to pull him toward me and kiss every inch of his body was intense and it was almost a relief when Max's dad came out to tell us it was time to get changed for dinner.

∞)(∠

The following day was New Year's Eve and Max, Lexie, Simon and I spent the day skiing at Breckenridge. I was surprised at how well Simon could ski considering Ireland wasn't exactly known for their ski resorts. He said he had been on a few skiing vacations with Finn and Erin and was able to keep up with the rest of us without any trouble. He only wiped out once. We had gone over a succession of three small jumps that were very close together and on the third jump Simon lost his balance and tumbled head-over-heels for several yards.

"You had quite a yard sale," Max teased him as he brought Simon's poles to him.

"Yard sale?" Simon asked, confused.

"A big wipe out. You know – because your skis and poles and gloves and hat were spread across the slope like you were getting ready to sell them in a yard sale."

Simon nodded in understanding, then held out his hand to Max so that Max could help him up. In one very quick motion, Simon yanked on Max's arm and caused him to tumble to the ground beside him. "I'm thinking I'll sell *your* hat in my yard sale, as well," Simon teased as he pulled Max's hat from his head and threw it across the slopes. When the two boys finished laughing at each other's jokes, we picked up their gear and continued with our skiing.

Later that evening, we met Max's parents and Jessie and Abbey (his brother and sister) for dinner before heading to Keystone to go night tubing. When the sun went down, the temperature dropped significantly, but the resort had set up portable heaters and there were several large, stone fire pits at the bottom of the slopes where we could warm up after each run. It was a clear night and the stars twinkled brightly above us as we raced down the hills on our tubes. On some runs, all eight of us would link up and go down in one mass. Some runs we would race each other to the bottom, throwing any sense of fair play out the window in our pursuit to be the first to cross our predetermined finish line. On other runs, I would sit between Simon's legs, his arms wrapped around me, and the two of us would go down the hill together. Those were my favorite.

Just before midnight, the eight of us gathered around one of the stone fire pits with hot chocolate and waited to count down to the New Year. At midnight, Simon pulled me to him and kissed me. He tasted like hot chocolate and marshmallows and that just made his kiss even sweeter than it normally was.

"Happy New Year," he whispered as he rested his forehead against mine.

"Happy New Year," I told him, and I made a wish as we stood there together that the end of my year would be as wonderful as the beginning.

Chapter Nine

We were all exhausted New Year's Day. We had skied for seven hours before tubing for four hours and when we got back to the cabin, it was almost two in the morning. We spent a good portion of the day in the hot tub and later in the evening Simon, Lexie, Max and I decided to go into town and walk around. The Christmas decorations were still up, making the whole town look like a winter wonderland. Lights were draped across the main street and big bows of evergreen were wrapped around the street lamps. It started to snow as we were walking and that made the whole scene even more magical.

We were sitting outside drinking hot chocolate on an outdoor patio when I noticed Simon and Max looking at each other in a strange way. It was almost as if they were trying to communicate without actually saying anything and they both looked very anxious.

"What's wrong?" I asked Simon.

Simon looked at me with an odd expression and hesitated. "Let's head back to the condo."

"We just got here," I said, a little stunned that he would want to leave.

"I think we should go," Max said as he stood up.

"Why?" Lexie asked, annoyed. Lexie didn't like it when she didn't understand something, and I was pretty certain she was just as clueless as I was as to why Max and Simon had started behaving like a couple of fugitives confronting a group of burly FBI agents.

"I have a headache." Simon doubled over in pain as he said it, gripping his head and grimacing. Max shot him an odd look, like he was deeply impressed with what Simon had said, and at the same time incredulous and horrified.

We all stood up and started to walk toward the condo. Simon wrapped his arm protectively around my waist and guided me through the crowded sidewalk. He seemed nervous and jumpy, but the pain he had experienced had apparently abated. Periodically, he and Max exchanged meaningful looks, which in turn caused Lexie and me to exchange meaningful looks. As we continued to walk, I realized both Simon and Max were walking very close to me, Lexie a few steps behind us.

"Don't worry about me," she said sarcastically. "I'm good. Not that anyone's asking."

Max fell back to put his arm around her, kissing her on the cheek and mumbling an apology, then pulled her with him so he could walk next to me once again. Neither he nor Simon left my side until we walked through the front door of the condo.

∞

I listened to the voices coming from downstairs while Lexie slept in the bed beside me. It was late—at least three in the morning—so it surprised me to hear anyone up. I pulled a warm cardigan on over my pajamas and walked downstairs to find Simon, Max and Max's parents all sitting in the living room having a very serious conversation. When Simon saw me enter the room, he became silent and stood up quickly.

"Did we wake you?" he asked quietly, coming over to stand in front of me.

I nodded.

"I'm sorry. I'll walk you back upstairs."

"Actually, can I talk to you first?"

He hesitated before nodding. "We can go to my room. I think Max is going to stay down here for a while."

We walked up the stairs and headed in the direction of the room Simon was sharing with Max. Both of the beds were very neatly made and it was obvious that neither of them had been to bed at all that night.

"What's going on?" I asked when he had closed the door behind us.

"We lost track of time. I didn't realize it was so late," he told me.

"Not just now, but in town, too. You said you had a headache, and it really seemed like you were in pain, but by the time we got back here you were fine. And you and Max are acting really weird and you keep giving each other funny looks."

He sat down on one of the beds, leaning over with his elbows resting on his thighs, his hands clasped in front of him. He looked down at his hands for a few minutes, then looked back at me. "You don't miss a thing, do you?" he said with both pride and annoyance. He took a deep breath. "I have a condition that causes me to get headaches at certain times."

"You mean like migraines?"

"Something like that."

"Have you seen a doctor? Maybe it's something serious."

"It's not."

"Simon—" I started to protest, but he interrupted me.

"Maggie, I promise it's nothing serious. I just need to avoid the cause of them, that's all."

"It looked pretty serious, Simon. You looked like you were in a lot of pain, and then it just went away."

"I'm fine."

"If it happens again will you go see a doctor?"

"Yes," he promised, standing up and wrapping his arms around me. "You know," he said, kissing my forehead, "We're alone."

I looked up at him and he moved his lips to mine, kissing me intently. I moved my hands to his chest, then slid them around his neck, pulling him closer.

Someone knocked on the door and Simon pulled away, shaking his head and smiling. "There's always a knock."

I chuckled as he reached over to open the door. Max stood in the hallway looking uncomfortable.

"Mom says we should all go to bed," he said.

"Your OWN beds," she said as she walked by, wearing a teasing smile. She stopped to kiss Max, and I followed her out into the hallway and down to my room with Lexie where she still slept, oblivious to my late night wanderings.

෯ଓ

My life chugged along as usual after we got back from our trip to Breckenridge, but there was some background noise in my brain that kept reminding me that things weren't quite right. I made a list of all of the weird things that had happened since the start of my junior year—Creepy Dude at the football game, the book Simon had given me for my birthday, the way Simon and Max were acting in Breckenridge—and when I looked at it all together, all in one place, I got a little freaked out. I decided I had to talk with Simon about it. I had to figure out a way to make it all seem perfectly normal so I could go back to being happy and carefree.

I sat with Simon in the four-story atrium at the Museum of Nature and Science, waiting for Lexie and Max to join us for a movie in the IMAX Theater. We were each sitting in one of the black armchairs overlooking City Park, and I was struck by how beautiful the view was. Snow bunched in small piles, but the sun was shining brightly, and the view of the Denver skyline with the Rocky Mountains in the background was spectacular.

"A lot of weird stuff's been happening," I said. There was so much information swirling around in my head that seemed unrelated, but there was one factor connecting everything. Simon.

He sat back in his seat, keeping one of his hands entwined with mine. "Do you ever think about the world and wonder what we don't know?" he asked reflectively, staring out the window. "It's just massive, and sometimes I wonder about the secrets it still holds." He turned his head slightly to look at me. "The beliefs people have had, even over the past few hundred years, have changed dramatically. Do you think that someone two hundred years ago could have possibly comprehended the idea of a television? Or computers? What's out there that *we* can't conceive?" He squeezed my hand lightly. "You're right. There are some things I need to explain to you, and I *will* tell you what I can't tell you today. Soon. Much sooner than I probably want to."

Before I could ask him to elaborate, Lexie and Max entered the atrium and I sighed heavily as I stood up, frustrated that my attempt to talk with Simon had been aborted.

ഇന്ദ

Simon spent the week after our visit to the planetarium in a foul mood. He was quiet and irritable, and we spent little time together beyond our one common class and the ride to and from school. He said he needed to talk with Finn and Erin most days when I suggested we do something or that he hang out at my house for a while after school. His smiles had become forced and his kisses perfunctory.

"Simon, do you want to break up with me?" I finally asked after several days of this behavior. It was Friday afternoon in late January, and we were sitting outside my house in his car after school. He'd been staring distractedly out the front window.

He snapped his head quickly to look at me. "What? No. That's the farthest thing from my mind. Why would you ask that?"

"You just aren't yourself lately, and we rarely see each other beyond school, and when you kiss me—it's not the same. I just wondered if that's why. It's okay if you do want to break up with me. I understand. I don't want you to be with me if you don't want to be."

Please don't want to break up with me!

The defeated look in his eyes made my heart melt. "I don't want to break up with you, Maggie, but I do need to tell you something that may make *you* want to break up with *me*." My heart did a few summersaults before it slid down my ribs to plop sluggishly into my stomach.

He took a deep breath and looked out the front window again, his forehead crinkling with worry. "I need to explain everything to you. I really wish I could put it off forever, but that's not possible." His expression was grim. "I think it would be better to go to my house, though. I'd prefer to tell you there."

My heart was still sloshing around in my stomach, twisting itself into a heavy, painful knot. I was certain Simon was taking me to his house to break up with me, even though he said he didn't want to. Nothing else made sense, and the thought of it caused such a penetrating pain.

"Have a seat," he suggested as we walked into his living room. I sat on the sofa, and Simon took a seat across the room in one of the armchairs. I didn't like the distance he'd put between us. It felt like a bad sign.

"I would love to never explain any of this to you, but I find I really have no choice at this point." His face was dark and troubled.

"Okay," I said, trying to steady myself.

He hesitated and took a deep breath and stared at me, the furrow in his forehead deepening. "Maggie," he said, his voice and hands shaking, "I'm a faery."

Chapter Ten

I took a moment to process what he had just said. What did that mean? A faery? Like Tinker Bell? Then it hit me hard. He was trying to tell me he was gay. Calling a gay person a faery seemed derogatory, but maybe that's the word they preferred in Ireland. *Great!* I thought. *He's gay. Of course he's gay. I like him too much for him not to be gay.* So, he *was* breaking up with me after all. He'd figured out he was gay and was breaking up with me so he could start dating boys. Would he want to start being friends with me? Would he want to help me with my hair and my clothes? Was that just a stereotype? Maybe not all gay boys liked that sort of thing.

I took a few deep breaths. Yes, it was heartbreaking to hear the news. I really liked Simon and wasn't sure how I'd be able to manage going back to being his friend without my heart breaking into a million pieces, but first and foremost, Simon was a friend of mine and I needed to be supportive of his choices. I'd watched enough *True Life* on MTV to know my reaction to his decision to "come out" to me was very important, so I chose my words carefully.

"Okay," I said slowly. "Okay. I'll support you no

matter what, Simon. It doesn't matter. I'll do whatever you want me to do. I think there's a gay and lesbian organization at school. If you want me to go with you, I will."

He looked at me for a long moment with complete confusion, but then I saw understanding spread across his face. He stood up quickly. "I'm not gay, Maggie," he said quietly before he started to pace.

"I don't understand."

"I'm a faery. As in an *Irish* faery."

His confusion must have been contagious because I was becoming just as confused as he looked. "Do they call it something different in Ireland? I'm sorry. I didn't know. I didn't mean to offend you." I was fighting off tears at this point, upset that I was losing my boyfriend and upset that I was upsetting him.

"Maggie." He looked at me, his eyes pleading. He stopped pacing and came and sat beside me. "I don't like men—not like that. I am sexually attracted to women—to *you*. I'm not gay. I'm a faery."

"What does that mean?" I asked, feeling as if we were having two entirely different conversations.

He stood up again, obviously agitated. "It means, among other things, that I have certain abilities that other people don't have." He took a few more deep breaths. "Maggie, I'm going to show you something that you're going to find shocking. Something you believe is an impossibility."

I didn't say anything. I just looked at him and waited, and as I looked into his eyes, he vanished. Really. One second he was there, then he wasn't, and after about two beats, he was back.

"Wha—" I couldn't even finish the word that was

the beginning of my question. This was absolutely insane. People couldn't make themselves invisible. "Wha—" I tried again, but still couldn't get the words out.

"Maggie." He walked back to me and took my hand, his eyes and voice pleading. "I can make myself invisible at will—because I'm a faery." He vanished again, but I could still feel his hand on mine. He reappeared, a look of concern on his face. I stared at him, my eyes wide, my mouth hanging open, but too dazed to speak.

"There's more," he said. He hesitated, but seemed to feel a need to move forward with the demonstration. "Watch the TV remote on the table."

I moved my gaze to the spot on the small table across the room and watched as the remote lifted up and moved quickly through the air to his waiting hand about fifteen feet from where it had started.

"There are no strings, Maggie. No tricks. I can move anything you tell me to in the same way." I shook my head vigorously and noticed that my whole body had started to shake. This. Wasn't. Normal. This went against the laws of nature, and I was very afraid.

"It *is* a trick. It has to be a trick. It's not funny, Simon. You're freaking me out."

He shook his head solemnly. "No trick." As if determined to get me to believe in this sick game he was playing, he raised his left hand in front of him and I watched as small flames flickered on his fingertips. "Do you want to see more? I can show you more, but I need you to believe me."

I stood quickly and moved further away from him. "Stop it, Simon!" I yelled. I could feel the tears stinging my eyes and I wondered why he was so determined to make me believe in something so ridiculous.

He crossed the room and took my hand in his. I pulled it away. I didn't know why I didn't want him to touch me. He was Simon—that hadn't changed—but he wasn't the Simon I thought I knew.

"I can fly, too, Maggie. Do you want me to show you? Will that make you believe?"

"Stop it, Simon!"

"I can make it rain from this ceiling. I can put a person in so much pain that they'd want to die—just with a flick of my finger. I can make every light in every house on this block extinguish without moving from this spot."

"Stop it, Simon! Stop it!"

Waves of trembling shook my body. Simon stood in front of me, unable to soothe me.

"I want to go home," I said, my voice now a whisper.

He nodded, his eyes glistening, and we walked to his car.

ഔൠ

"Faeries aren't real," I mumbled softly as we drove to my house. Simon looked at me sympathetically, but said nothing. "Am I going insane, Simon?"

"No," he said with tenderness. "You're not going insane. Everything you saw tonight—everything I told you—is real."

I think I'd prefer insanity.

He walked me to the front door and I noticed that

all of the lights were off in the house. I'd forgotten that my parents had planned to take Brandon to his basketball game and then out to dinner, but I suddenly saw it as an opportunity.

"Come inside," I told Simon. "Do all that stuff here."

"They're not tricks, Maggie. I can do that stuff anywhere."

"Prove it."

I unlocked the door and pulled him inside and up to my room.

"Okay," I said once we were inside. "Show me."

He rolled his eyes and disappeared. A moment later, he was back.

Okay, so it hadn't gone as I'd planned. I'd thought he had somehow rigged his house to make it look like he could do those things, but if he could still make himself invisible in my room, then that meant—no! No! I couldn't believe it. I *wouldn't* believe it.

"Take your clothes off," I said, another idea coming to me.

His eyes widened in shock.

"It's not what you think," I explained. "I just want to make sure you haven't done something to your clothes that makes it look like you're invisible. I'll go and get some of my dad's stuff for you to put on."

Simon started to unbutton his shirt and I hesitated, forgetting my plan and focusing on the idea of seeing Simon shirtless. I gave my head a shake, then left to get some of my dad's clothes.

"Here," I told Simon as I handed him a pair of gym shorts and a t-shirt through the small opening in the doorway. While seeing Simon naked on any other day would have been appealing, I knew I had to keep my head clear.

A few moments later, he opened the door and handed me his shirt, jeans, socks and shoes. "Do you want to inspect them?" he asked.

I shook my head, but left his things in the hallway before I went back in my room.

"Okay, so—"

He nodded and disappeared again.

"How are you doing it?" I demanded, unable to keep the anger out of my voice.

"I was born able to do this—because I'm a faery."

"Stop saying that. It's just a trick."

"No trick."

He held out his hands and I watched as a pillow from my bed and a shirt that I had left crumpled on the floor flew across the room toward Simon. He dropped them both immediately and held up both hands, all ten fingers on fire. He extinguished them with a flourish before raising his left hand above the open palm of his right. Little droplets of precipitation flowed from one hand to another, and when he flourished his hands again, I watched as the water turned to ice, then to mist, then to little blue flowers that floated to the floor of my room.

"I can do this anywhere you'd like," he said. "I can take off all of my clothes so you can make sure I don't have any wires or devices that might make it look like something it's not. I'm a faery, Maggie, and I need you to believe me."

"Why? Why is it so important? Why are you telling me this?"

"Because you're in danger."

"What kind of danger?"

"Remember when your grandfather told you about the other Margaret O'Neill—your great-great-grandmother?"

I nodded my head.

"The stories she used to tell your grandfather were true. There *is* a prophecy about a girl born with the name Margaret O'Neill who changes the course of the world. There are faeries that don't want the world to change. They want to keep doing things that will destroy humanity and they think that if they get rid of the Margaret O'Neill mentioned in the prophecy, they'll gain power and take over the world."

"They think I'm the Margaret O'Neill from the prophecy? And they want to get rid of me? Kill me?"

"Yes," he said, answering my question quietly.

"Do *you* think I'm the Margaret O'Neill from the prophecy?"

"Yes," he said, quieter still.

"And they're going to try to kill me?" I asked, too incredulous to believe what he was saying.

"Yes." Barely a whisper.

"Does this have anything to do with your headache when we were in Breckenridge? And the guy at the football game?" I asked, the insignificant pieces of information forming a line and marching together toward the front of my brain.

"Yes. The guy at the football game wasn't a faery, but there were two faeries in the tunnel, and I saw some faeries in Breckenridge that I thought might want to hurt you. I wasn't sure what their intentions were and I didn't want to take any chances."

"There are *more?*" I was trying very hard to get the

shaking under control, but the more he told me, the more I shook.

"Yes."

"How many more?"

"Thousands."

Well that's fantastic!

"Maggie," he said softly, tentatively taking my hands in his. "I can't help who I am. I was born this way and I'd love to tell you that I wish I *hadn't* been born this way—that I'd been born normal just like you. But the thing is, if I were normal, I wouldn't have lived long enough to meet you, and that, to me, would be the biggest tragedy imaginable."

My head snapped up and I looked at his face. "How old are you?" I demanded.

He took a deep breath and seemed to be resigning himself to the inevitability of having to answer my question. "I'm two-hundred-and-eight."

"Years?" I asked, hoping that maybe I was mistaken and he measured his life in smaller increments.

"Yes, years," he said wryly.

"What? So you're immortal?" I stood up to pace the room.

"I'm not immortal. I just age a lot slower than normal people do." The way he kept saying "normal" was a constant reminder of the rapidly widening divide between us.

"Are there other things you can do?"

"All faeries can fly, and we can talk to each other without speaking. We can make ourselves invisible, although it takes a tremendous amount of concentration to stay invisible for longer than a few minutes. Hot and cold don't bother us like it does other people and we don't have to eat or drink or sleep as often. I, specifically, can find lost objects—and people—and I can move objects without touching them."

My boyfriend could fly and he could talk to people telepathically. *Well that's just great!*

I thought back to all of the strange things that had happened since I'd known Simon, and everything started to make sense. Then I thought about all of the things that should have seemed strange, but hadn't, and I felt foolish. Evidently, I was very good at burying my head in the sand.

"Why didn't you tell me? Why did you lie to me all this time?" My voice was rising in anger and fear.

"The only time I've ever lied to you, Maggie, was when we were in Breckenridge," he said calmly and quietly. "And yes, I should have told you sooner. I wish now that I had told you sooner. But when would have been a good time? The first day we met? The first day we were alone? The first time I kissed you?"

I couldn't process what he was telling me. Was I going crazy or was he? Faeries weren't real. Invisibility was not possible. Summoning objects was not possible.

"Please leave," I said, needing to put some distance between me and this crazy story Simon was telling me.

He nodded his head slowly before picking up his clothes in the hallway and walking down the stairs.

Chapter Eleven

I sat on my bed and tried to think of some way to calm myself. Unless I wanted a one-way ticket to the loony bin, there was nobody I could talk to about this—even I didn't believe it.

At that point, I saw three possibilities. First, I was insane, and none of this was really happening. Second, Simon was lying to me. Maybe it was just an elaborate prank and Simon would call, laughing, at any moment. I held out hope for that possibility, but it didn't seem likely. Third, everything Simon was telling me was true. That was the option I liked the least.

I paced back and forth in my room for hours, unable to stop my brain from thinking about what I'd seen Simon do. I went downstairs and tried to eat dinner, but the difficulty I had swallowing made me give up on that idea. I went back to my room and checked Facebook and my email, trying to go back to the normalcy I'd taken for granted. I tried to sleep. I paced some more. I rechecked my email. I tried again to sleep. At three-thirty, I got up once again and started pacing the floor. I thought about calling Lexie, reasoning that just hearing another human voice might calm me down, but three-thirty was way too late—or too early. I wanted to call Simon but decided against it. I wasn't ready to talk to him. As a compromise with myself, I sent him a text.

R U asleep? I typed before hitting the "Send" button.

Within a few short seconds, my phone vibrated. **No.**

I hadn't thought about what to say after that and while I sat on my bed trying to figure out what to type, my phone chimed again. **Are you ok?**

No, I typed.

Do you want me to come over?

Yes, I thought. **No,** I typed.

Can I call you?

No.

Several minutes passed before I got another text from him. **I don't know how to help you, Maggie. Please tell me what to do.**

I don't know what will help. I'm afraid.

I know. I'm sorry.

I didn't respond to his last text. I turned the phone off and crawled back into bed, curling into a ball of protection against everything Simon had told me. Eventually, I drifted off to sleep.

I bolted into a sitting position, my breathing still rapid from the nightmare I'd woken from. Simon was a monster and was trying to kill me (*my subconscious wasn't being very subtle that night*), when the old woman made an appearance.

"Ask your grandfather," she said soothingly. It was the first time I'd ever heard her speak. The shock of her voice, rather than the nightmare itself, jolted me awake.

I could see the faint light outside through my window and knew it was close to dawn. I looked at the clock near my bed. Six o'clock. I'd only slept for a couple of hours. The weight of everything Simon had told me pressed me down into a pit of despair. Was he a monster? Was he evil? Either he could do some pretty incredible things that I didn't want to think about, or he was just plain mean, trying to make me believe something that he knew was upsetting me. I needed more information—impartial information.

I grabbed my computer and composed an email to my grandfather. I lied and told him I was working on a presentation about folklore and that I wanted more information about Grandma Margaret to use as part of the presentation. I pressed "Send," but didn't know how long it would take to get a response. It seemed like my grandparents didn't check their email very often.

I wanted to keep my mind occupied while I waited to hear back from him, so I decided to do some research. I typed "Irish faeries" into the Google search bar and hit the "return" button on my keyboard. The web pages I visited seemed to depict faeries as running the gamut from ornery to downright wicked. I found it disturbing that most of the web sites talked about faeries in a clinical sense, as if they were real. Were there people who actually believed in faeries and the magic they could do? According to one web site I found, they could fly, shift their form, cast spells, and inflict disease. I also read about ways to repel faeries. All of the websites said they had an aversion to iron and stale urine. *Well, doesn't everyone have an aversion to urine—stale or not?*

Without consciously thinking about it, I logged on to Facebook and did a search for "Margaret O'Neill." There were pages and pages of Margaret O'Neills from all over the world. There were pictures of young girls, and older women, happy and goofy, with friends and by themselves. I wondered if Simon had ever considered that one of *them* had been the Margaret O'Neill in the prophecy. Had he met any of them? Checked them out? Why did he think it was me, and not one of them?

I tried to type in another search topic but realized my hands were shaking and decided it was best not to overload myself with information. I closed my computer before curling back into a ball underneath the thick comforter I'd pulled from my closet. I didn't want to think about what all of this meant. I didn't want to think of Simon as anything but the perfect human I thought he was. I didn't want to think about losing him. I didn't want to think about the prophecy he said I was a part of and the faeries that wanted to hurt me. I didn't want to think about all of the things I thought I knew, but was now certain I didn't. I felt so small and helpless. Home used to be a place of safety for me. I'd always believed that there was nothing my parents couldn't protect me from. I think they believed that, too. Now I understood how vulnerable I'd been all along.

My mom poked her head into my room at some point in the middle of the day. "Simon's on the land line. He said your cell's turned off."

"Can you tell him I'll call him later? I don't feel well."

"What's wrong?" she asked, starting to walk toward

my bed.

"Cramps," I lied. I knew it was the only thing that would make her go away and not fuss over me. It was the only cause of discomfort I could have that didn't require further investigation.

"Do you want me to tell him you'll call him later?"

"Yes, please." I pulled the comforter back over my head and sank deeper into my depression.

&)(&

My mom came into my room later in the day with a tray of food.

"How're you feeling?"

"The same."

"Hungry?"

"No."

"Simon called again."

"I'll send him a text and let him know I'm okay," I promised.

After she left, I turned on my phone and saw that I had twelve messages from Simon, each one expressing his concern and regret.

I'm ok, I typed into my phone. I pressed "send" and powered it off again.

It was starting to get dark by the time I decided to get out of bed. I took a shower and got dressed before going downstairs where my parents and Brandon were clearing the table from dinner.

"Do you want some spaghetti?" my mom asked when she saw me.

I nodded, feeling the hunger and realizing I hadn't eaten more than a few bites since lunch the previous day. My mom made me a plate with spaghetti and garlic bread and put salad in a small bowl. I sat at the counter in our kitchen and ate, then headed back to my room and grabbed my computer.

I had emails from Lexie, Simon and Katie Bell, but I clicked on the only one that mattered to me at that moment. My grandfather had returned my email.

Maggie Girl! So good to hear from you. In response to the question you didn't ask, but the one I know was foremost in your mind when you composed your email, your grandma and I are both doing well and we miss having you guys around.

In response to the question you did send in your email...

Grandma Margaret was born in Ireland in 1888. She and my grandfather married when she was 17 and moved to the states in 1907. They had 5 children, all of them born in the states. She held onto the old ways of Ireland, though, long after she'd moved here. She was very superstitious about faeries and told us stories about how they could cause disease and do horrible things to people.

She also talked about a prophecy that had to do with a girl named Margaret O'Neill. I think I told you about that when you were here. She said this girl would change the course of history. We used to tease her and tell her to get busy saving the world, but she told us she was the wrong Margaret.

She was a great storyteller. When I was a child,

we would sit and listen to her stories for hours. Sometimes she scared the bejesus out of me with those stories. I'd have nightmares for weeks!

She died in 1979 in her sleep. Never seemed to be sick a day in her life. She was a hardy woman.

Anyway, I'll send more if I think of anything that might help. I also put a few pictures in the mail for you. I thought they might be good for your presentation.

I love you, sweet girl.

Grandpa.

It really wasn't much more than he'd told me over Christmas, but I saw it differently when I looked at it through the lens of what Simon had told me.

ഇൻൽ

By Sunday, I'd convinced myself that the entire situation was absolutely ridiculous and that Simon was just playing a sick game with me. Unfortunately, that didn't make me feel any better because that meant my boyfriend was a really huge ass. He'd seen how upset I was, but he still kept up the game. Why was he doing it? What did he stand to gain?

"So, you want to tell me what's really going on?" my mom asked when she came to check on me later in the day.

All the emotions I'd been trying to hold back bubbled to the surface, and I couldn't stop the tears from falling. My mom lay down next to me on the bed and rubbed my hair the way she had when I was a little girl.

"Did you and Simon have a fight?" she asked after a long silence.

I nodded. It wasn't the complete truth, but it was the closest I could come to the truth without making her really angry with Simon.

"Do you want to tell me about it?"

"No," I whispered.

"Do you want me to stay with you?"

"No," I whispered again.

ഏരോ

By Wednesday afternoon, I was exhausted from avoiding Simon and Lexie and my parents and anyone else who wanted to talk to me about my feelings. I grabbed my bag from the back of Simon's car after school and walked into the house. Simon got out of the car and tried to walk me to the door, but I was already inside before he'd reached the porch steps. He hadn't brought up any of the stuff he'd done, and I hadn't yet decided how to talk to him about it. He'd hurt me and I worried I wouldn't be able to go back to the way things were before. Simon had seen how upset I was and he hadn't stopped and that meant he wasn't the person I thought he was.

"Is that you, Maggie?" my dad called from the kitchen.

"Yes, Dad."

"There's a letter for you on the front table. It's from Grandpa."

I looked on the table near the front door and saw the small white envelope. I picked it up and walked sluggishly to my room before opening it.

"Hope this helps, Maggie Girl. Love you, Grandpa."

Folded inside his note were three pictures. The first was a picture of a young woman with her hair in a loose bun and wearing a long black skirt and a white shirt. She was leaning against a stone wall and the inscription on the back of the photo said, "Margaret O'Neill, Co. Donegal, Ireland, 1906." My great-great-grandmother.

I laid the picture on my desk and looked at the next photo. It showed three people—the same woman who was in the first picture with a man and a young boy. My hands started to shake when I looked at the picture more closely. The boy in the picture appeared to be about ten years old and he looked a lot like Simon. The man in the picture was a dead ringer for Finn. I turned the picture over. "Margaret O'Neill, Simon Brady, Finn Brady, Co. Donegal, Ireland, 1906." I placed the picture on my desk with the other one. I couldn't think about it. I didn't want to understand it. I didn't want to know.

I reluctantly looked at the third picture of an older man and an older woman. The picture caused painful knots to form in my chest, but it took me a moment to figure out why. The woman in the picture was the woman in my dreams—the woman who had been a figment of my imagination for as long as I could remember. I flipped the picture over to read the inscription, touching it like it was poison. "Sean and Margaret O'Neill, 1951." The woman in my dreams was my great-great-grandmother.

My hands were shaking uncontrollably. I grabbed my cellphone from my bag and called Simon, very thankful in that moment that I had him on speed dial and only had to press one button with my trembling fingers.

"Maggie," he breathed my name with relief.

I tried to talk to him, but violent sobs choked at my throat.

"Maggie, what's wrong?" he asked, alarmed.

I worked really hard to calm myself enough to talk to him, but couldn't manage it.

"I'm coming over," he said before hanging up.

I put my phone back in my bag, grabbed the pictures from my desk and walked outside to wait for Simon.

"What happened?" he asked when I was in the car. I shoved the pictures at him in lieu of an explanation. He looked through each one before turning to me. "I'm so sorry, Maggie." He reached over to hug me.

I pushed him away.

"What does this mean, Simon?" I asked angrily through the tears. "You knew my great-great-grandmother?"

"Yes. I met her."

"It's all true, isn't it? Everything you told me. The stories she used to tell my grandfather. All of it." Anxiety and fear started a very painful wrestling match in my chest.

"I'm taking you to my house," Simon said as he started the car. I didn't argue with him. There wasn't a good place to be at that moment. There wasn't a place left on earth where I could feel safe anymore.

I was prepared to talk with Simon about the pictures, to demand answers from him, but he pulled me to sit with him on the sofa, and when I felt his arms wrap around me, all desire to have an uncomfortable conversation left me. Instead, we sat together and watched TV like two very normal teenagers. Simon had his legs propped up on the ottoman in front of him, and I rested my head on his chest, listening as the air went in and out of his lungs, the rhythm of it soothing me.

I'm guessing I wasn't able to stay awake for more than ten minutes. I'd only slept for a couple of hours at a time since Simon had shared his secret with me five days ago. I'd been a walking zombie. When I finally woke up, I was alone on Simon's sofa, a blanket over me, memories of dreams and reality mixing together in my head. I heard faint voices coming from another room.

I walked toward the back of the house. As I got closer, I realized the voices were coming from the back deck. I stood in the open doorway leading from the kitchen and watched Finn and Simon.

"She is seventeen years old, Finn!" Simon said quietly to his brother, and though he wasn't yelling, his anger was apparent. "You're expecting too much from her!"

"There's a good chance she won't live to see her eighteenth birthday if we don't act now," Finn said firmly.

I registered Finn's words, but I couldn't allow my mind to accept their full meaning. It was too much.

Simon started pacing, his hands resting on top of his head with his fingers laced together. "We don't even know if she *is* the Margaret in the story," he pleaded.

"Simon," Finn said gently. "We both know it's her. And we both know that if it's not her, countless lives will be lost. Balor's getting stronger and becoming more violent, and it's not long before he—" Finn looked up and saw me standing in the doorway. Simon turned to see what had made Finn stop talking.

"Maggie," Simon said, walking toward me. "Did you sleep well?" I knew he'd tried to switch his anger toward Finn off, but his words to me were still strained.

I wanted to ask them about Finn's words—about how I would die before my eighteenth birthday—but I was too afraid. "I must have slept well," I answered. "I had a lot of dreams."

"Let's go inside," he suggested. "It's cold out here."

It *was* cold. I wasn't wearing shoes or a coat and I shivered, but the cold felt good. It was waking me up and helping to clear my head. Reluctantly, I let Simon lead me inside. Finn came with us, and we walked back into the living room at the same time that Erin was walking down the stairs.

"I want to know what's going on. I want to know—" My voice cracked, and fear kept me from going on. They all looked at each other apprehensively, but nobody said anything. "I have a right to know," I choked out.

Chapter Twelve

Simon sat next to me on the sofa and took my hand in his. Finn took a deep breath and sat silently for a moment.

"Simon and Erin and I are all faeries," he finally began. The knot in my chest twisted. "Over the years, faeries have developed a code of conduct. Part of that code says faeries must obey all laws for the community where we live, we must never harm a non-faery, and we can reveal that we're faeries only when absolutely necessary."

I nodded. Made sense. Good rules.

"These rules were put into place in order to protect both non-faeries and faeries. Non-faeries are at a disadvantage because they can't do magic and don't have certain skills faeries have—thus the rule that says faeries must never harm a non-faery. The other two rules are to protect faeries. From time to time, people have captured faeries and tried to figure out what makes us able to do what we do. Unfortunately, many faeries have died because they were subjected to experiments designed to isolate and replicate their skills. By concealing our true identities, and blending in as best we can, we're protecting ourselves against harm.

"There are some faeries who believe we shouldn't follow human laws and others who would do away with the other two rules as well. One man, in particular, is leading a group of faeries that want to do away with this code of conduct entirely. They're hoping to wipe out humanity all together so that the faerie race—the fey—can control the world. This group resents the laws non-faeries have written and don't think they should have to follow such laws. They also don't want to continue to hide who they are and what they can do. If all of the non-faeries are gone, faeries would be free to develop their own laws, and there would be no need to hide that we're different.

"This group of faeries has already started their goal of eliminating non-faeries. Some faeries have the ability to create earthquakes and hurricanes and disease and they can also trigger warfare, and they're using these skills to kill people at a staggering rate."

I interrupted. "Faeries cause earthquakes and hurricanes?"

"Not all disasters are faery-made, but some are," he said. "The group of faeries creating these types of events is led by a man named Balor."

I felt Simon's grip tighten around my hand.

"Balor has unprecedented magical abilities and he's able to cause disasters that can kill hundreds of thousands of people in a very short time. He encourages his followers to aid in his destruction, and there are many who believe that taking him down would help to bring down all of the faeries following him. Some believe his followers only do his bidding out of fear or because he's put them under a spell.

Balor's made his intentions to end all of humanity very clear, and removing Balor from power may stop this otherwise inevitable outcome. He's the cause of a lot of mass destruction, including the floods in China last fall."

I thought about the footage of the floods I'd watched. One person had caused all of that misery? "Balor and his followers have the power to end humanity—to kill everyone?" I was trying to stay in control, but it was hard.

"Yes," Finn answered. "We do what we can to stop them, but we're not always successful."

"But why are they doing this?"

"Balor wants to get rid of anyone without faery powers in order to eliminate any obstacles in his path toward leading the world."

I couldn't help but make a face. It sounded so "double-oh-seven" and I could almost hear the maniacal laughter from James Bond's nemesis as he made plans that would lead him toward world domination.

"How will killing people help him?"

"The faeries have special abilities that give us an advantage over people without faery blood, but the faeries are outnumbered—by a long shot. If people found out about us, they could do a pretty good job of killing us off. Balor and his followers are killing people without making them suspicious. They're causing "natural" disasters and inciting war and everyone thinks the deaths are therefore inevitable. They don't know to blame faeries because they don't know faeries exist. Once everyone without faery blood is gone, there will be no need to hide what we are."

"So what do I have to do with all of this? What does the prophecy have to do with it?"

"Some stories in Irish folklore are retellings of things that have already happened and some stories are about things that will happen at some point in the future. Maggie, we believe Balor is the giant in the story of Simon and Margaret and we believe that you—" he paused and looked at me with a greater intensity, "—are Margaret. *The* Margaret. We believe you'll need to—play some part—in defeating Balor."

I laughed out loud. It was completely and totally ridiculous—more ridiculous than Simon's ability to make himself invisible. "I have to help defeat a giant," I scoffed.

"Well, Balor's not a giant in the literal sense," Simon said. "He's a giant in a figurative sense."

"So, what? I'll help defeat him and then you'll fall in love with me and want to marry me?" I asked, remembering the ending to the story in the book he'd given me. This was getting better by the minute.

I could see the hurt on Simon's face before I heard it in his words. "Well, we don't know which parts of the story are true and which have been embellished through the years."

"Then how do you know I even have a part in all of this?"

"We don't know for certain. We have some clues, though," Finn explained

"What sort of clues?"

"Your name, for one," Simon answered. "Not just Margaret, but also O'Neill. And your physical description. In early retellings of the prophecy, a physical description is given of Margaret. One part of the description says that Margaret will be the only person in her family with red hair and the rest of her family will have black hair. And your birthday— November 1st. Faeries are more powerful during November than any other time, and we think your birthday might be significant. But really, we don't know anything for certain."

"Then why are you telling me this? Maybe I don't have any part in it at all. Maybe it's just part of the story that was embellished or it's just a coincidence that I have the name and the look."

"You're right. It might be a coincidence, but we have reason to believe it's not."

"Do you realize how insane all of this sounds?" I demanded. "Look at me. I'm no match for *Brandon*, but you're expecting me to fight off a faery? A very powerful faery?"

"I know how impossible it must all seem," Simon answered. "I know we're challenging your core beliefs about the world, and if there were any way to keep all of this from you, I would."

A crushing reality hit me. "Is that why you're here? Is that why you're dating me? Because you wanted to find out if I was the person in the story?" I looked directly at Simon, not caring that Finn and Erin were there to witness this very private part of our conversation.

He looked down at me, grief in his eyes. "We *are* here because of you. We've been tracking the genealogy of Margaret O'Neills for a long time and we did come here to watch you and to see if you were the one, but Maggie, please do not believe that my actions toward you are false. In the process of figuring all of this out, I've developed very strong feelings for you. I didn't need to date you to get the information we're looking for. Actually, this all would have been a lot easier if I didn't have feelings for you. But I do. I can't change that. Please believe that nothing in my touch, my kiss, my words to you, is false. I can bear a lot of things, Maggie, but I *cannot* bear the thought that you would believe I've lied to you about that."

My head was spinning and my heart ached. There was too much to take in. Too much to process. Too much to understand.

"And the pictures?" I asked.

"We met your great-great-grandmother before she left Ireland," Finn said. "It *is* Simon and me in the picture with her."

"The other picture—the one where she's older—she comes to me in my dreams." As soon as the words were out of my mouth, I worried that I sounded as unbalanced as they all sounded to me, but they looked like I had just confirmed something they already knew.

"What do you mean?" Erin asked.

"When I have nightmares, she's in my dreams. She never talks to me, but she stands there and I feel better. Well, she talked to me the other night, but that's the first time."

"What did she say?"

"I was having a dream about—a monster." I left out the part about Simon being the monster. "And she told me to ask my grandfather. Then my dream was over."

"That's part of the prophecy," Finn explained. "It says the Margaret we're looking for will be visited in her dreams by her ancestors."

"But you don't know for sure that it's me. How do we know for sure?" I wanted to eliminate myself from the running of this particular race as quickly as possible.

"There's a ring—it's in Ireland—that will fit the Margaret we're looking for," Simon explained. "That's how we'll know for sure."

"But there're millions of people with the same ring size as me," I reasoned.

"It won't fit in a physical sense," Erin said. "It will be more of a metaphysical thing."

Well that's not vague or anything.

"So, let me get this straight," I said trying once again to gather my thoughts, "If I do nothing—if I don't try to defeat Balor—I will probably die, along with all of my family and everyone I know, because Balor wants to kill them all. But, if I do try to defeat him, I may die in the process, but I may succeed and everyone gets to live. My only chance at survival is to go after Balor and kill him." I could feel the tension flooding out of Simon, stretching out and reaching deep inside of me. The three faeries in the room looked at each other uncomfortably, but said nothing.

"Me," I continued. "*I* have to be the one to kill an evil faery? *I'm* responsible for the lives of seven billion people living on the planet? I can't even keep a pet goldfish alive! And has anyone bothered to *look* at me? I would lose in a fight against a strong wind, but you think I can defeat Balor? What skills do all of you think I have that could possibly make me the right person for this job? How is it that you can look at me and say, 'This is her. This is the person who's going to save the planet'? Do you get how totally and completely insane all of this sounds?"

"Yes," Simon said solemnly.

I sighed heavily. "So what's your plan?"

"You need to try on the ring. The Guardians won't allow it to be removed from its current location, so we'll need to go to Ireland. Once you've tried it on, we'll know if you're the one or not."

"The Guardians?"

"Sort of a faery army," Simon explained. "The faeries know that regular people can't defend themselves against magic, so the Guardians have devoted themselves to protecting them."

"So you want me to go to Ireland?"

"We're thinking Winterim," Erin said. Winterim was a two week period in February when students were free to pursue activities that interested them, or, in the case of students who were struggling to keep up with the coursework, a time to receive some remedial attention. Some of the luckier students took trips to Paris to study art. Lexie and I were going to a science center in the mountains with a group of other students from school.

"But Winterim is less than three weeks away!" I protested. "There's no way my parents will let me go to Ireland in three weeks."

"Well," Erin began after a quick glance at Finn. "We might be able to persuade them if they think it will be an educational experience for you. We can tell them you'll be doing a Winterim experience there, and it won't be a lie if we actually do some planning ahead of time. If not, Finn has certain *persuasive* abilities."

"What sort of persuasive abilities?" I asked, thinking of mob movies where "persuasive abilities" meant that the bad guys cut off the fingers of the good guys or threw them in a river after outfitting them with a pair of cement boots.

"It's one of my special gifts—as a faery," Finn explained. "I'm able to convince people of things. We'll start by asking your parents to allow you to go on a Winterim experience with us to Ireland. If they won't agree, I'll use my abilities to persuade them. They won't be aware of what I've done. They'll simply believe it was a decision they came to on their own." I wondered why Finn didn't use this ability on Balor to convince him not to wipe out humanity, but I figured it was something he'd already thought about.

"Will you go to Ireland, too?" I asked Simon. He nodded.

"Maggie, please know we don't tell you all of this without a tremendous amount of consideration and discussion," Erin said. "If we thought there was another option, we would let you go on with your life, oblivious to the dangers Balor presents. But if Balor isn't defeated, all of humanity could die." *Yeah. That much I got.* "But it's more than that. We want to keep you safe. If Balor suspects that you're the Margaret mentioned in the prophecy, he won't hesitate in killing you. The Guardians are working to stop Balor, and our hope is that you won't have to do anything, but we have to keep you safe until Balor is no longer a threat."

"Why should I believe any of this? How do I know these stories are true? How do I know you don't have some sick agenda that involves telling me a bunch of lies?" I wanted desperately for them to talk me out of believing all of the information I'd gotten over the past few days, but the evidence supporting their story was mounting.

"I know this is so much to take in, Maggie," Erin said, coming to hold my hand in hers. "We wouldn't blame you if you decided to walk away from us and never look back, and we will *never* ask you to do something you don't want to do. Whatever you do, it will always be your choice, and whatever you decide, we *will* support you."

"Why me?" I asked, voicing the question that had been rattling in my brain for a very long time.

"We honestly don't know," Finn answered gravely.

Chapter Thirteen

"Simon, I did some research about faeries on the Internet," I said as he pulled to the curb in front of my house later that night.

"And you're wondering which parts are true and which aren't," he prompted.

I nodded.

"I imagine you read that we can't touch iron," he started. I nodded again. "That's a myth."

"And urine?"

"Myth. My aversion is no stronger than yours. And salt doesn't bother us either."

"Spells?"

He nodded thoughtfully. "Was there a particular spell you were wondering about?"

I shook my head. "But you can do spells?"

"Yes. You saw some of them."

"Is that what we're calling all the crazy ass shit you did in my bedroom?"

He laughed.

"What?"

"Well, first of all, I've never heard you use that kind of language. It sounds a bit odd coming out of your mouth." I rolled my eyes. "And second, I'm really glad your dad didn't hear you say that sentence. He would have jumped to some conclusions that would probably get me deported—or worse."

"I don't think there's anything even remotely funny about this entire situation," I said, not in the mood to joke with him.

He reigned in his smile. "No, of course not."

"So, you can make yourself invisible. You can fly. You don't feel the cold or the heat."

"I feel it—I'm just not as sensitive to it as you are."

"And you can find something that's lost."

"Well, that's just me. Not all faeries can do that. Faeries have some special abilities that most other faeries don't. I can find lost objects and people. Finn can persuade people."

"And Erin?"

"She's a healer. She can heal most faery wounds, and some human-inflicted wounds and illnesses, by just touching us."

"Are you human?" It was a hard question for me to ask, mainly because I was afraid of the answer.

"It's a gray area," he said.

"A gray area?" I asked with my best are-you-kidding-me tone.

"I'm basically human."

"Basically?"

"Mostly."

"Mostly? What are we talking about here, Simon? Do I have more chromosomes in common with you or with a chimp?"

His expression was pained as he answered. "I'm not certain. I haven't done the research."

I decided not to let that particular response sink in

and planned to push thoughts of Simon's divergent DNA from my mind.

"Is that it?" he asked after a few silent minutes. "You don't have any more questions?"

"Not right now," I confessed. I was certain I would have a barrage of questions in the coming months, but at that moment I was on serious information overload.

He walked me to my door and wrapped his arms around me. "You should go in. It's cold out here."

I pulled myself closer to Simon, not ready to leave him for the solitude of my room.

"I have to kill him," I said simply, the reality of the last few days coming to me in one tsunami-sized wave.

"My hope is that you'll never have to do it."

"But what about the prophecy?"

"The Guardians can do it."

"What if they can't?"

"They will."

"What if they can't?"

He paused for a long time and let out a long breath before answering. "If the Guardians can't figure out a way to do it, then it will have to be you. But not today. Today, you're safe."

He pulled me tighter, and I was overwhelmed by the safety I felt in his arms. At that moment I wasn't Margaret O'Neill, protector of the universe. I was just Maggie and I was with a boy and I had a curfew and a pesky little brother who might tell on me if I were late and parents who might ground me, and for all of that I couldn't be happier. I had a biology test and a dentist appointment and a best friend who would want to know why I wasn't returning her phone calls. As long as I had all of this in my life, I felt like I could ward off the nightmares and monsters being forced upon me. As long as I was normal, I couldn't possibly be extraordinary.

And that's when I really lost it. Tears flowed from my eyes and pretty soon I was sobbing and gasping. Simon rubbed his hand up and down my back slowly, rhythmically, trying to help me calm down. It was a full fifteen minutes before I was able to croak out one word—the question that was weighing heaviest on my mind.

"When?" I asked him.

He took a deep breath and hesitated. "Not now," he finally answered.

I pulled away and looked him in the eye before I repeated more firmly, "When?"

He took both of my hands in his and closed his eyes for a moment, resting his forehead gently against mine. When he pulled back from me and opened his eyes, I could see his pain and fear. "We're going to hold him off as long as we can while we try to develop a plan. It could be a year. It could be a decade."

I had to kill him. And if I didn't kill him, he would take over the world. And that would be a bad thing. It would mean I would die. It would mean *everyone* would die. My family. My friends. Simon?

I felt my knees give way under the weight of the puzzle I was starting to put together. Simon scooped me up before I hit the ground, cradling me in his arms, and carried me to sit on one of the rocking chairs. He held me on his lap, opening his coat and pulling it around me. I rested my head against Simon's chest and breathed in the smell of him—earthy, like a field after a hard rain—and it calmed me down. In that one moment, everything felt right.

Unfortunately, that good feeling was short lived, and a distance formed between Simon and me after that day. He still picked me up each morning and took me home each afternoon. He still sat with me at lunch and called me every evening to wish me sweet dreams. He still played video games with Brandon and had dinner with my family. He still hugged me and kissed me, but only in an obligatory way. He was being cautious, not certain as to whether or not my feelings for him had changed, and to be honest I think my feelings toward Simon *did* change. I didn't want him to touch me or kiss me the way he had before.

I still liked Simon, but I was afraid of who he was and of the changes he brought to my life. I suppose he picked up on those feelings. I felt a tremendous amount of guilt for pushing Simon away. I knew he couldn't help who he was, nor could he help what I might have to do. I was certain that if it were his choice, I wouldn't have to risk my life and defeat Balor. He was merely the bearer of bad news, and I was punishing him for that.

Lexie had started to pick up on the change in my relationship with Simon and in my overall attitude. The distance that formed between Lexie and me was worse than the distance between Simon and me. Simon knew the cause of the strain on our relationship. Lexie didn't; I wasn't able to explain it to her. I wasn't able to explain the changes that had come over me to anyone.

"You know," Lexie said one afternoon after a study session in the library, "seeing a therapist is nothing to be embarrassed about."

"What?" I asked, confused. "Who's seeing a therapist?"

"I was thinking maybe *you* should. Something's going on, Maggie, and you don't seem to want to talk to me about it, and by the looks of things you're not talking to Simon about much of anything, so maybe you should go see a therapist. Seriously."

The image that idea brought made me laugh out loud. I imagined myself sitting in a therapist's office, talking about faeries who can make themselves invisible and how I might be the "chosen one" who had to defeat the evil faery, Balor, in order to save humanity. I'd end up with a one-way ticket to the psych ward. "I don't think that's a good idea," I said, putting my books in my bag.

"Then talk to me or talk to Simon," she pleaded. "I want my friend back."

I felt the tears pooling in my eyes and fought to keep them from dripping pathetically down my face. I turned my back on Lexie and made a big production of rearranging everything in my bag.

"What's going on?" I heard Simon ask. He must have walked over when I'd turned my back.

"I was just recommending to Maggie that she seek the services of a professional counselor since she's obviously not willing to talk to you or me about whatever it is that's bothering her." I could hear the hurt in Lexie's voice and hated that I was the cause of it.

"I'll see you guys tomorrow," she said glumly. I still didn't turn around when she walked away, but continued to rearrange my bag, trying to fight off the tears.

Simon placed his hand gently on my back. "Maggie—"

"Don't," I said tersely, brushing his hand away and slinging my bag onto my shoulder. I walked toward the exit, not bothering to look behind me to see if he was following.

"Maggie, I'm sorry," he said after he'd started the car and pulled out of the student parking lot. The fact that he was apologizing when I was the one acting like a spoiled brat was really too much, and the tears I'd been fighting started to flow freely down my face. He pulled over to the side of the road and drew me into his arms, but if his intention was to stop me from crying, he'd sadly missed the mark. Having him hug me this way—the way he had before—made me cry even harder.

"I'm so sorry. I'm so sorry," he kept saying, over and over.

"Stop," I said, pulling away from him. "Stop apologizing to me. It's just making it worse."

"Then tell me what will make it better," he pleaded.

"I DON'T KNOW!" I said, far louder than I'd intended.

"I'm sorry. I am. I know I should have told you sooner, but I couldn't bear the thought of hurting you. It was a mistake to let myself care about you so much."

"A mistake?" I whispered. The hard lump was back in my throat, and the tears threatened to start falling again.

"Yes, Maggie, a mistake," he said gently. "I think, on some level, I knew you were the one, even before I met you, but I was so busy sheltering you that I wasn't being fair to you."

I thought frantically for something to say but came up empty. I wanted to say that it was okay, that it wasn't his fault. I wanted to say I still cared about him and wanted to be with him. I wanted to remind him that I was acting like a big baby and blaming him for something that wasn't his fault. But I didn't say any of that. After sitting in silence for a few moments, I quietly gathered my things and got out of his car without another word. He didn't try to stop me when I started the walk home. A few seconds later, I saw him drive away.

Chapter Fourteen

My days became a fog of classes and people. I rarely talked to anyone or did my homework and I became trapped in my own world of depression and self-pity—the new world I'd discovered the night Simon told me he was a faery. I knew I'd never feel safe again. If the stories about the faeries were based in truth, I knew there were other stories—other faery tales—that were based in truth as well. Was Frankenstein real? Dracula? The Boogey Man? The Big Bad Wolf?

When I was very little—maybe five or six—my parents took me on a hike in Rocky Mountain National Park. At one point on the hike, we were surrounded by hundreds of huge pine trees that towered far above us, and while we walked along the path, a wind blew through the trees, and they all swayed and bent, groaning and creaking in unison, and I wondered if they'd fall on me. I felt so small beneath those trees and so breakable. Every time I thought about the faeries and what they were expecting me to do, I felt very small again, like I had that day surrounded by hundreds of massive pine trees, and just as I had that day when I was young, I knew I was breakable.

෫෬

Mr. Warner handed back our project folders with a rubric stapled to the front. I hadn't worked on our project for a week and a half and wasn't even aware we'd turned it in.

I looked at Simon with confusion. He shook his head, a plea to wait until later to talk about it.

"I didn't finish the work for our project," I told him in the hall after class.

"I finished your work. The group doesn't know," he explained.

"I can't take credit for work I didn't do," I told him firmly.

"Maggie, under the circumstances—"

"So I'm no longer accountable for my own life?" I asked. "I have a free pass because the only thing in my life worth accomplishing is killing Balor?"

He was silent.

"I have to tell Mr. Warner." I turned to walk away.

He reached for my arm and pulled me back to him. "Let's take a walk."

"I have a class," I said. "So do you."

"We can be late." He didn't wait for a response before taking my hand in his and pulling me with him toward the parking lot. We went to his car, and he turned it on to warm us up—to warm *me* up.

"You don't have to tell Mr. Warner about the project," Simon told me after the vents had started blowing warm air. "He already knows."

"What do you mean?"

He reached over and fidgeted nervously with the buttons on the instrument panel. "He's a faery."

"Mr. Warner? Our history teacher?"

"Yes."

"He's a faery?" I asked, incredulous.

"Yes."

I thought about our Western Civilizations teacher, but had a difficult time picturing him as a faery. Then it occurred to me that my experience with faeries was too narrow for me to be developing stereotypes.

Simon lowered his hand from the instrument panel and moved it to tap his index finger on the center console. "He's been assigned to watch over you for a long time now."

"What?" Mr. Warner had been my history teacher in middle school and had moved to the high school when I had. Lexie and I joked about my bad luck when he'd made the move. He had taught every social studies class I'd had since sixth grade. I never thought much about it because he was such an inconsequential part of my life. "Oh," I whispered lamely.

"No one blames you or thinks less of you for not finishing this project, Maggie. The fact that you're able to get out of bed every day and make it to school is pretty impressive under the circumstances."

I chuckled humorlessly to myself. The only reason I got out of bed every day and went to school was because I knew my parents would kill me if I didn't, and since my own death might mean the death of all of humanity, staying alive seemed like the responsible choice.

I made a move to leave the warmth of Simon's car and go to class, but he stopped me.

"There's something else I wanted to mention," he said.

"Great," I said ruefully.

Finn's thinking about doing some persuading with your parents."

"Why?"

"They're worried about your change in behavior. Your mom's called Finn a couple of times wondering if it has anything to do with me."

I had foolishly believed that my parents hadn't noticed any changes. "Ask him to wait. I'll try to do better with my parents."

"Don't make things harder on yourself than they need to be, Maggie. Your behavior right now isn't a sign of weakness."

"Ask him to wait," I repeated firmly.

I was determined to do better—to act normal.

I got out of the car and headed back to the building, a new image of my history teacher forming in my mind. Mr. Warner looked like he was about forty or so, but how old did that make him in faery years? If Simon was two hundred and eight, Mr. Warner must be at least twice as old as that, if not more. The stories he told were no longer remote accounts of things that had happened to someone else long dead. The stories he told could have been his own stories, or the stories of someone he loved; the stories of people who still walked the earth and looked like everyone else.

∽✺∾

Lexie talked me into going to a party at Cameron and Connor Martinez's house the weekend before Winterim. She told me Max and Simon were having a guys night out, so it would just be the two of us. I knew it wasn't a good sign that Lexie knew my boyfriend's plans better than I did.

I regretted going to the party the moment we walked through the front door. I wasn't in the mood to be around happy people, and I was on the road to being angry with the fifty or so students in the house when something shifted inside of me, and sadness replaced the anger. None of them knew that Balor intended to kill millions of people, including every person at the party. They didn't know. I felt sad for them because I knew they were targets, but I was also jealous. They could live the rest of their lives, however long or short they might be, oblivious to the danger. I missed oblivion.

"Hey, Maggie, I wanted to thank you for doing all that work at the last minute on the project," Cameron said as I sat in a chair and tried to will my body to beam itself into my bedroom so I could escape the party and go to sleep. "You really saved our grade."

I mumbled, "You're welcome," knowing I couldn't tell him that it had actually been Simon to do all the work.

"The website actually looks amazing," he said. "I can't believe we pulled it off. Did you read the comments Mr. Warner wrote on our grade sheet?"

I shook my head. I hadn't actually looked at anything more than the final grade.

"He said it was some of the best work he'd seen on a group project. He said it was a professional-quality website. I guess we should thank your dad for that."

"Yeah. He's definitely good at what he does," I said.

"I'm glad Simon suggested the website," Cameron

went on. "It was a good idea. Hey, where is Simon?" He looked around.

"He didn't come," I told him. "He and Max are hanging out or something. Can you excuse me? I'm going to get something to drink."

I walked away, not waiting for a response from Cameron. I didn't want to talk anymore—to anyone.

"I'm going to get something to drink," I told Lexie. "Do you want anything?" She was in the middle of a dancing video game with a group of three other students. She moved gracefully on her four-inch heels, and as always, a group of guys surrounded her, staring at her and wishing, I'm sure, that she would break up with Max and go out with one of them.

"Water," she said without taking her eyes from the television screen. "Thanks."

I walked into the kitchen and was surprised to see Luke standing next to the keg that was sitting on the floor of the kitchen.

"Hey," he said as a greeting, thrusting his chin up slightly in a way I knew he thought was cool. He was dressed in his usual slovenly chic—wrinkled and worn t-shirt, frayed jeans and dirty DC skate shoes.

I ignored his greeting and opened the refrigerator door next to his left shoulder.

"How'd you manage to get your boyfriend to let you come to a party without him?" Luke asked. He had a red plastic cup in his hand, and I didn't need to look to know it was filled with beer.

"He didn't *let* me. I do what I want."

"Well, do you *want* a beer?"

A voice in the back of my head said that drinking was the most idiotic thing I could do. A voice closer to the front told me that *any* kind of interaction with Luke was self-destructive. I told both of the voices to shut the hell up. I was angry at the entire world for the turn my life had taken and wanted to punish everyone—including myself.

"Sure," I finally said—ready to use alcohol to get back to the state of total oblivion I was craving.

Luke smiled triumphantly and walked away to fill one of the red plastic cups with beer from the tap.

"To your health," he said after handing me the cup.

I took a sip, my face twisting as I tasted the bitter drink. "How do people drink enough of this stuff to get drunk? It tastes awful."

Luke laughed. "You develop a taste over time. It's best to just down it quickly without tasting it."

I looked at the full cup in my hands and decided to give it a try. I took a deep breath and held the cup to my mouth, letting it pour down my throat without stopping long enough to taste the bitterness of the beer.

"Good girl!" Luke said, laughing again. "I'll get you some more."

I lost track of how many cups I downed. The room started to take on a distinctly distorted quality. I loved the feeling the alcohol left me with—warm and confused. I liked confused the most. I couldn't keep a coherent thought going to completion, and that felt really good. I drank more, not wanting the confusion to go away.

After an undetermined number of beers, I looked up to see Lexie standing in front of me, her mouth wide with shock.

"What in the hell are you thinking?" she asked

quietly, dumbfounded. "You're drinking? With Luke? I knew you were being self destructive, but this is a new low."

"Drinking's fun, Lex! Try it!" *Was that me talking?* My tongue felt thick and my words distant.

"No. I don't think so. Come on, Maggie. Let's go."

"Really, Lex. Why didn't anyone tell me how fun drinking was? This is really fun. I wanna do this all the time."

"Yes, well, you may not be quite so enthusiastic when you wake up in the morning. *Let's go.*"

"No. I want to drink some more. It's really fun, Lex."

"So you keep telling me. Maggie, let's go. Now!"

"It sounds like Maggie wants to stay here." Luke was beside me, his arm suddenly wrapped around my waist. Lexie said something I didn't understand before turning to walk away, her silver stilettos clacking across the tile of the kitchen floor before being silenced by the carpet in the living room. Luke led me to a sofa and pulled me to sit on his lap. I registered the synapse firing in my brain that reminded me that Luke was not a nice guy, but I quickly dusted away that thought, not willing to think of anything that got in the way of my attempts at self-preservation.

"I've missed you, Maggie," Luke whispered seductively in my ear. I knew sitting with him was wrong, but I wasn't willing to acknowledge my reasonable and logical side long enough to move away from him. I liked being the girl I'd been when I was with him. I didn't want to be brave or responsible or noble. I wanted to be an impulsive seventeen-year-old who dated someone for no other reason than because it was fun in that one moment.

Luke tried to kiss me a couple of times, but even in my drunken state I knew I couldn't. I hadn't completely forgotten about Simon, but Luke was determined I should kiss him and he eventually put his hand around my neck and pulled me to him, pressing his lips roughly to mine. I tried to move away, but his hand kept my neck firmly in place and eventually I felt myself respond to him and returned his kiss. I knew he'd hurt me and that he was capable of hurting me again, but I still kissed him as if I were trying to pull everything I'd lost out of him. Luke was a link to my old life when things were simple and innocent and easy.

"Maggie." I turned quickly on Luke's lap to see Simon standing in front of me with a look that was murderous, but even in my drunken state, I saw something else. Sadness. The most profound look of sadness I'd ever seen in my entire life. It broke my heart and mesmerized me at the same time and I stood up to go to him.

Chapter Fifteen

Luke grabbed my hand before I could take my first step. "I don't think she wants to go with you. She seems pretty happy to sit here with me."

"Let her go," Simon said through gritted teeth.

"No," Luke said as he stood up and pulled me toward him.

"I thought we had an understanding the last time we talked, Luke," Simon said calmly, anger flittering at the edges of his words.

"I agreed never to hurt her. She doesn't look hurt to me," Luke responded, tightening his grip around me.

Wait a minute. They'd talked? When had they talked? Luke had agreed not to hurt me? That didn't sound like Luke.

"Then we have a very different idea of what hurting Maggie looks like," Simon said.

"It looks to me like you're the one hurting her. She was very happy to sit on my lap and kiss me a few minutes ago."

Simon shoved Luke away from me. "Get away from her and stay away from her."

Luke punched Simon in the face. Simon's hand

went instantly to the spot where Luke had made contact, and I watched as he fought to regain control of himself, the muscles in his jaw tensing and relaxing rapidly. I knew he wanted to punch Luke back, but he was battling hard against that desire.

The floor moved underneath my feet and I felt myself flying through the air. Simon had thrown me over his shoulder and was carrying me out of the house. He said nothing as he carried me out to his car and sat me roughly in the passenger's seat.

"Buckle your seat belt," he said angrily when he was sitting in the seat beside me. "Or are you too drunk to manage that?"

"We can't leave Lexie," I said, proud of myself for remembering my best friend in my drunken state.

"She's with Max."

"I thought you were having a guy's night."

"We were," he said with frustration, "but that was interrupted when Lexie called to tell us that you were drunk and hanging out with Luke. Now buckle your seatbelt so we can leave."

I fumbled with the buckle, determined to show him that I wasn't so drunk I couldn't attach my own seat belt. After several near hits—and not-so-near hits—I felt Simon grab the buckle roughly and press it in with a loud click. He then turned away and started to drive, his determined silence saying more than a string of profanities ever could.

He drove to his house, and when I got out of the car, I felt as if the world were turning back flips. My stomach dropped abruptly and rose again quickly, and I turned toward the nearest bush to throw up while Simon stood next to me and watched. I was grateful he hadn't decided to hold back my hair like a cheesy character in a bad romance novel. There was nothing romantic about throwing up, and the thought of Simon—or anyone else—touching me at that moment made my skin crawl.

When I had finished depositing my dinner on the Brady lawn, we started to walk into the house. After I stumbled a few times on the pristinely smooth and flat concrete of the sidewalk, Simon grabbed me and lifted me into his arms. It might have been an endearing act if it weren't for the complete lack of tenderness.

₨⃣

I woke up on the sofa, a blanket draped over me, and sat up, still feeling a little loopy, but not nearly as drunk as I'd felt when we'd first gotten to Simon's house. It was dark, but I could see Simon sitting in a chair across the room, staring at me, a mask of forced calm.

"Hi," I said. He didn't respond. "I should probably go home." I knew it was well past my curfew.

"You're spending the night here," he said after a long pause. "Finn'll go over to your house and convince your parents of something or other so you won't be in trouble."

"No, I'll go home and face my parents. I don't want Finn to mess with their minds." I knew it was the right thing to do. I did the crime and I had to face whatever punishment my parents decided to dole out.

"Unfortunately, you created a situation with your actions last night that requires him to 'mess with their minds' in one way or another. Either he does it now and they're oblivious to your actions last night or he does it later so they allow you go to Ireland for Winterim, despite your actions. We can't put the fate of the world on hold while you throw a tempter tantrum."

Ouch!

"I'm sorry, Simon." My voice filled with the contrition I felt.

"What were you thinking, Maggie?"

"I wasn't. I think that was the whole point."

"You didn't give a single thought to anyone but yourself and you didn't care who you hurt in the process."

"I'm sorry. I know. You're right."

"Which part are you sorry about, Maggie?" His voice was rising with anger. "The part where you drank beer with your ex-boyfriend—the ex-boyfriend who attacked you? Or was it the part where you completely disregarded my feelings when you kissed Luke?"

Oh god, oh god, oh god! I'd forgotten about the kiss, and of course Simon would have seen it. He was standing right there. Whatever indecision I was feeling toward my relationship with Simon, kissing Luke was inexcusable.

"You're right, Simon. You should be angry with me, but it wasn't what you think."

"It never is in these types of situations."

I ignored his snarky comment and continued with my explanation. "He kissed me, and I should have stopped him, but I wanted my life to go back to the way it was before, and I thought kissing him would bring it all back. It was stupid. I know that. But I wasn't thinking."

"It sounds like you put a *tremendous* amount of thought into it," he said darkly.

"Simon—"

"Don't bother, Maggie. I thought I could expect more from you. You've obviously proven me wrong."

Finn walked into the living room and looked pointedly at his brother.

"Simon, that's enough," he said. "Let her sleep."

Simon looked at Finn for a long moment, then nodded his head and sat silently. I think I liked it better when he was yelling.

ഇറ

When I woke up in the morning, I was alone. I stood up to look for Simon, and nausea overcame me. I ran to the bathroom, barely making it to the toilet in time. I threw up for several minutes and sat back on my heels, waiting to see if I was done or if I should stick close to the toilet for a while. I noticed a pair of denim-covered legs at the door to the bathroom and a hand—Simon's hand—reached down to hand me a toothbrush.

"Thanks," I mumbled.

"Come to the kitchen when you're done and I'll get you some tea. I think we need to talk." His voice was quiet and strained, but he didn't sound angry anymore.

I nodded, the movement causing severe pain in my head.

After brushing my teeth and downing a couple of ibuprofen that I found in the medicine cabinet, I walked to the kitchen. Simon had a cup of hot tea waiting for me, and I sat down at the table to drink it. Simon sat down across from me with a mug for himself.

"Maggie, I know you're not happy," he said after a few minutes.

"Simon—" I interrupted, wanting to tell him he was wrong, but knowing we'd both know it was a lie.

He looked at me for a moment before he continued. "I hate that you kissed Luke, but I also understand that I need to take at least part of the blame."

"How on earth could you think this was in any way your fault?" I was completely incredulous. I knew Simon was a good guy, but this was taking it a bit too far.

"I tried to keep a distance between us, Maggie. I tried so hard. I knew it would just complicate everything for you, but I wasn't strong enough. I kissed you before I told you who I was. I hadn't given you all of the information you needed to make an informed choice. I didn't tell you I was a faery and I didn't tell you about the prophecy. Those two things are such a huge part of who I am and I didn't tell you about them until after I'd kissed you."

"It doesn't matter. It doesn't change who you are."

"Can you honestly say that me being a faery doesn't make you uncomfortable?"

I didn't answer. The only answer I could truthfully give was not one I was willing to admit to him.

He understood my silence and continued with what he wanted to say. "I know what it's like to fight against a lack of free will. I hated my role in the prophecy, not because I didn't want to be a part of it, but because I'd never been given a choice. I won't do that to you. I won't make you do anything you don't want to do—and that includes dating me."

He paused, but I didn't say anything.

"I worry about you every second of every day," he said. "I worry that we're taking away all of the good in your life and I worry about the future we're creating for you and the risks we're asking you to take. I don't want to have to worry about whether or not you want to be in a relationship with me."

"You're breaking up with me," I said, the realization of where this conversation was going hitting me hard in the gut.

Chapter Sixteen

"There's so much you have to face, even if you're not ready. I want you to have a choice about us. I only want to be with you if you're certain it's what you want."

Was I certain? No. Did I want to lose him? No. Our relationship had been teetering on the precipice of a cliff since I found out that Simon was a faery, and he'd just walked up and knocked it over the edge. I wasn't completely happy with Simon, but I also wasn't ready to live without him.

"I can't do this without you," I whispered.

"You won't have to. I'll stand beside you, no matter what."

I wanted to lie to him, to tell him what he wanted to hear, but I couldn't bring myself to do it. Tears stung my eyes, fighting to run down my face.

"I'll always be your friend, Maggie." It was the worst thing he could have said to me. He was no longer my boyfriend. He was my friend.

I couldn't hear anymore. I walked out of the kitchen and grabbed my shoes before going out the front door, wanting to walk home alone. It would be a long walk, but I hoped it would wake me up and make me feel better about what had just happened. Simon didn't try to stop me. He understood. He always understood, sometimes more than I did myself.

When I got home, I went to my room and closed the door before letting the life drain out of me completely and falling to the floor. I was shaking and crying and miserable and I wasn't able to gather the energy needed to move myself to the bed. By the time darkness fell in the room I had finally cried myself out, numbness overtaking the pain I'd been feeling.

I fell asleep on the floor and had a nightmare too fragmented to piece together. Grandma Margaret came to me in the end. She didn't say anything, but she did reach out her arms to me and held me close until it was time for me to wake up.

ഇരുഃ

I avoided Lexie in the week between the party and Winterim. I wasn't mad at her—if the situation had been reversed, I would have done exactly what she'd done—but I was embarrassed. Of all the stupid things Lexie had seen me do in the years we'd been friends, getting drunk and kissing Luke had been the worst, and I wasn't certain she'd forgive me. Avoiding her was easier than being rejected by her—at least for the moment.

I didn't see much of Simon in the few days left before our trip to Ireland, and I never knew if he continued to come to my house to pick me up because I made sure to get up and leave the house in time to walk to school. I didn't want to see him or talk to him. It hurt too much.

Word that I'd kissed Luke spread quickly around the school. On Monday morning in Western Civ class, Katie Hill twirled her hair furiously around her index finger while she giggled at everything Simon said—funny or not. After class, she pulled him aside, taking the hem of his shirt in her fist as she coaxed him back into the room. I have no idea what she said to him, or did to him, and I stopped going to Western Civ class after that. I had enough to deal with at the moment, and didn't need to watch while Katie Hill moved in on my ex-boyfriend.

I was so hurt about losing Simon, but I tried to focus on our trip and the ring. I had no doubt Simon would keep to his word and be a friend to me while we were in Ireland and I had to resign myself to accepting that it would have to be enough. After I had tried on the ring, after we were back from Ireland, only then could I think about Simon and trying to repair the damage I'd done to our relationship. For now, I needed to focus on everything that trip meant to me and to my future.

ℰ◌ℛ

It came as no surprise that Finn needed to persuade my parents to let me go to Ireland. My mom had actually laughed out loud when I'd first mentioned the idea to her, and no amount of pleading on my part would convince either of my parents to let me go. Finn made them believe they *wanted* me to go on the trip so that I could do a Winterim experience with Simon, studying the culture and history of Ireland. I really worried about messing with their minds like that. They knew they shouldn't let me go, and were probably pretty confused about why on earth they were saying yes to such a ridiculous request.

"Are you doing okay?" Simon asked as we sat on the plane. Things were still pretty tense between us. We hadn't talked since the day he broke up with me, and it hurt every piece of my body to be sitting next to him, knowing he wasn't my boyfriend anymore.

I nodded in response to his question.

"Maggie—"

I stuck my headphones into my ears and folded my arms around myself as I moved away from Simon and toward the window next to my seat. Sitting next to him was hard enough. Talking to him as if my heart hadn't been pulverized would be impossible.

"Do you think you'll ever forgive me?" I heard him whisper before I increased the volume on the music playing in my ears.

I wanted to be kind to him. I wanted to let him know that I still cared about him—that I always would. I wanted to sit on his lap and kiss him passionately, but at the same time I was angry for everything he'd taken away from me.

"There's nothing to forgive," I said coolly before making the ever-so-mature decision to ignore him for the rest of the fifteen-hour trip.

I was still angry when we landed at the small airport near his home in Northwest Ireland, and the heaviness of the fog just depressed me. Falling asleep for the ride from the airport to his house seemed like the best option for everyone involved.

I woke to Simon unbuckling my seat belt. "Hi, sleepyhead," he said softly. "We're home." His lips were close to my ear and his hand was on my knee and the closeness of him caused a physical ache that started in my chest and moved down toward the palms of my hands.

I took a moment to compose myself before stepping out of the car. The obscured moon sent little light our way, but I could see a very large stone house in front of us. When I looked around I didn't see any other buildings, or lights from other buildings. I could hear ocean waves crashing nearby, but I couldn't see the water from where I stood.

"Welcome to Ballecath," Simon whispered as we walked through the massive front door.

"I'm going to show her to her room," he told Finn and Erin. They'd flown out of Denver a couple of days before us but were at the front door to meet us when we walked in. "I'll be back down in a little while." I knew Simon wouldn't sleep. He was too excited about being home and since he didn't need as much sleep as I did, he'd be able to stay awake with no trouble at all.

He led me down a long hallway at the top of the stairs, toward the two doors at the end.

"You're actually going to be staying in Finn's room," Simon explained. "We thought you'd be more comfortable if you were staying across from me, and Finn and Erin moved to another room in the house when they got married, so it's been vacant anyway."

Simon led the way into the room on the left. "This will be *your* room now," he said.

The room was beautiful. A large, wooden, four-poster bed stood in the center of one wall, the fluffy down comforter already pulled down and waiting for me. There was a fireplace on the opposite wall with an inviting fire already lit, and two overstuffed chairs sat facing the fireplace with a small table separating them. On one side of the fireplace was a large armoire. On the other was a small desk and chair.

"You'll have to share a bathroom with me," Simon said. "Is that okay?"

I nodded

"Do you want me to stay with you until you fall asleep?" he asked, sounding a little shy.

"No."

He looked at me for a moment and nodded his head slowly before he walked out of the room, leaving me alone with all of the monsters in my head.

Chapter Seventeen

When I woke up the following morning, it took me several languid moments to remember where I was. The fire was still going in the fireplace, so I assumed someone had been in at some point to stoke it. Despite the fire, there was a definite chill that hit me when I kicked back the comforter that had been keeping me warm throughout the night. I pulled some fleece socks and a fleece sweater out of my suitcase and put them on before I went into the bathroom to brush my teeth. I noticed the door to Simon's room was open and his bed looked like it hadn't been slept in. I wasn't surprised.

I went back to my room and sat at one of the chairs near the fireplace. I was hungry and wanted to go in search of the kitchen, but I was worried I'd run into Simon. Spending the entire day next to him on the airplane had drained me and I needed some time away from him. My stomach was saved by a knock on the door. Erin came in with a tray of food for me.

"I wasn't sure if you'd be hungry or not, but decided to bring you a tray anyway."

"Thank you," I told her as I took a bite of the scrambled egg on my plate.

"Do you have everything you need?"

I nodded, wanting to make my mom proud by not talking with my mouth full.

She sat with me and talked about the weather and Ireland and Lexie and school while I ate my breakfast, then she suggested that we go for a walk. I hesitated, knowing that I wasn't quite ready to run into Simon.

"Simon went into town with Finn," she said, interpreting my hesitation.

"Okay," I said.

"I'll meet you downstairs in a few minutes then," she said as she picked up my tray.

A light rain was falling so Erin grabbed a couple of raincoats from hooks by the backdoor, handing one to me before we headed out. We walked through a courtyard behind the house. It was closed almost completely on three sides by a U-shaped building. Erin explained that there were three small apartments in the building for staff and anyone else who might need a place to stay. My guess was that there were probably twenty bedrooms in the house and couldn't imagine that they would ever have enough guests to fill all of them, plus the three apartments.

We walked through the archway that separated the courtyard from the rest of the estate. Beyond that courtyard was another courtyard—garages, Erin told me. Beyond that was a third courtyard—the stables. We continued past the stables and into a lightly wooded area. It was cold, but the fresh air felt good, and I felt more alive than I had in weeks.

"A few faeries are coming for dinner tonight," Erin said as we walked back toward the house. The rain had slowed and as we walked up the hill behind the last courtyard, I could see just how massive the Brady home really was. In front of the three courtyards stood a large brick house with two long wings extending beyond the main part of the house. It reminded me of the buildings they used for estate homes in movie adaptations of Jane Austen stories.

"How many faeries?" I asked.

"Simon, Finn and I," She began "Aidan will be there—you met him at the airport last night. Liam and his daughter, Keelin. Sloane and her husband, Quinn, another old friend of ours, Alana. And you."

"Great. Nine faeries and me." Sounded like a fun evening.

"Quinn's not a faery, so only eight faeries," Erin clarified.

I turned and looked at her, shocked. "Faeries and regular people marry?"

She nodded. "Quite regularly, actually."

"And he knows you're all faeries?"

"Mm-hmm."

"And he's okay with that?"

She smiled. "Yes. He's okay with that."

"Why is everyone coming for dinner?"

"They're good friends of ours and they wanted to meet you before everyone else gets here. They're all members of the Guardians."

"What exactly *are* the Guardians?" I remembered Simon had mentioned them the night they told me about Balor, but I didn't really know what their role was in the faery world.

"It's a sort of faery organization—kind of like being in the army. We train for several decades to use our skills to defend what we believe in, but we also spend a lot of time learning about our history and culture."

"You're one too?"

"Yes."

"And Simon?"

"Yes."

"Erin, can I ask you something? About Balor?"

"Of course."

"Simon gave me a book of Irish folklore for my birthday."

"Yes, I know the book."

"Well, I was just wondering if all the stories are true, or just the one about Margaret and Simon."

"They're all based in truth, but all have been exaggerated and embellished over the years."

"The one about Balor?"

"It's based in truth, but exaggerated."

I'd read the story of Balor before we left Denver. I'd opened the book and flipped through it for answers to this impossible fate that had been thrust upon me. I found Balor's name in the index and turned to the story that told of this horrible monster. It described an evil god—the god of death. He had one evil eye that had the power to kill anyone he looked at and he had to keep it covered so he didn't kill everyone simply by looking at them.

"But in the story of Balor, it says his grandson will kill him."

Erin nodded. "The same woman who wrote the prophecy about you wrote that one, as well. Balor's grandson didn't survive, though. Her prophecy about you said that if the grandson wasn't alive, then you would defeat Balor."

"Are you sure he's dead?" I asked.

"Yes."

"How did he die?"

"Balor drowned him when he was a baby because he knew about the prophecy and he knew that without a grandson, that particular prophecy couldn't come true. I think that when he weighed the two prophecies—the one where his faery grandson killed him and the one where a human girl killed him—he decided that his grandson was the biggest threat and got him out of the way first."

Fantastic.

„′›‚

Erin told me that dinner at their house was always casual. In the Jane Austen movies, people who lived in houses that looked like the Brady house always wore tuxedos and ball gowns to dinner, and as I hadn't thought to pack any ball gowns—or tuxedos for that matter—I was relieved to hear that I could just wear jeans. I decided to wear a fitted sky blue blouse and a black cardigan with blue and white flowers embroidered around the neckline.

There was a knock on my door and when I opened it up to a waiting Simon, I felt a burn spread across my face. I hadn't expected to see him until I was downstairs in a room full of people. It would be easy to avoid him with others around, but there was no dodging him when we were one-on-one.

"You look nice," he said. "Your eyes and shirt are the same shade of blue."

"We match," I said, looking at him. He was wearing dark blue jeans that made his long legs seem even longer and a soft black t-shirt with an unbuttoned oxford shirt over it, the sleeves rolled up to the elbows. The oxford shirt was almost the exact same color as the blouse I was wearing under my black cardigan. Simon looked down at his own outfit, then looked at mine and smiled.

"Can I walk you downstairs?"

I nodded.

"Simon?" I asked as we walked down the long hallway from our bedrooms.

"Mm-hmm?"

"I was wondering something about dinner tonight."

"Yes?"

"Well," I began, a little embarrassed by my question, "when faeries get together do they talk to each other in their heads or out loud?" I knew fairies could communicate telepathically and wondered if Simon, Finn and Erin only talked out loud for my sake.

I watched as Simon fought a smile. "We generally talk out loud," he said. "Speaking to each other inside of our minds can be useful, but it's not as satisfying as speaking out loud. And trust me—faeries love to talk!"

We'd reached the dining room by that time and when we walked in, it looked like everyone was already there. I had heard a lot of conversation before we entered the room, but once I was through the door, everyone became silent. A girl with coal black hair and vivid green eyes ran at Simon and flung her arms around him. Simon stepped away from me and wrapped both of his arms around her. She looked like she was probably the same age as Simon, and it was clear that the two knew each other very well.

"Simon!" the girl exclaimed as she hugged him.
"I've missed you so much."

Chapter Eighteen

Simon let his arms fall to his side and turned to look at me. "Maggie, this is Keelin, a very old friend of mine."

"Who're you calling old?" Keelin demanded. "I'm four months younger than you yourself."

"I stand corrected," Simon said with a bright smile. "My *young* friend, Keelin."

"Better," she said, returning his smile. "Very nice to meet you, Maggie," she added as an afterthought before turning back to Simon, but the way she said it made me think it wasn't as nice as she might like me to believe.

"And this is Liam," Simon continued, "Keelin's father."

"Howya, Maggie?" Liam said. "Welcome to Ireland." Liam looked like he was a little older than Finn and Erin and he had the same green eyes and black hair that Keelin had, but there were thick streaks of gray running throughout his hair.

"This is Sloane," Simon continued, "and her husband, Quinn."

They both came to me and shook my hand warmly. Sloane was tall, with broad shoulders and brown hair that fell across her back. Quinn was even taller than Sloane, with strawberry blonde hair and a lot of freckles.

"And of course you remember Aidan from last night." Simon motioned to the man who had picked us up from the airport the night before.

"Are you settling in okay?" Aidan asked.

"Yes, thank you."

"Are you going to forget about me, Simon?" A young woman stepped toward us.

"Of course not, Alana. I was saving the best for last. Maggie, this is my friend Alana. Alana, this is Maggie."

The strikingly beautiful, blonde haired woman stepped toward me and took me into a tight hug. She looked like she was a few years older than Simon and she had a smile that lit up her eyes. "So good to finally meet you. I feel like we've been friends for years." I blushed a little, not sure how to respond to her effusiveness.

We all sat down at the long table. Food had already been set out in large bowls and on platters, and everyone started to serve themselves and pass the dishes around. True to Simon's word, the faeries did speak out loud to each other during dinner, but I understood very little of what they said. They would slip into another language occasionally, which I assumed was Irish Gaelic, but even the words they spoke in English didn't make sense to me because they talked about people and experiences that were completely unfamiliar. As I watched them, I realized Simon and the others shattered my image of faeries as sweet, glittery little people with colorful wings and pointed ears. It would be impossible to distinguish the faeries sitting at the dinner table from anything but completely human.

I sat next to Simon, with Keelin on the other side of him, and any time he tried to talk with me, Keelin interrupted with a question about his life in Denver or to remind him of an event from their childhood. Evidently, Simon and Keelin had known each other since they were babies and had seen each other regularly in the past two hundred years. They had *a lot* of shared experiences, and Keelin seemed determined to talk with Simon about each and every one during dinner.

After sitting at the table for several hours, listening as the others joked and laughed and talked about things that were completely foreign to me, I decided to go to bed. I touched Simon gently on the arm to pull his attention away from Keelin long enough for me to let him know I was leaving the table.

"I'm going up to bed," I said when he turned around to look at me.

"Are you okay?" he asked, slightly alarmed.

"Yeah. Just tired. I don't think I've adjusted to the time change yet."

He nodded and started to stand. "I'll walk you upstairs."

"No. Stay here and catch up with your friends. I'll be fine."

I said my goodnights and as I turned to leave the room, I caught a glimpse of the smug look on Keelin's face.

I pulled on my pajamas and brushed my teeth and thought of Keelin's beautiful black hair and her long legs and the two hundred years of history she shared with Simon. I knew that under the best of circumstances, I'd be no match for her, but especially now—when my relationship with Simon was so tenuous—I didn't stand a chance if she decided she'd like to take Simon away from me for good.

I got into bed and pulled the thick comforter over my head, trying desperately to block the images my imagination had conjured of Simon and Keelin locked in a passionate embrace, kissing each other with all of the intensity that had been in my own kisses with Simon, but were now a distant memory.

As I lay there whipping myself into a jealous frenzy, I heard a soft knock on the door and Simon's voice asking if he could come in. The petulant four-year-old who seemed to have taken up permanent residence inside of me decided to ignore him. I pulled the comforter over my head and cried myself to sleep.

☙❧

"Good morning," Erin said cheerfully when I walked into the kitchen the following day. Several of the faeries I'd met the night before were in the room with her, and while a heated conversation had been taking place before I'd opened the door, everyone was silent when I walked in. "How about some breakfast?"

I nodded and went to stand in front of the fireplace to warm myself after the long journey from the fireplace in my room. I hated that I was the only one bothered by the cold. It made me feel weak and it emphasized the gap between the faeries and me. I wasn't one of them.

"Is Simon around?" I asked, trying to sound indifferent as visions of Keelin wrapped in his arms flittered through my head.

"He's out riding," Erin said. "With Keelin. They left a couple of hours ago, so I imagine they'll be back soon."

Great. He's with Keelin.

"We wanted to talk to you about the meeting tonight," Finn said as he prepared my breakfast.

"Let the poor girl eat before you start in," Erin chastised Finn playfully.

"Probably best to wait for Simon, anyway," Liam said. "Why don't we meet in the front drawing room in an hour? Simon and Keelin should be back by then and that'll give Maggie time to eat and get dressed." His words reminded me that I was still in my pajamas, and I realized I should probably be embarrassed about that, but then I decided I had much bigger things to worry about—like Simon and Keelin on a private horse ride. Oh yeah, and the whole ring thing and the evil faery.

When I came back downstairs for the meeting, I heard angry voices coming from the drawing room. I stood outside for a moment to listen, knowing it was incredibly rude, but too curious to pass up the opportunity to hear something really good.

"You need to give her time, Liam. This has been quite a shock for her," Erin was saying.

"We should have taken her away from her family when she was an infant and raised her among us. We're wasting valuable time waiting for this girl to reconcile herself to her fate," Liam responded.

"So we were to take every Margaret O'Neill born

with red hair and raise them among the faeries?" Sloane asked. "We were to ruin the life of every child born with the description mentioned in the prophecy? Even you must hear how ridiculous that sounds."

Everyone was quiet, and I decided to take advantage of the momentary silence to walk into the room before I was caught snooping. Simon and Keelin were back from their ride, and the other faeries stood around the room looking somewhat uncomfortable.

Simon came over to me and kissed my cheek—the epitome of a friendly gesture. "Sorry I wasn't here when you woke up." My skin tingled where his lips had touched my face and I wanted to reach up and press my hand to the spot so that I could hold the feeling to me, but I restrained myself, knowing I'd look like an idiot.

"It's okay," I lied to Simon. "I hope you and Keelin had a nice ride," I lied again.

"It was great. I haven't ridden for so long!"

Fantastic!

"So, Maggie," Sloane said as everyone sat down around the room, "we just wanted to talk with you about this evening. We'll share all we know and hopefully we can answer any questions you might have."

Simon, who was standing next to me, put his hand in mine and squeezed it lightly. It felt both painful and comforting and I had to fight away tears because having his hand in mine reminded me of everything I'd lost, but I didn't pull away. I left my hand in his and tried to ignore the pain so I could focus on the comfort.

"There'll be faeries here from all over Ireland, and a

handful from outside the country. We'll meet in the great hall here at the house, and after everyone's gathered, Liam will present the ring for inspection. When any faery who chooses to has inspected the ring, you'll put it on the index finger of your right hand." She stopped there.

"What happens after I put the ring on?" I asked.

Sloane paused and looked away from me, and when I tried to make eye contact with one of the other faeries, they all looked away too. Evidently there was something super interesting on the floor that all of them had to look at right away.

"Well, the thing is, Maggie, we don't really know," Sloane said when she finally looked me in the eye again. "The ring will either identify you in some way as the Margaret O'Neill in the prophecy, or it won't. We have no idea how we'll know it. The prophecy says only that the ring will fit the rightful wearer."

Well that clears things up! I wondered why they had called a meeting to pass on so little information. It seemed like someone could have filled me in as they passed me in the hallway.

"Nobody knows what will happen?" I asked, more than a little shocked. Simon tightened his grip on my hand. "So it could melt my hand off for all we know. Or kill me."

I was expecting Sloane to tell me how ridiculous either of those scenarios would be, but she didn't.

"Maggie, we're asking you to take a tremendous risk—"

You think?!

"—and we would all understand if you chose not to try the ring on. None of us would blame you for walking away and leaving here right now."

"Have any of *you* tried the ring on?" I asked.

"We all have," Liam spoke for the group. "It's something we've all done in the course of studying the ring and the prophecy."

"And what happened?" I asked.

"Nothing," Liam said, "because none of us is the rightful wearer."

"And what if I am the 'rightful wearer?' What then?"

"Then it will be up to you to kill Balor," Liam said bluntly.

"But how do we even know this prophecy is real? What if it's one of those things that's been twisted through the years? What if it's all just a bunch of crap?"

There was another uncomfortable shifting among the faeries in the room.

"The woman who made the prophecy is very reliable. Every prophecy she ever made was completely accurate," Sloane explained.

"Who is this woman? Is she still alive? Can we talk to her and make sure we understand it correctly?" I was looking for the loophole that would take me back to the quiet life I'd been living a few weeks before.

"We're not able to talk to her," Sloane said evasively, "but please be assured that the prophecy is very accurate."

Simon put his hands on my waist and turned me around to face him. "Maggie, nothing changes after you try on the ring. You don't have to do anything you don't want to do. Nobody will make you do this if you don't want to."

"Really, Simon?" Liam's voice was tinged with anger. "You're willing to risk the lives of every human on this planet—possibly even our own lives—so that this girl can go back to her silly life in suburbia?"

Hey!

"What's your plan then, Liam? How do you propose forcing her to kill Balor?" Simon's anger shot up instantaneously.

"If the alternative is less pleasant, she will see reason," Liam said, his voice menacing.

"Our goal is to protect her from Balor," Simon responded. "We will not put her in danger."

"Jaysus, Simon," Liam said as he threw his arms in the air. "You want to protect the life of one girl at the peril of millions. Maggie may lose her life if she fights him, but what's one life?"

Simon was breathing heavily, and his hands hung in fists at his sides.

"This is *her* choice," he demanded tersely. "We'll not force Maggie to do anything she doesn't want to do."

"So we'll just allow Balor to follow through with his plans? Simon, you of all people should know what he's capable of doing."

Simon's face was turning an ominous shade of red, and I could see his chest rise and fall deeply as he fought to control his anger.

"Enough," Finn said as he walked between them. "Liam, this is Maggie's choice. Nobody will force her to do anything. And I would ask you to please remember Simon's wishes, as well."

Liam still looked angry, but he didn't say anything else.

"I need to go for a walk," I said, standing up. I suddenly felt like I couldn't breathe, and the four walls of the large room were closing in on me.

"I'll go with you," Simon said as I started to walk toward the door.

"No, Simon," I said, turning to face him, my tone harsh. "I don't want you to go with me." I registered the hurt look on his face and walked out the door.

There was a fine mist falling when I walked outside. The fog was dense, and I felt like the moisture was hanging in the fog more than it was falling from the sky. I hadn't brought out a rain jacket and knew the mist would start to permeate my clothes if I stayed out long enough, but I decided wet skin was preferable to walking back into the house and having to face faeries.

"You might need this," Alana said, materializing through the fog with a red raincoat in her hands. "This mist seems innocuous enough, but it accumulates quickly."

I thanked her for the jacket, put it on over my sweater and continued on my walking temper tantrum. Alana walked with me.

"No one can blame you for the way you're feeling right now, Maggie," she said as we walked. "What you're doing is very brave. We'd understand if you decided to leave here right now after telling us all to stuff it."

"Tempting," I admitted. "The telling you all to stuff it part, I mean."

She laughed, and I started to cry, the pressure I'd been feeling since I'd arrived in Ireland overwhelming me once again. Alana led me to a wooden bench away from the house and held my hand in hers.

"Do you want to talk about it?" she asked.

I barely knew Alana, and somehow that made talking to her easy.

"I miss Simon," I began. "I screwed things up with him and I don't think it will ever be right again."

She looked at me and I could see the sympathy in her eyes.

"It was hard in Denver," I continued, "but at least there I didn't have to see him. It's hard having him so close to me all the time." I wiped the rain and tears from my face with my free hand. "And I'm scared. I don't want to try on the ring. I don't want to face Balor. I know Liam's right. I know my one life isn't worth the life of millions, but I'm afraid to die. And I know I will. I know Balor will kill me. I can't fight him. And if I can't fight him, then so many people will die, and I can't face that pressure. It's too much." The pain in my chest was back and I found it hard to breath past the lump in my throat. "It's so unfair. It's all so unfair. Not just for me, but for everyone—for all the people that are going to die because I'm not strong enough to fight Balor."

Tears were streaming down my face and the rain was falling harder, chasing them away as fast as they fell, but I didn't make a move to go back to the house. Alana pulled me to her and let me cry myself out in her arms.

"I'll try on the ring," I said when I had recovered enough to talk. "I don't know what I'll do beyond that. I don't think I'm strong enough to be the person you all want me to be."

"Somehow we find strength when we most need it. It'll come to you."

"I don't know if I want it to come to me. I still just want my 'silly life in suburbia.' I don't want the fate of the world on my shoulders. It's too much."

Alana said nothing, but I felt that she understood. She stayed with me until I was ready to go back to the house, but neither of us said anything more.

Chapter Nineteen

I sat on the window seat in my room that evening, thinking about Simon and the faeries, and everything they believed, and everything they thought I could do. It all seemed so unbelievable, and I still held out hope that this was just an elaborate joke. To be honest, I actually favored the idea that I was crazy and all of this was happening in my unbalanced mind over the idea that it was actually true.

Even if it were true—if Simon and the rest really were faeries and there was an evil faery that needed to be defeated—it didn't mean I was the one mentioned in the prophecy. There were a lot of Margaret O'Neills out there, and the right Margaret O'Neill might not have even been born yet. I could go downstairs and try on the ring, and nothing would happen, just as nothing had happened when the rest of them had tried it on. But what if the ring did fit me? Would I be able to find strength when I needed it? It didn't feel like I had enough courage inside of me to save myself. I definitely didn't have enough to save the entire world.

And then I thought about my family. About everyone I loved. Was I willing to risk their lives and the lives of every non-faery on the planet because I was too afraid to come face to face with evil? Was I willing to walk away and watch as Balor killed each and every one of them? What about Simon? Would Balor kill Simon too?

Simon came to my room when it was time to go down for the meeting. I was still sitting in the window seat looking down at the vast lawn that spread out at the front of the house, the Atlantic Ocean churning in the distance. Keelin was walking toward the front door and she looked so beautiful with the wind blowing her black hair, making her look like she was in the middle of a photo shoot. I felt the sting of jealousy flowing through me, knowing it would be so easy for Simon to be with Keelin, and so hard to be with me.

"How're you doing?" he asked.

"Fine," I lied. I seemed to be getting really good at lying to Simon—to everyone.

"Can I sit down?"

I pulled my knees up to my chest and wrapped my arms around them, giving him room to sit on one end of the window seat.

"Did you and Keelin ever date?" I asked. He looked confused by my question. "I know," I said. "I should be thinking about the meeting and the ring and Balor and not something as silly and trivial as romance."

"Romance is not silly or trivial," he said.

"Did you ever date her?" I asked again, not wanting to let him off the hook.

"Yes," he answered. My heart nose-dived toward my feet.

"Would you still be dating her if you hadn't moved to Denver?"

"I don't know," he said quietly.

Before he could say anything more that might increase the number of fractures in my already breaking heart, I stood and told him it was time to go.

"Maggie—" he protested.

"I don't want to be late for my first ever ring-trying-on ceremony," I said as I walked out the door, leaving him to follow behind.

Simon caught up with me in the hallway and took my hand as we walked down to the great hall. I gripped his hand so hard it hurt, my nerves starting to come through as we got closer to the ring and everything it meant, but Simon didn't complain.

The large hall was filled with at least a hundred faeries. The ones I knew stood at the front of the room, waiting for me. I was a little overwhelmed at how many people had gathered and intimidated knowing they were all there to see me.

"Are you ready to start?" Sloane asked as I stepped into the room.

"Yes," I said, the word catching in my throat. Simon stood next to me and placed his hand protectively on the small of my back. I was scared and felt better knowing he was next to me, even if he were only there as my friend.

Liam took a small, black velvet box from his pocket and opened it, revealing a silver ring inside. I noticed with surprise that it was a Claddagh ring, very similar to the ones Simon, Finn and Erin wore, and I thought back to the time when Simon had said he was pretty certain someone would give me a Claddagh ring at some point. This one looked older and more worn than Simon's, but it still had the two hands coming together to hold a heart with a crown above it.

Once everyone had an opportunity to inspect the ring, Sloane turned to me. "It's not too late to change your mind," she said.

I shook my head, ready to get it over with once and for all. I tried not to think about everything this ring meant—about how dramatically my life might change in the next few moments—because I knew if I did I wouldn't be able to go through with it. I could still feel Simon's hand on the small of my back and the heat from his skin reached through the cloth of my shirt and up to my heart, and knowing he was there with me made what I had to do a little easier. My heart was pounding wildly against my ribs as I took the ring from Liam's extended hand, and after a moment's hesitation, I slipped it on my right index finger. As soon as the ring touched my skin, I felt as if I'd been punched in the chest. I plummeted to the ground, sitting on my heels, my hands braced in front of me on the floor, trying to steady myself against falling any further. I was experiencing an extreme sense of vertigo and I felt like I was capable of falling well beyond the boundaries of the floor. I could hear Simon and the others asking me if I was okay. I could feel their hands on me, but they felt so distant. The room was getting darker and darker, and I was finding it hard to breath. I closed my eyes against everything I was seeing, too afraid to face whatever was happening to me.

"Don't fight it, Maggie Girl," I heard a woman call to me, using the nickname my grandfather used. "Don't fight it. Let yourself come to us. Open your eyes."

When I opened my eyes, I didn't see Simon or the other faeries. Instead I saw a dark room filled with people, young and old and each wearing clothes from different time periods. My great-great-grandmother approached me and put her hand on my face affectionately. Her hair was completely white and tied into a braid at the back of her neck. Her eyes were the same blue as mine, and she looked peaceful and kind.

"We've been waiting a long time for you," she said, smiling gently.

"Grandma Margaret?" I asked. She nodded, still smiling.

I looked around at the other people in the room.

"Your ancestors," she said, answering my unasked question. "The O'Neills and the Breslins. Come. Sit."

"I can't," I protested. "Simon. He'll be worried."

"That, my dear, is an emotion Simon is going to get to know very well. He'll spend a lot of time worrying about you in the days to come. Besides, he's waited two hundred years for you. He can wait a bit longer."

I saw Simon's face swim before my eyes and felt that he was simultaneously close and distant.

"Do something, Erin!" I heard him say frantically. "She's feverish. Something's happening to her." I felt his hands on my face. My own hands ached to reach out to him, to assure him that I was okay.

Then I felt Grandma Margaret's hand on mine, and the feel of Simon's hands on my face faded away. "Come," she said, pulling me deeper into the room. I felt myself teetering between the two worlds—the one with the room full of faeries and the one with the room full of my ancestors.

"Simon," I said through the fog of my consciousness, "don't leave me."

He rubbed his hand across my cheek and

whispered, "Never. I will *never* leave you."

I closed my eyes and slumped in a heap to the floor, and as I did I felt Simon's tears falling on my cheeks.

"Get the ring off her!" he yelled to someone I couldn't see. "It's going to kill her."

I felt myself being lifted off the floor in Simon's world and realized he had me in his arms, carrying me out of the room and up the stairs, and for a moment I was lost in the feeling of being so close to Simon. I could feel his arms around me, cradling me, the warmth of his hands reaching through layers of clothes and warming the skin beneath. I didn't want to leave the circle of their protection, but the pull was so strong.

"Come," Grandma Margaret urged, and Simon slipped a little further away.

"Am I dead?" I asked her as I sat down at the table with the group of strangers who were each a part of me—the strangers whose DNA ran through every cell of my body and made me who I was.

"Finn, please!" Simon was growing more and more frantic, and more and more distant. "Do something!" I was in my bed in Simon's house, but I didn't feel his hands anymore. I tried to open my eyes, to see his face, but he was slipping away from me.

"No. Not dead. Just taking a much needed mental vacation." My grandmother chuckled. "It's the ring," she explained. "It was meant to pull you here with us for a while."

"Then it *is* me," I confirmed, dread filling up in the pit of my stomach. "This is how we know that the ring 'fits' me."

Simon was gone. Everything in his world was gone

from my sight. My touch. I could no longer hear his frantic insistence that someone help me.

"Yes," she said, putting her hand gently on my face. "The ring fits you, Maggie. It was made to fit you."

"Why me?" It wasn't a complaint, but a genuine question.

She didn't respond.

I tried to pull Simon back to me. I'd started to tremble with the knowledge of what was happening and wanted to feel his protective embrace, but he was gone.

"So, what happens now?"

"Now you spend some time with us getting used to the idea of what's to come," she said. The others in the room—the rest of my ancestors—had faded away. I was alone with Grandma Margaret.

Chapter Twenty

Time didn't seem linear while I was with my ancestors, and I often felt like I was in a dream where I would jump from one scene to another with seemingly no transitions. I talked with so many of them about my life and their lives and the lives of everyone we knew and loved. Mostly though, I talked to Grandma Margaret.

"You know," she told me as we stood on a steep cliff overlooking the ocean below, "I knew your Simon before I left Ireland."

"I know," I said. "I saw a picture of you with Simon and Finn."

"He was a young boy then. Maybe ten or eleven in human years. I was an old lady of nineteen at the time." She smiled playfully.

"The prophecy could have been about you," I pointed out.

"It could have been, but it wasn't. I knew it would need to be a Margaret O'Neill that was born with that name. And, Simon doesn't love me."

"What difference does it make if Simon loves you or not?"

"The prophecy says Simon will fall in love with *the*

Margaret O'Neill."

I looked at her, dumbfounded. "Why should it matter? It won't help me do what the prophecy says I need to do—it won't help me kill Balor."

"It won't help you any more than having red hair will help you. It was just part of the description given in the prophecy. Your name. Your physical description. That sort of thing. But it also said Simon would fall in love with the Margaret he was looking for. He doesn't love me. He loves you."

"No he doesn't," I said, knowing even before the words left my mouth that he did. Grandma Margaret smiled knowingly.

"It's me," I confirmed once again.

"It's you."

I took a brief step back into Simon's world and when I opened my eyes, I saw that I was in my bed at Simon's house and he was sitting in a chair next to me. When he saw my eyes open, he jumped up and came to me, taking my hand in his.

"Maggie," he breathed, relief wrapping around him, sheltering him.

I stepped back into Grandma Margaret's world, straddling the two times and spaces.

Simon called for Erin, not moving his hand from mine.

"How about a walk?" Grandma Margaret asked.

I stepped out of Simon's world completely again, not ready to face what waited for me there.

"You need to stop being angry with that poor boy," Grandma Margaret said. "None of this is his fault."

"I know," I said miserably. "I just don't know how to stop blaming him. In my head, I know he's done nothing wrong, but I'm still angry."

"You're angry with Simon because it's safe, but the time has come for you to stop playing it safe, Maggie. You know Simon will tolerate your tantrums and your fits and he'll still love you." I was embarrassed by her candor and in the truth of what she was saying. "But the person you're really mad at—now *that's* dangerous."

I knew she was talking about Balor. His name seemed to be on the minds and lips of every faery and dead ancestor.

She stopped and put her hand gently on my cheek. "You need to harness that anger and direct it all toward its rightful owner. You need Simon's support, and shutting him out will only make what you have to do much more difficult than it needs to be. Don't waste that emotion on Simon. Use it against Balor."

"Simon lied to me. He told me so many lies."

"He's lied to you only once, Maggie Girl. Simon is unable to lie without causing himself considerable pain."

I looked at Grandma Margaret and tried to process what she had said. I thought about our trip to Breckenridge. The time when Simon had said he had a headache.

"Yes," Grandma Margaret confirmed what I was thinking, as if she could hear the thoughts in my head. "The ironic thing is that he was telling the truth about having a headache, but he could only get a headache of that scale from telling a lie."

"Why can't he lie?" I asked.

"It's a faery thing," she explained dismissively. "A faery can choose to not answer a question or a faery can choose to give only part of the whole truth, but if a faery tells an outright lie, they experience incredible pain. Only a handful of faeries have been able to master the magic necessary to lie without pain. What Simon did was very difficult and took a tremendous amount of willpower."

I laughed out loud. I'd dated a guy who couldn't lie. Who wouldn't want to date someone incapable of lying? Ironically, it was my own lack of honesty that had broken us up, and I wondered if we'd still be together if telling a lie would cause *me* extreme physical pain.

"If it was so hard, why did he do it?" I asked. "Why did he lie? Why did he cause himself so much pain?"

"To protect you, of course," she said.

I hated that Simon had caused himself pain for my sake. He would do anything to keep me happy and safe, and I'd taken all of his sacrifices for granted. "I've acted so badly," I admitted.

"Do you think Simon didn't rebel against his destiny exactly as you're rebelling now? You have more in common than you think, Maggie Girl."

∞∞

I pushed my way into Simon's world for another moment. It was dark, but I heard voices.

"Give her time, Simon," Erin said in a comforting and reassuring tone.

"There must be some way to get the damn thing off her finger!" Simon's voice was angry, but quiet.

"She's fine right now. Her pulse is steady. Her fever is starting to come down. Her color is good. Anything we might do to get the ring off could change that."

Simon didn't respond.

"If things change for the worse, we'll try again to get it off," Erin assured him. "For now, let her rest."

℘ᓚᘏ

"So, you're pretty angry about your place in this prophecy," Grandma Margaret commented as we sat on a low stone wall overlooking a creek that wound through the green hills surrounding it.

"Yes," I admitted. "And I just don't understand it. I'm not the best person to do this. I don't have special powers. I don't even know how to shoot a gun. I've never hit anyone or been in a fight. I can't do this. I don't stand a chance against Balor."

"And you're angry that you have to be the one to kill him."

"Yes," I said in a way that indicated my response should have been obvious. "There are seven billion people on this planet. Why couldn't any of them kill Balor? Why can't one of the faeries do it? Why does it have to be me? I had a good life and I was happy. Why did I have to have all of that taken away?"

"Let me ask you something, Maggie. How would you feel if you got to the end of your life and discovered there was something you could've done to prevent your death and the death of everyone you loved, but by the time you found out, it was too late? Which is worse? Right now, you know things about the world you don't want to know. You have to go and kill a very powerful faery and risk your own life doing it. But, if you got to the end of your life before you got this information, would that be worse or better?"

I thought about what she said and hated to admit to myself that it made sense. If I found out at the end of my life that there was something I could've done to save myself and everyone I loved, I would be so angry that I hadn't been given the chance to do what I needed to do. It was better to know. It was better to have a chance at survival—even if that chance was minuscule. I didn't like my place in this prophecy, but I would like it even less if there was nothing I could do—that anyone could do—to save the world.

"But why me?" I asked, hearing a slight whine in my voice.

"It's not like she *chose* you—the woman who made this prophecy. She didn't *decide* it would be you. She saw the future and saw you killing him. It was a prediction, not a decision."

"So she could be wrong."

"She's never been wrong before."

"But she could be—this time."

"Only *you* can decide if believing in this prophecy is worth the risk."

⚭

"I'm here if you need me," Grandma Margaret said as we sat in the kitchen of the stone cottage in her world. "You won't go through this alone."

A small boy of about six sat with us, cheerfully snapping peas. He was my grandfather's brother, William, who had died when he was six, and I wondered if I'd ever be able to tell my grandfather that I'd spent time with his brother who had died sixty years earlier.

"Granny says we're your investors," William told me importantly.

Before I could think too much about what he meant, Grandma Margaret chuckled and said, "Ancestors, William, not investors. We're not giving the girl money."

I smiled at William, and he came to sit on my lap, wrapping him arms around me before turning around and leaning against my chest.

"I have to kill Balor," I said, stating the obvious once again.

"Your destiny is only what you choose it to be."

"So I don't have to kill Balor if I don't want to?"

"Oh, no," she said, smiling enigmatically. "You have to kill Balor. But only because you've already chosen to make it a part of your destiny." Her riddles sometimes gave me a headache.

"You'll never be alone, Maggie Girl. Remember that. You'll never be alone."

"Okay," I said, not really certain about what she was telling me.

"You need to go back now," she continued. "They're waiting and they've worried long enough."

"But I don't have any idea what I'm supposed to do. How am I supposed to kill Balor? I don't even know where he is or how to get to him. How do I keep him from killing me?" I wasn't ready to go back. I wanted more information that might help me.

"The pieces of the puzzle will all come together when they need to. Trust in that."

I nodded reluctantly, not wanting to leave her.

"Grandma," I said before I left her world, "you

come to me in my dreams."

"Yes dear, I know. I've always looked after you and I always will."

"Thank you," I said, tears forming in my eyes. I wasn't ready.

She smiled again and said gently, "Go back now."

I hugged William tight before lifting him off my lap and standing up. Grandma Margaret and little William started to fade away from me, and in their place I saw Simon sleeping in the chair beside my bed. I waited for a few minutes, expecting to float back to Grandma Margaret again, but I didn't. I was back in the real world and knew I should be happy about that, but it just made me feel more vulnerable. Being with Grandma Margaret had allowed me to put off the inevitable, but once I'd left her, I'd have to move forward with the waking nightmare that had become my life.

I sat up and pulled my knees to my chest before wrapping my arms around them. Simon looked so seraphic and peaceful as he slept, and I didn't want to wake him. When he finally opened his eyes, he looked at me, confusion crossing his face.

"What's wrong?" I asked him.

"I'm trying to decide if you're really awake or if I'm dreaming."

"You're not dreaming. I'm here. I'm staying here now."

He came to me and wrapped me in his arms. "Maggie," he murmured into my hair. The relief in his voice was strong; sharp little ice crystals of worry melting away.

"I'm okay." I wrapped my arms around him. I felt

like I hadn't slept in days, and it occurred to me that maybe I hadn't. I didn't remember sleeping while I was with Grandma Margaret, and while it felt like I had been sleeping in Simon's world, maybe it only appeared that I had.

"How do you feel?" Simon asked, pulling back to look at me.

"Tired."

He laughed, the relieved expression on his face palpable. "You've been sleeping for three and a half days."

I felt my eyes go wide in shock and jumped out of bed, grabbing my purse from the desk and rummaging through it to find my phone.

"Oh god, oh god, oh god," I mumbled nervously as I pulled it out of my bag. Simon was next to me, pulling the phone from my hand. "I told my parents I'd call every day. They've probably already called the FBI, and the CIA and the Irish equivalent of the FBI and CIA."

"G2," he said calmly as he led me back to the bed.

"What?"

"G2. The Irish equivalent of the FBI."

"Whatever. My parents are freaking out by now. I'm surprised Navy SEALs aren't already repelling down from helicopters or something."

"Finn took care of it," he said—still annoyingly calm.

"What do you mean he took care of it?"

"He worked his magic," Simon said with a pointed look.

"Ah, literally."

"Yes. Everything's fine. They think you've been

working hard on your Winterim project but have found time to call them twice every day that you've been here."

My heartbeat slowed somewhat, and I found myself able to take a deep, calming breath.

"I can't believe I was asleep for three days." I walked back to the bed and sat down on the edge.

"It felt like an eternity," he said softly. "You did wake up and look at me once."

"I remember. I woke up another time, but it was dark and you didn't notice. I don't think I was sleeping, though." His expression turned to curiosity and concern. "I was with Grandma Margaret."

"*Your* Grandma Margaret?"

"Yes. You know, the one my grandpa told me about over Christmas. You met her. The one in the picture."

Simon's face became ashen.

"I was in her world while I was gone," I explained. "A bunch of my ancestors were there, but I mostly talked to her. I went back and forth, though. Between here and there."

"What did your grandmother say?" Simon asked.

"She told me you can't lie," I began. "She said it's a faery thing. And she said that I should stop being angry with you and funnel my anger toward Balor. And," I hesitated, not wanting to deliver this last blow, "she said it *is* me who has to kill him, Simon. I'm the one."

Simon looked at me, but said nothing.

"What's wrong?"

"We guessed as much when we couldn't get the ring off," he said. "It seems to have chosen you."

I hated the expression I saw on his face and knew the conflict of his emotions had to be torturous for him. He'd been looking for me his entire, very long life. He'd finally solved an incredibly difficult puzzle, but he didn't want it to be me because he loved me. He knew the dangers I would face and he didn't want it to be me.

"I'm the one, Simon," I said as gently as I could. "It has to be me." He moved to sit beside me, pulling me to rest my head against him, his cheek nestling into my hair. I heard the air move in and out of his chest and the thu-thump of his heart pounding. He wrapped his arms around me, and I didn't fight him. Grandma Margaret had changed the way I felt about so many things—including Simon. I knew she was right. I knew he loved me. I knew he was in just as much pain as I was and he was just as afraid. I let him hold me and soon fell into a dreamless sleep.

When I woke up, I was lying down and Simon still had his arms wrapped around me. I moved my arm to rub his side, letting him know I was awake. I still felt groggy, but I also felt like I needed a shower and some food, and while Simon insisted on waiting in my room until I was ready to go downstairs with him, I assured him that I could manage the shower and toothbrush on my own.

After I had dressed, I walked downstairs, surprised at how completely normal I felt—not like I'd been sick or anything. One moment I was in a coma-like state and the next I was back to my old self.

As I approached the door to the kitchen, I heard angry voices.

"You're expecting too much from her!" It was

Simon making the big fuss. "Every one of you seems to forget that she is a seventeen-year-old girl! Do any of you understand that?"

"Yes, Simon, we do," Liam said, "but what choice do we have?"

"We don't know, do we?" Simon said, his voice still agitated. "We actually have no idea if this is the solution to the problem. All we have to go on is an old story."

"You know it's more than that, Simon." Sloane this time. "You know that every one of her prophecies has come true. Are you willing to risk all of humanity and the world as we know it in the off chance there is an alternative plan?"

"There has to be another option!" Simon insisted. "For now, let's just keep protecting her. Let's keep her alive while the Guardians work to defeat Balor. It's our job, not hers."

I wanted to go into the room full of faeries and tell Simon he needed to stop protecting me, but I didn't actually want him to stop. Not really. It felt good knowing that he was pulling me back, keeping me from getting any closer to Balor.

I opened the door and looked at the small group gathered in the kitchen. Finn, Erin, Keelin and Liam were standing with Sloane and Simon, and they all fell silent when I walked into the room. Simon turned quickly to look out a window, and I guessed he probably didn't want me to see that he was upset.

"We should head out if we're going to get some dagger practice in," Keelin told Simon.

Simon turned to face her and nodded, his expression still grim.

"I'll go with you," I told him. "I want to learn how to use a dagger." It would be great if the Guardians could take Balor down before I got a chance to do it myself, but I knew I'd need to develop some skills in case they didn't.

Keelin let out of snort of laughter at my suggestion and coughed to cover it up.

"You don't need to learn how to use a dagger, Maggie," Simon protested. "We're going to protect you."

"And what if you can't?" I asked him. "Are you expecting me to fight Balor with my good looks?"

Keelin snorted again and didn't even try to cover it this time. Simon shot her an angry look, and I stalked out of the room, prepared to sulk for a long time.

Chapter Twenty-One

Simon didn't return to the house all day, and I wanted desperately to go and look for him, but I was still angry with Keelin for laughing at me and angry with Simon for so many things. Late in the afternoon I positioned myself in one of the drawing rooms at the front of the house in a comfy armchair, hoping to see Simon when he returned. Erin came into the room and sat next to me.

"Put yourself in his shoes, Maggie," she said, curling her legs to her chest and wrapping her arms around them. "He loves you, and it hurts him to know how much danger you're in now."

"He broke up with me, Erin," I reminded her.

"I know he broke up with you, but he does love you. He was ready to love you before we even came to Denver, but it's more than that. He also feels responsible for the position you've been placed in. He's spent his entire life looking for you, but if he hadn't succeeded, you'd be carrying on with your life in Denver, oblivious to our world. Because he found you, you're here, with a bunch of faeries, plotting ways to save humanity."

"But if he hadn't found me," I protested, "I would

definitely die—along with everyone else."

"Yes, but if he hadn't found you, he wouldn't know you, and the thought of losing you wouldn't hurt so intensely."

Ah. I could feel the light bulb in my brain turning on.

"I feel so out of control, Erin. Simon seems so sure of his place in this world and what's expected of him, but I can't seem to stop fighting against it."

"There was a time when Simon fought against who he was," she assured me. "He went through a pretty rough rebellious phase. He was a bear to live with for the better part of fifty years."

"Fifty years? Are you kidding me?"

"No. I'm very serious. I was there to experience it first hand, although his anger was mainly directed toward Finn. Ironically, I think it brought them closer together."

"What finally snapped him out of it? How did he stop being so angry?"

"You'd have to ask him to be sure, but I think it occurred to Simon that had he been given a choice, he would have picked this life. He would have made the decision to fight Balor. It was the lack of choice that was the biggest problem for Simon."

"Why doesn't he have a choice?"

She hesitated a moment before answering. "The prophecy isn't just about you. It's about Simon, as well."

I nodded. "It's not something I would have chosen for myself."

"You may see things differently in time."

"I hate that he broke up with me," I confided.

"Do you understand why he did?"

"He wanted me to have a choice, but I did choose to be with him. I *wanted* to be with him."

"Did you? Honestly?"

There was that word again— "honestly." It took on new meaning after learning from Grandma Margaret that Simon and the rest of the faeries couldn't lie. Simon had always known that the people closest to him were completely truthful at all times, but I hadn't been. I had lied to him and lied to myself so much that it was difficult to sort out the lies from the truth. I *had* been angry with him and I *had* questioned whether or not I wanted to be with him. Simon saw through my lies the night I kissed Luke, and I felt horrible for hurting him. Had he ever been lied to by someone he loved before? I doubted it. There were many firsts I wanted to share with Simon, but being the first person he cared about to lie to him definitely wasn't one of them.

⋙⋘

I started to get restless as the sun set and decided to walk out to the courtyard, knowing that I'd see Simon return a good three seconds sooner than if I waited inside. Aidan walked through the archway, a yellow lab following behind him.

"Woudja want a fire?" he asked as he walked toward me. "It'll fight off the chill."

I nodded and he started to pull wood from the pile beside the outdoor fireplace in the middle of the courtyard.

"I can do it," I said, taking the logs from him.

"You sure?" he asked. "I'm happy to help."

"Thank you, but I can do it."

"Okay, then. I'll leave you to it. Let me know if you need any help. There's some dried kindling in the box there." He gestured toward a wooden box that sat next to the fireplace, then walked toward the house.

"Oh, that'll be Jake," he said before going through the back door. "Simon's dog."

Jake walked to a corner of the courtyard, picked up an old watering can in his mouth and carried it back to me, dropping it at my feet.

"Gee, thanks," I told him as I picked up the can and set it next to the fireplace. He wagged his tail wildly.

I piled logs into the fireplace and stuffed some of the kindling beneath them before looking for a match. There didn't seem to be any in the box of kindling, so I walked to the house to look, Jake following close behind.

Aidan was in the kitchen and I asked if he knew where I could find matches.

"Oh, uh—" he started opening and closing drawers and cabinets, but didn't really look in them carefully. He finally turned around and looked at me, shuffling from one foot to another. "Well, the thing is, Maggie, we don't really need 'em you see."

My eyebrows knit together in confusion. He lifted one hand bashfully, as if he were ashamed of it, and in a moment, fire licked at his fingertips, then extinguished itself.

"I'll go out and light it for you," he offered.

I nodded, feeling stupid for some reason, and followed him back outside. Flames licked at his fingertips once again, and I watched as he tossed a small ball of flame toward the firewood piled in the fireplace. Within seconds, the logs were blazing with fire.

"Thanks," I muttered.

"My pleasure," he said before leaving me with Jake.

I took the blanket that was draped across the back of the outdoor sofa and wrapped myself in it while I waited for the fire to warm me, finding myself oddly comforted by the woodsy smell of the smoke. Jake tilted his head to one side in a way I chose to interpret as, *Look, Maggie. Fire.* He then trotted over and sat down in front of me, burrowing his nose under my hand in an attempt to communicate his desire for me to pet him. It was so peaceful to sit outside with Jake, watching the fire burn and crackle.

"Do you think Simon will ever forgive me?" I asked Jake.

He tilted his head again, and this time I decided it meant, *Of course he will. He loves you.*

"Do you think *I* love *him?*"

Another head tilt. It looked like Jake was trying to say, *Yes, you idiot, of course you love him. You're never going to be happy unless you admit that to yourself.*

"What if he doesn't really love me? What if I tell him I love him and he laughs at me? What if he doesn't want to be my boyfriend again?"

Jake tilted his head again, and this time he seemed to be sending an increasingly hostile message. *Maggie, you are so stupid. If you don't suck it up and tell him you love him, you're going to lose him to Keelin. I mean have you seen her? She's absolutely gorgeous. I'd date her if I walked on two legs.*

"Oh, shut up," I told Jake.

He barked once, and I'm pretty sure that meant, *You asked.*

I was profoundly relieved when I saw Simon walk through the darkness and into the courtyard. That relief turned quickly to pain, however, when I saw Keelin walking beside him. Had they spent the entire day together? The wedge that had formed in our relationship—the wedge that had started to dissipate after my time with Grandma Margaret—was suddenly back and bigger than ever.

Jake jumped up from his spot near me and ran to greet them. I turned to leave quickly, before either of them could see me, and went to my room, wanting to put the mental images I was having of Simon and Keelin out of my head.

I heard a knock, and before I could respond, Simon had opened the door a few inches and peeked in at me. "Can I come in?" he asked.

"Yeah," I said, that one word completely devoid of enthusiasm.

He came and sat on the bed next to me. "I'm sorry about this morning. Keelin was out of line."

I didn't say anything, still fuming from the sight of Simon and Keelin walking together toward the courtyard, and after several long moments of the silent treatment, he stood to leave.

"Simon, I don't want to be friends with you anymore," I blurted out, pushing past the hard lump that was forming in my throat.

He turned back around to face me, and when I saw the hurt look on his face, I knew he'd misunderstood.

"I want us to date again," I said quickly, trying to

clear up his misinterpretation. "I hate that we broke up. I think I understand *why* you broke up with me and I think maybe I'd thought about breaking up with you too, but I know what I want. I want to be with you."

He took a few deep breaths in a way that made me think he was trying to steady himself, and I thought about Keelin and wondered if it was too late. Maybe I'd lost him forever to the girl he'd known for over two centuries. "If you've changed your mind and want to date Keelin instead, I'll try to understand."

"Keelin?" Simon asked, confused.

"You said you used to date her."

"I did date Keelin and I do love her." My heart twisted miserably in my chest with those last words. "But," he continued, (*Oh thank god there's a "but."*) "I love her like a sister. We grew up together. At one time we tried to be more than friends, but it didn't work out."

So, I had one obstacle out of the way. Simon had just confirmed that his relationship with Keelin wouldn't be something that would keep us apart. That just left the one thing neither of us wanted to talk about—the one thing that had been the impetus of our break up. It hung in the air, translucent and indefinable, and that made it harder to battle. I had to say it out loud. I had to give shape to the ugly monster coming between Simon and me, because it was the only way for us to stab away at it and defeat it.

"Simon," I said, unable to look at him, "I kissed Luke." There it was. It was out. I could almost feel it taking shape in front of us, filling every crack and crevice in the room.

He was painfully still for a heartbeat. "I know, love.

I was there." His tone was rough and quiet, and I knew the thought of Luke and me kissing was difficult for him.

"I was an idiot."

He smiled. "Since I can't lie, I won't disagree." He was teasing me, and it felt familiar and good. "But you kissed Luke for a reason, and that reason hasn't changed. I'm still a faery. I will always be a faery."

"It doesn't matter."

"What's changed, Maggie? Why did it matter then but it doesn't matter now?"

"I know what I want. There's no doubt in my mind anymore. I want *you*. I kissed Luke because I wanted everything to go back to the way it was before, but I don't want to go back to that life if I can't take you with me."

"I think you want the guy you thought I was but you don't want who I really am. I will always be a faery," he repeated. "Nothing can change that."

I felt my heartbeat quicken and a painful flush crushed my ribs. He was still rejecting me, and it hurt, but I couldn't give up. I needed to be strong enough to push past the pain so I could tell him how I felt. "You told me once that you don't regret being a faery because if you were human you would have died a long time ago and you never would have met me."

"Yes."

"Well, it's the same with me. I'd prefer to have an ordinary life *with* you, but if I have to choose, I pick the crazy life *with* you over the normal life *without* you."

"I think now is not a good time to be making that decision. You have so much to think about and to worry about and any decision you make about me right now will be clouded with fear and anxiety, but I'm not going anywhere, Maggie. I'll be here for you every step of the way, no matter what."

"You're right. Everything that's happening with the ring and Balor *is* affecting my decision. It's making me realize what's important, and I know I can't assume I can put off the things that are important until tomorrow because I have no guarantee that there will *be* a tomorrow." I took a few steps closer to him, hoping that if I shortened the physical distance between us, it would shorten the emotional distance, as well. "You've been a great friend to me since we met, Simon, and I have no doubt you'd continue to be a great friend to me if that's what I asked of you. But it's not what I want. What can I say to make you believe that?"

He didn't respond, and I could see the battle going on behind his eyes. It was the same battle I'd seen on the first day he kissed me. He wanted to be with me as much as I wanted to be with him, but he was worried that it wasn't the right thing. He was trying so hard to fight his true feelings for me in order to do what he thought was right, but I knew he was losing that battle with himself.

I moved closer to him and gently reached up my hand and brushed his cheek. He shuddered slightly but didn't move. I lowered my hand and looked into his eyes. "If you can honestly tell me you don't want to be with me, then I'll back down right now."

"It's not what I want," he whispered, his voice unsteady. "But I need to do what's best for you."

"Being with you *is* what's best for me."

The battle behind his eyes intensified. I wanted to

make this easier for him but I didn't know how. I'd only known Simon for seven months and when I compared that to the two hundred years he'd been alive, it was such a minuscule amount of time, but I still had a pretty good grasp of who Simon was. He was selfless. He'd been taught to sacrifice his own happiness and his own wellbeing in order to do what he thought was right. Us being apart wasn't right, and I didn't know how to make him see that, but pushing him was just causing him pain, and I couldn't do that to him. I had tried, but I had failed and I knew it was time to accept defeat. Reluctantly, I turned away from him and walked toward the window, keeping my back to him. I felt the tears in my eyes but worked really hard to keep them from falling. I didn't want him to see. I didn't want him to know how much pain I was in because I knew that would just cause *him* more pain.

We stood apart, the room separating us for a long time. When I heard him walk toward me, I felt a fluttering burn in my chest that made it hard for me to breathe. He took my hands and turned me to face him, and the touch of his skin on mine was almost unbearable. Reaching up, he tenderly placed a hand on either side of my face, encouraging me with his fingers to look into his eyes.

Chapter Twenty-Two

"**Y**ou hurt me," he said simply, his pain pushing through his words, his fingers and every breath he took.

I nodded and forced myself not to cry.

"You have the ability to lie to me," he said, "but I'm begging you not to lie to me now. Please, promise me that this is honestly what you want." His voice was soft, kind, and patient.

I nodded my head, unable, at first, to say anything. I took a few deep breaths to chase away the ache in my chest and whispered, "I promise."

He kept his hands on my cheeks, and I could feel the heat and longing and confusion coming through his fingertips, forcing the hurt away. He looked intently into my eyes for several long moments before pulling my face toward him for a kiss—the kind of kiss that mends everything that's been broken, fusing together all of the damaged pieces. As he kissed me, a wonderful thought snuck into my brain and settled over all of the worry and frustration and fear: I did love him. I'd probably loved him for a long time, but had fought against it because I was an idiot. Now that one thought brought me so much peace and joy, and I wanted to tell him—I wanted him to know how wonderful it felt to love him—but I stopped myself. Almost as soon as the thought popped into my head, my brain started to strengthen the already existing walls of steel that protected my heart.

"I missed you," I whispered instead.

"Oh, Maggie, I missed you too," he sighed. He moved his hand to rest at the back of my neck, his fingers tangled in my hair, pulling me closer to him as he kissed me again. I found the bottom of his shirt and moved my hands beneath it to rub the bare skin of his back. I could feel him shiver with my touch, and his kiss became more intense.

I heard a knock on the door and wanted to ignore it, but Simon pulled away from me and walked over to open it.

It was Erin. "I just wanted to check on Maggie before I went to bed. How're you feeling?"

"Great," I said, blushing.

She smiled knowingly. "I'll leave you to it, then." She walked out of the room and Simon closed the door behind her and pulled me to lie down with him on the bed. I rested my head on his chest and enjoyed the closeness of him, knowing I'd never take a single moment with him for granted.

"Saved by the knock again?" I whispered to Simon, knowing that Erin's interruption had prevented each of us from getting lost in the moment. I felt his chest move as he chuckled.

We were both quiet for so long that I thought maybe he'd fallen asleep.

"Simon, are you awake?"

"Yes." He started rubbing my hair gently and kissed

the top of my head.

I waited for a long time before asking him the question on my mind. "Have you every *been* with anyone?"

He continued to rub my hair but didn't immediately answer. "No," he finally said.

I was more than a little incredulous. "You mean," I began, pulling away from him so that I could see his eyes, "in over two hundred years, you've never been with a woman?"

One corner of his mouth turned up, and I could tell he was fighting a smile. "I can see that two hundred years without sex probably seems unbearable to you," he said, "but to me, two hundred years is a relatively short time." He hesitated again, and I knew he was thinking very carefully about what to say to me. "Fairies age about one year for every twelve human years, so in human years, I'm about the same age as you are, both physically and emotionally. You wouldn't be too surprised to know someone of seventeen was still a virgin."

I curled myself back into the crook of his shoulder and tried to wrap my mind around all of that.

"What about Keelin?" I asked, voicing the inevitable.

"I never had sex with Keelin," he said carefully.

"Were you intimate at all?" I asked, knowing I was taking advantage of his inability to lie.

"We kissed," he admitted.

"Anything else?"

"Not much else," he said quietly.

"What does that mean?" I asked, my heart beating furiously with the possibilities.

"There was one time when I thought...I thought we might do more than kiss."

"What happened?"

"I was reminded of who I was and of my responsibilities."

"What reminded you?"

"Finn. He interrupted us and slapped me soundly on the side of my head."

I liked Finn a little more knowing he had aborted any intimacy between Simon and Keelin.

"And nothing happened after that—between you and Keelin?"

"No."

We were silent again, interlaced in each other's arms and enjoying our rediscovered intimacy.

"Maggie?" Simon asked after about ten minutes.

"Hmmm?"

"Have *you* ever *been* with someone?" he asked carefully.

"You know what happened that night with Luke," I answered. "He got a few bruises for trying to 'be' with me."

"Yes, but that doesn't mean there hasn't been someone else."

"No," I assured him, "there's been no one else."

He sighed heavily and kissed the top of my head.

"Simon?" I asked after another lengthy silence.

"Hmmm..." he murmured into my hair.

"Do you ever think about *being* with me?"

He laughed softly. "Only every minute of every day."

"Oh," I said. "But you only ever kiss me."

"I'm thinking that one of my faery gifts must be

extreme levels of self control," he teased.

"You don't want to do more than kiss me?"

"Yes, of course I do. I just want to make sure we're both ready. It's a huge step and not one I take lightly. Besides, the two times I thought we might do more, we were interrupted by a knock on the door."

I chuckled, knowing exactly which times he was referring to.

"Maggie," he said before I could fall asleep.

"Yeah?"

"Do ever think about *being* with me?"

"Every minute of every day," I admitted, echoing his words back to him.

He sighed deeply and rubbed his hand against my back. "Sleep well, *cushla macree.*"

The words were foreign to me, but I heard the tenderness in his voice, and it made them sound somehow familiar and right.

"What does it mean?" I whispered.

He smiled. "Sleep well, *pulse of my heart.*"

And I did.

ℴ℞

"Hi," Simon muttered sleepily the following morning. He was still fully clothed, including his shoes, and he was lying on his side, his arm draped across my torso.

"Hi," I said, smiling at him. I pushed a strand of his hair back from his forehead and rubbed my fingers along his temple. "You must have been really tired."

"Mmm," he murmured in assent. "I was shattered."

"Shattered?"

"Exhausted."

"Do you want to go back to sleep?"

"No. Finn's yelling at me to wake up," he said groggily. I gave him a questioning look, and he touched his index finger to his forehead absently.

Ah, yes. Faery Phone.

He kissed me briefly and sat up on the bed. "You coming down?" he asked.

"I'm going to brush my teeth first."

He nodded while suppressing another yawn, and walked toward the door, turning around before he left. "Finn just told me we have some guests. He thought you might want a warning."

"Guests?"

"Mmm." He nodded, finally giving in to the yawn. "People who heard the ring fit. They want to celebrate."

When I went downstairs after I'd showered and dressed, about a dozen people I didn't recognize were talking with the faeries in the house. By dinnertime, there were at least a hundred. Tables were set up outside in the courtyard, and food and drinks were brought out from the kitchen. People wandered around, talking and laughing, and occasionally someone would slap me on the back or hug me and offer congratulations. Simon stayed close to me the entire day, rarely taking his hand from mine.

Jake wandered around the courtyard all day, tirelessly dropping a variety of objects at people's feet—sticks, old shoes, work gloves, tennis balls.

"What's Jake doing?" I asked Simon.

He smiled brightly, obviously very proud of his dog. "He likes to bring people gifts when they come to the house."

I smiled too, thinking of the old watering can he had dropped at my feet the first night I'd met him.

"So, is Jake a faery dog or a regular dog?" I asked. I had no idea if faery dogs even existed, but my new worldview didn't exclude the possibility.

Simon laughed openly. "A regular dog. Faery dogs aren't this friendly." *Unfriendly faery dogs. Awesome.*

As the night wore on, a band formed and people began to dance. Sometimes everyone would sing along with the band, interrupted only when a toast was made—to me, to Ireland, to friends and love and hope. Everyone seemed so happy, but I couldn't help but feel like the sacrificial virgin being led to the mouth of the volcano.

Simon pulled me out of the crowd to dance with him during a slow song, taking my hand in his, moving expertly across the dance floor, the hand at my waist coaxing me gently to move to the destination in his mind. I felt as if our bodies were made for each other, made to move together. It was just the two of us out there—just the two of us in the world. The other dancers and people milling about faded away, and nothing in that moment was important except Simon and his hand holding mine and the belief that being with him was the most important thing I'd ever done. I heard the music change tempo, something faster, and Simon stopped dancing, both of his hands moving to my face, his lips reaching down to mine, and I felt like our lives were twining themselves together, everything from inside of me flowing into him through that kiss, and everything inside of him flowing into me, mixing and blending until it couldn't be separated into mine and his anymore.

"That kiss felt like magic," I whispered when he pulled away.

He smiled and rubbed his fingers along the side of my neck. "It was just a normal kiss. No magic."

"There was nothing normal about that kiss," I teased. He reached down and took my hand again, leading me away from the dance floor, both of us still smiling in the afterglow of something magical that wasn't magic.

"Just one dance, then," Aidan said, pulling me away from Simon, his exuberance making his offer hard to resist. I went with him and let him twirl me around to the fast tempo, but I was anxious to get back to Simon, anxious to keep the connection I was feeling with him from fading away.

When the dance finished, Aidan kissed my hand and said, "Thank you, Margaret." Hearing the formality of my full name made me blush inexplicably.

I looked around for Simon and saw that he was standing away from the crowd, talking with Liam, Finn and Sloane. Even before I could hear what they were saying, I knew it was a heated conversation. I walked toward them, curious and worried.

"There is no reason why Simon shouldn't remain as her primary Guardian," Sloane was telling Liam. "Maggie trusts Simon. That trust makes him the best person to guard her."

"Maggie may trust Simon, but I'm not so certain I do," Liam spat caustically.

"What's that supposed to mean?" Simon asked, anger in his voice.

"It means we would all do well to remember who you are," Liam responded.

In an instant, Simon had pulled back his fist and punched Liam, sending the older man to the ground.

Chapter Twenty-Three

"Go cool down, Simon," Finn told him. Simon looked at Finn for a moment and turned around to leave the party.

"This just proves my point," Liam reasoned.

"It proves nothing, Liam," Sloane said, "except that you can be an insensitive ass. Simon will continue to work as Maggie's primary Guardian. My decision is final."

"So we're just going to forget whose blood runs through those veins?" Liam asked.

"*Dun do chlab. Anois,*" Finn said to him quietly, menacingly. I didn't know what the words meant, but Finn's threatening tone went a long way toward translating for me.

Liam stood up and looked at Sloane and Finn scathingly.

I turned away, wanting to find Simon to make sure he was okay. I walked toward the stables, thinking he might seek out Jake for comfort, but didn't see him. I was heading back toward the house when I saw Alana.

"Looking for Simon?" she asked. I nodded. "He walked toward the strand."

"The strand?"

"The beach."

I hadn't had an opportunity to go past the tennis court during my stay and wasn't sure how to get down to the vast expanse of beach that ran along the Brady property. I started to open my mouth to ask, but Alana had already raised her hand to point out the direction. "There's a path just there—between the trees. You can't miss it."

I walked in the direction she'd pointed out and found the path. It twisted downward between the trees and came to an end when it reached sand and grass. Simon was leaning against a boulder that rested in the sand, his legs pulled up with his arms wrapped around them, his chin resting against his knees. He stared out at the churning of the ocean, and the luminosity of the moon created a reflection on the water that made it look alive.

"Hi," I said softly as I sat down next to him. I knew Simon was having a difficult time coming to terms with my place in the prophecy, and my heart broke for him. "Simon—" I began gently, rubbing my hand against his shoulder and back.

"I didn't want it to be you," he said, his voice rough. "I've looked for you my entire life. I was born knowing about you and I've spent my life searching for the girl in the prophecy but now that I've found you, I don't want it to be you. I don't want you to be in danger and I don't want you to face what you have to face."

"I know," I murmured. "I don't see any way around it though, and I think I'm ready—or at least getting there."

We were silent, Simon glancing over his shoulder at

the party in the courtyard.

"How can they celebrate this?" he asked, finally looking at me. "I know we're one step closer to killing Balor, but in the process we're putting you in a tremendous amount of danger. I don't see how that's something to celebrate."

I wanted to take his pain away, to feel it myself so he wouldn't be unhappy anymore. I realized Simon's happiness was just as important to me as my own, and the walls I'd built around my heart started to crumble and I wasn't afraid anymore—not of Simon and the way he made me feel—but at the same time, I felt my heart twist in pain. The walls I'd built around my heart had sheltered it, and now that the walls were falling away it was exposed and vulnerable in a way it had never been and I felt naked and unprotected.

Simon reached over and rubbed his hand against my cheek, his thumb gently caressing my jaw. The love in his eyes made the twisting in my heart ease a little, and I knew everything would be okay. I knew I could trust Simon to be gentle with my newly exposed heart.

"I love you, Simon," I said as his fingers pushed a strand of hair out of my face.

He stopped abruptly, his fingers still twined in the strand of my hair. He smiled before leaning in to kiss me. "I knew you'd get there eventually," he said as he rested his forehead against mine. "I've loved you from the first moment I saw you."

I sighed in exasperation. "So competitive," I admonished playfully. He moved his lips to my forehead, then down my nose and to my mouth. His kiss was soft and loving, and the tenderness of it made me believe that he really had loved me for a very long time.

"Just remember who said it first," I reminded him as his lips moved to my jaw.

"So competitive," he whispered against my ear. Then, moving back to look at my face, he said, "I love you, Maggie." He kissed me again, sweet and full of the love we felt. In that moment I felt luckier than any person on the planet. I smiled to myself—my life was in danger, as were the lives of everyone I knew, but I was lucky because Simon loved me.

I felt the quickening of my heart and the warmth that spread through my chest and the rest of my body. I raised my head so I could look into his eyes and placed my hand on the side of his face. He stared at me intently before leaning in to kiss me again. I wanted to kiss him and never move my lips from his, but I also wanted his lips available to tell me again that he loved me. It was the first time that I was envious of his faery powers. If we could communicate telepathically, he wouldn't need to speak.

After several wonderful minutes of kissing, Simon leaned back against the boulder, and I rested my head against his chest. His arms were wrapped around me, his hands rubbing my arms and shoulders.

"Are you cold?" he asked.

I laughed at the familiar question.

"What?" he asked, confused by my response.

"It just suddenly makes sense. All those times you asked me if I was cold. I never understood why you would ask me since I probably wasn't cold if you weren't, but you don't feel the cold as much as I do. That's why you always asked."

"Mm-hmm," he admitted as he removed his jacket

and wrapped it around my shoulders.

I settled back into his arms and watched the water moving across the sand, twisting through the large rocks that littered the beach.

He took my hand in his and touched the ring on my index finger. "You need to always wear this, no matter what," he said. "Liam put a protective charm on it before you tried it on and he also thinks the woman who made the prophecy put some sort of protection on it. The magic Balor and his followers can do is very powerful, so we don't know how much protection it will actually give you, but you need to never take it off. You'll be safer with it on than you will be without it."

"I thought you guys couldn't get it off when I was sleeping. It seems like it might be stuck for eternity."

"Maybe," he agreed, "but Liam thinks you might be able to take it off yourself."

"Should I try now?" I asked, nervous about the result.

Simon looked nervous too, but in the end nodded for me to try. I pulled the ring off my finger without any trouble and easily slipped it back on. I didn't notice any change during the two seconds it took to accomplish the task.

"So," I said, "now we know."

"Now we know, but don't take it off again. Please."

I took a deep breath and curled myself closer to him, starting to feel the chill of the humid Ireland air.

"There's something else," Simon said after kissing the top of my head and wrapping his arms around me, "Until he's...defeated, you won't ever be alone. There will always be several Guardians with you, although they'll generally make themselves invisible."

"I heard you talking to Liam. He said you're my primary Guardian."

"Yes, I'm your primary Guardian. I have been since we first moved to Denver last August, but I can't always be with you, and now that we know you're *the one*, it'll be even more important to protect you. Balor will eventually find out and he'll come after you, so you'll have several Guardians with you at all times."

I hadn't considered the idea of bodyguards. "*All* the time?" I asked, sitting up to look at him.

He looked at me and with complete seriousness said, "*Always.*"

"Well that's going to be annoying," I murmured.

"Yes," Simon said with an ironic smile, "but maybe not *quite* as annoying as dying and taking all the hopes of humanity with you."

"No. Maybe not *that* annoying," I agreed. "What about..." I started.

"Yes?" he prompted.

I looked at him and worried about asking him my question. "It's not important," I mumbled, dropping my head in embarrassment.

He put his hand under my chin and lifted it until I was looking at him. "Maggie," he said sweetly, "You should know by now that you can ask me anything."

"It's not important. You'll think it's stupid anyway," I mumbled.

He kissed me gently. "Ask me your question," he encouraged, his lips moving against mine. It took me a minute to remember what the question was, but as the kiss became more passionate, it came back to me.

"Will you and I ever be alone, or will someone always be with us?" I asked, unable to look him in the eye.

"I'm a Guardian, so you'll be protected when I'm with you, but there will generally be at least one other Guardian nearby, even when I am." He smiled and kissed me again. "But, if we request it, they'll give us some privacy."

"Are we alone now?" I asked. I knew faeries could see each other, even when they made themselves invisible to humans, so Simon would know if there were any faeries with us.

"We're alone. There are enough Guardians at the house and on the grounds tonight to keep Balor away. Alana followed you down here but left when she saw you were with me."

I started kissing him again, not holding back any of the physical longing that had been building for the past few weeks. We had a lot of catching up to do in the passion department, and I didn't want to waste any time getting to it—especially if our time alone was going to be scarce. I caressed his hair roughly, running it through my fingers. He kissed me back, nibbling gently at my lower lip before pulling away to move his mouth to my jaw, then my neck, kissing me just below my ear. I moaned softly, moving my hands under his shirt, running them against his stomach and chest.

He pulled me to sit in his lap and I wrapped my legs around his waist, all the while placing soft kisses along his jaw and neck and finally on his lips, opening my mouth and touching my tongue to his. He moved his lips from mine and started to kiss my neck again, sending shivers through every nerve in my body. I lifted his shirt and moved my hands up and down his back. His left hand caressed my side, stopping at the top of my hip.

"I love you, *cushla macree*," he whispered into my ear.

Chapter Twenty-Four

Simon and I sat alone in the kitchen Monday morning eating our breakfast. Simon had cooked it himself, and as I ate my salmon and eggs, I realized that Simon cooked as well as Finn did. I was surprised they could both cook since, by the looks of their house, they could hire a staff of fifty just to do the cooking.

"By the way," I said, the thought triggering a question that had been on my mind since we'd arrived at Ballecath. "Why didn't you tell me you were rich?"

Simon laughed and the sound was so resonant and wonderful that it flowed through me and wrapped around me and I didn't want him to stop. "I guess I just don't think about it much," he admitted with a shrug. "I grew up this way. It's what's normal to me."

"Yes," I teased. "A house the size of Kentucky is quite normal."

He smiled and reached across the table to take my hand in his.

"Do you feel like being a tourist today?" he asked as his thumb traced lightly along my open palm.

"A tourist?"

"Mmm," he said distractedly. "Your parents think you're here on an educational vacation." He looked at me and smiled. "We spent an entire week of your vacation with the whole ring business, so I was thinking we could spend this week being tourists and working on your project—unless you want Finn to do some convincing, but I think it'd be fun to see some of the sights around here."

"What did you have in mind?" I asked. I hadn't left the grounds of Simon's home since I'd arrived in Ireland and was excited at the prospect of a change of scenery.

"I thought we could drive down to the Belleek factory and take a tour. That's a pretty touristy thing to do."

"What's Belleek?"

Simon shook his head in disbelief. "Maybe you're not as Irish as I thought," he joked.

We left Simon's house with enough Guardians to fill three SUVs. Simon, Erin, Finn and I rode in one car, and eight other Guardians rode in the two others. I was a little unsettled about the number of faeries joining us, but Simon explained we wouldn't have as many protections around us when we left the grounds of his estate.

Erin did a wonderful job describing the history of Belleek pottery during the two-hour drive and had even brought along some books with pictures of different pieces that had been made at the factory since its opening in the nineteenth century. The tour itself was fairly short, but I was absolutely amazed as I watched the artisans mold and cut the clay into beautiful flowers and basket weaves. I took pictures of the pottery in every stage and stopped in the gift shop to buy my mom a small candy dish with the signature

Belleek shamrocks painted on the side.

Our tour guide informed us that Belleek didn't sell "seconds," and any piece of pottery that was less than perfect was destroyed before it had an opportunity to leave the factory. He asked if anyone on the tour would like to smash a few pieces, and my hand went up in the air immediately. It felt fantastic to drive the wooden stick down on the delicate pieces in the small wooden box, shattering them until they were small shards of nothingness. After hammering away at the pottery for a full minute, I looked into the wooden box with the broken pieces. Finished pottery and unfinished clay mingled together in a small heap. Even though the pieces were completely broken and irreparable, I could see the beauty of what they had been. I could see the potential that had been in each and every piece, now lost forever. While it felt so cathartic to shatter the pottery, it also felt tragic. Even something that was less than perfect had the potential to be wonderful, but now that the pieces lay shattered, that potential was forever lost. I felt sadness for those broken pieces of pottery, knowing they were so like the broken pieces of my life. The ring and the faeries and everything I'd learned from them had torn my life apart and there wasn't a bottle of super glue large enough to fuse the pieces together.

"Getting in touch with your violent side?" Simon mused as we walked out of the factory.

"Something like that," I said.

After our tour of the Belleek factory, we drove to a small pub. I sat at a table with Finn, Erin and Simon, while the rest of the Guardians sat at three different tables around us. I laughed when our food was brought to the table, and three sets of eyes looked at me as if I'd gone off the deep end.

"The Irish really do take the potato seriously, don't they?" I offered as an explanation for my laughter. I looked pointedly at the plates that had been put in front of me. I'd ordered the Irish stew and saw that my meal consisted of three different types of potatoes. There were potatoes cut up in the stew and the stew had been poured over mashed potatoes. My meal had also come with a side of French Fries—which Simon informed me were called chips in Ireland. Everyone laughed freely, and it felt so good to be a normal teenage girl again, carefree and doing something as ordinary as poking fun of the food in a foreign country.

෨෬

"I've been thinking about something my Grandma Margaret told me while I was with her."

Simon and I were walking along a stream that flowed through the vast open lands around his home. It was the morning after our trip to Belleek, and we'd decided to take a walk around the estate before we went back out on the tourist trail. Jake had come with us, leading the way with his tail wagging in complete satisfaction, a stick hanging out of his mouth.

"What's that?" Simon asked.

We'd come to a rough wooden bench that overlooked a stone bridge with a small waterfall flowing beneath it. We sat close to each other on the bench and I pulled my scarf tighter around my neck to ward off the chill before taking Simon's hand in my own.

"We were talking about how I was rebelling against my destiny, and she said you and I had that in common. That you would understand the tantrum I'd been throwing because you'd had a tantrum of your own."

He laughed. "She doesn't miss much, does she?" I was silent, waiting for him to elaborate. "From the day I was born," he began, "I knew about you. Your name was spoken daily in our home. I knew that, according to the prophecy, I'd fall in love with you and that the love we had for each other would be deep and unending. When I was little, it used to make me feel important to be a part of such a pivotal prophecy, but as I got older, I fought against who I was and the role I was expected to play."

"Erin said your rebellious phase lasted fifty years."

He laughed. "I have absolutely no secrets from you, do I?"

"Actually, I think you have *many* secrets that you keep from me."

He looked at me with an unreadable expression before he continued. "When I was the equivalent of about thirteen human years, I decided I would not, under any circumstance, allow some old prophecy to determine who I would or would not fall in love with. I began to resent my lack of free will concerning my love life and I convinced myself that I wasn't bound by destiny. That's why I eventually started dating Keelin." I tensed when he mentioned his relationship with her, and he responded by pulling me against him to rest my head on his shoulder.

"I decided I wouldn't love the person I'd never met,

but that I'd love the girl I'd known my whole life and, to be honest, I did love her. I *do* love her. But the love I feel for Keelin is nothing compared to the love I feel for you. I didn't understand how deeply and completely I could love until I met you.

"Finn tried to be tolerant of my rebellion. He never told me to stop seeing Keelin, but he did warn me to be responsible with her heart. I think he knew, even then, that I was going to love you so much more than I could love her, and he was concerned about Keelin."

He sighed heavily.

"The Guardians do everything they can to keep tabs on all of the Margaret O'Neills because of the prophecy. Most of them we can eliminate as possibilities pretty early on. The ones that look like they could have the potential to fit the qualifications in the prophecy are tracked more carefully. Guardians living close to them are assigned to observe them from a distance."

"Like Mr. Warner," I pointed out.

"Like Mr. Warner," he confirmed. "Eventually it became obvious that you were quite likely the one we were looking for, and Finn wanted to move to Denver so we could watch you more closely."

Jake trotted over and sat in front of Simon, the stick still hanging in his mouth. His head tilt in this case obviously meant, *Please throw the stick for me. I'm itching to chase something.* Simon took the stick from Jake's mouth and threw it far from us. Jake tore after it, then got distracted on the way by something in the grass that apparently smelled really good.

"I fought him, though," Simon continued. "I told him that he could observe you on his own and bring you back here if he thought it was necessary. There was no need for me to move to Denver. There was no need for me to leave my home—or to leave Keelin—but he insisted. In the end, he and the others convinced me that it was my duty to go to Denver, so I went, but most unwillingly. I was still determined not to love you and most of the time I convinced myself that I wouldn't even like you."

"Why wouldn't you want to love me?" I asked, hurt and offended.

He smiled wryly. "I've always known that the girl I loved—truly loved—would have a horrible fate. The prophecy says that the one I love will have to be the one to defeat Balor. The love between us is unequivocally the most wonderful thing I've experienced, but it's bound together with this horrible fate you're having to face."

"But why you? Why does the person *you* love have to be the one to defeat Balor?"

"I honestly don't know. It's something I've given a lot of thought to, but I just don't know."

"Grandma Margaret told me that the woman who wrote the prophecy didn't choose me, but that she just saw the future."

Simon nodded. "We'd talked about just letting everything play itself out. The prophecy doesn't say we have to find you. I suppose we would have found each other eventually, but we started to worry about your safety—and the safety of every Margaret O'Neill out there. If Balor found you first, he'd kill you without hesitation, and he probably wouldn't think twice about killing a few more Margaret O'Neills—just to be on the safe side."

I shivered and zipped up my fleece jacket. It helped to keep the cold from hitting my body but it didn't do much to keep the fear away.

Jake came back with the stick in his mouth and laid it at Simon's feet. His tail wagged wildly, and his tongue lolled in anticipation. Simon picked up the stick and threw it again.

"I didn't want to love you, but then I saw you. You walked into Mr. Warner's class on the first day of school last August, and I guess destiny took over. I fell in love with you the moment I saw you, and the two months that followed were agony. I had to watch you with Luke, and it took all the self-restraint I could summon to keep myself from punching him on a regular basis. I hated the way he treated you and I wanted something better for you—even if it wasn't me. Then, it took even more self-restraint to keep from taking you in my arms and kissing you the moment I found out the two of you had broken up, but I was still fighting my love for you. I knew loving you would mean that you'd have to take your place in this prophecy and I very foolishly believed that if I could resist you—if I could keep our relationship in the 'friend' category—you'd be safe from all of this, but fighting my true feelings toward you proved to be impossible. You and Luke broke up on the last day of October, and I was able to resist temptation throughout November, but once December hit, I was lost. I kissed you on December 1st."

"I don't understand," I confessed.

"Remember that I told you faeries are at their most powerful during November?"

I nodded.

"Well, I could fight the temptation to kiss you when I was at my strongest, but once November was over, I was putty in your hands." He smiled and pushed my glove down so he could kiss my wrist. "The day I kissed you, I suggested we go for a walk, hoping I wouldn't be tempted to kiss you if we were out in public. Unfortunately, I didn't think my plan through enough to realize that nobody would be out and about in a snowstorm."

"Ah," I said, finally understanding so much.

"I didn't want to pull you into my world, but then I realized that no matter what I did, you *would* be a part of this. I already loved you, and that told me you were almost certainly the Margaret from the prophecy. Whether I was your boyfriend or not, I would still love you, and you would still be the one, so I decided I might as well give in to my feelings toward you."

"So, you do understand my rebellion," I acknowledged.

"Yes, *cushla macree,* I do understand," he said. "At least I had the benefit of knowing about all of this for two hundred and eight years. You've had only a few short weeks to come to terms with it, and I'm absolutely amazed at how beautifully you've handled the whole situation."

I leaned away from him and gave him a withering look.

"You have, love. I anticipated much worse."

"I doubt you threw a fit nearly as big as the one I threw," I said thinking about the way I'd been acting the past few weeks.

He laughed loudly. "You and Finn should have a talk some time. I'm sure he could set you straight regarding the advanced level of my rebellion. My fit lasted a lot longer than yours did and involved a lot more yelling and breaking of things."

"You broke things?"

"A lot of things."

"I find that hard to believe."

"Sad, but true," he admitted. "You're seeing me after my angry, dark period. It was difficult, once I truly understood everything, to resolve myself to this life. I definitely have a dark side."

I was having a hard time imagining the dark side of Simon. He seemed so perfect and in control all of the time—well, except when he'd punched Liam.

Jake came back with his stick, and Simon threw it into the stream, sending Jake bounding after it.

"So," I said after a pause, "I guess I understand better why Keelin hates me."

"She doesn't hate you," Simon insisted. "I've talked with her since we've been back and I've tried to explain to her how I feel about you. Be patient with her. She needs that right now. Just as you and I both need the people around *us* to be patient."

"Simon, have you ever met Balor?" I asked, changing the subject to one that loosened its grip on my heart but made my skin crawl.

He looked incredibly uncomfortable, and darkness filled his eyes. "Yes."

"What's he like?" I asked, awestruck.

He hesitated. "He comes off as a normal guy. He looks normal and he walks through the world as if he's just a regular guy. The thing that sets him apart is his ability to convince people that his vision of the world is the only one that matters. He's able to get people to do things for him that they otherwise wouldn't do. He's incredibly charismatic, to the point that it's considered a special faery power rather than an aspect of his personality. His powers are also beyond what most faeries have been able to accomplish. He can do magic and use it in ways that have never been seen."

"The man at the football game. He was one of Balor's men."

"Yes."

"What happened?"

"Balor heard we were in Denver and sent some faeries to look into why we were there. They found out about you and were at the football game to kidnap you and take you back to Balor. The man who told you Brandon was in trouble was human. He needed to lure you to the others waiting in the tunnel since they couldn't lie to you."

"Why would a human help Balor, though? He wants to kill all the humans."

"I'm not sure. It could be that someone with powers like Finn's persuaded him to do it. It could be that they threatened him—or bribed him."

I tensed up, and Simon rubbed my shoulder.

"We decided the best thing to do would be to have Finn persuade him and the two faeries that you didn't fit the physical description of the Margaret O'Neill in the prophecy so they'd go back to Balor with the information, detouring him off your trail—for a while at least."

"Did it work?"

"It's not really much of an issue now. He'll find out soon enough. There were so many faeries here the night you tried the ring on, and again at the party. One of them is bound to say something that will eventually get back to Balor, but we'll never leave you unprotected."

"I need to learn to fight or something. I want to learn some way to defend myself when Balor comes looking for me."

"You don't need to defend yourself. We'll protect you."

"But according to the prophecy, I'm going to have to fight him eventually."

"The Guardians are working every day to defeat him. With any luck, you'll never even need to meet him."

"But what if I do? I want to be prepared."

"We'll keep you safe," he insisted. I could hear how worried and determined he was and leaned up to kiss him, wanting to distract him away from the dark possibilities that were a part of our future. He looked at me with a tender smile and placed one hand on the side of my neck, his thumb caressing my lips before leaning in to kiss me back. At that moment, Jake came running back from the stream and jumped on us, his entire body wet and muddy.

"Jake," Simon reproached, "get down!"

Jake responded to Simon's reprimand by licking his face. As Simon worked to control an over-excited Jake, rain started to fall, the drops speckling our clothes. It started out slow and easy, but turned into a deluge surprisingly fast.

"Are you kidding me?" Simon looked incredulous. "Let's get back to the house before you're completely foundered."

"Foundered?"

"Freezing cold," he interpreted.

I chuckled. "Have you ever noticed how we speak the same language, but sometimes we don't?"

He laughed. "Let's go, my non-faery friend, before you freeze to death." He took my hand in his and we ran toward the house.

Chapter Twenty-Five

Simon and I spent the rest of the week driving to various tourist sights near Ballecath. We went to an artisan fair in Donegal and to the Giant's Causeway along the northern coast. We went to the Ulster History Park. We took a boat tour of Lough Erne, stopping at Devenish Island, which had once served as a monastery. At the end of the week, Simon helped me put together a presentation binder for my project that included an interactive CD. For a guy that was born at the turn of the nineteenth century, I was really impressed with Simon's computer skills.

"There's one more place I want to show you," Simon said the day before we were scheduled to leave Ireland.

"Where?" I asked.

"It's a surprise."

Our entourage piled into the SUVs we'd used all week, and we drove toward Donegal, but instead of going into the city, we went northwest, driving along twisting dirt roads for over an hour.

"Are you sure this is worth the trouble?" I asked Simon after our SUV hit a series of jarring ruts in the road.

"I'm sure," he said, turning to me and smiling.

A few minutes later, the caravan stopped alongside the road. The only building I could see was an old stone cottage, the roof and windows long gone.

I looked at Simon with confusion, but he just kept smiling.

"This is where your grandmother grew up," he said.

"This house? My Grandma Margaret lived here?"

He nodded.

"Can we go see?" I asked, inexplicable tears welling up in my eyes.

"Of course," he said. "That's why we're here."

Simon and I got out the car, but the other faeries remained where they were. I walked through a large opening on one wall of the cottage, the place where a door had once protected Grandma Margaret's family—*my* family. The floor was covered in grass and fallen rocks, and vines snaked around the interior walls. There were two rooms, both of them smaller than my room at home, and it was hard to peel away the layers of disrepair to see a family sharing their lives here, but I felt them there. I felt *her* there. I ran my hand along one of the walls inside the main room, and my heart was full with the love I felt for them, and the strangeness of feeling love for people I'd never met confused and overwhelmed me. I could feel the family together in this room, eating their meals, telling stories by the fireplace, sharing the big and small moments of their lives, and I knew this was a family that loved each other above all else. I could feel the memories of them coming through the walls and the floor and every piece of that small building.

A large fireplace separated the two rooms. Intricate

Celtic knots were carved into the stone that surrounded the fireplace, running along both sides and across the top. I ran my fingers over them, wondering if they had any significance or if they were just meant to be decoration.

"They're shield knots," Simon explained. "They're meant to offer protection."

I wondered what Grandma Margaret's family had wanted protection from. Had she known, even back then, about Balor and the threat he would become?

I sat down on the hearth and put my head in my hands, letting my tears flow into them. I wasn't sure why I was crying. Maybe because it felt like I was back with her, in her world, in the world she knew and loved. Maybe because that pile of rocks felt as much like home to me as my house in Denver. Maybe because Simon had been so thoughtful in knowing that this was something I'd want to see. Maybe because it had been a really long couple of weeks and my sleep schedule was totally screwed up.

Simon came and sat beside me, pulling me to him to rest my head against his chest. "Was I wrong to bring you here?" he asked.

"No," I said. "No. I actually think I'm crying because it feels so right."

I felt his chest fall as he let out a heavy sigh, probably relieved that I wasn't angry with him.

"Do you want to take some pictures?" he asked.

I nodded and wiped my tears with the palms of my hands before standing up to take my camera out of my purse. After taking a few pictures inside, we walked out together to take some pictures of the outside.

"This is where your grandma, Finn and I stood for

the picture your grandfather sent you," Simon told me as we walked beside a low stone wall. "I'll get Finn to take a picture of the two of us here." He must have used faery phone, because Finn was getting out of one of the cars before Simon had finished the sentence. I handed Finn my camera, and Simon sat on the stone wall, pulling me to stand in front of him, his arms encircling me. Finn had only taken a couple of pictures when I heard Simon take in a sharp breath. He must have said something to Finn telepathically, because Finn's face looked shocked, or concerned, or angry—I couldn't figure out which.

"Let's go," Finn said.

"What's going on?" I asked.

Simon stood up and took my hand and pulled me toward the car.

"Simon!" I insisted.

"It's Balor," he said as he got into the back seat after me.

Chapter Twenty-Six

"Balor?" I asked, shocked and afraid. "Where?"

"Not here," Simon told me, "but we'd all feel better if we get you back to Ballecath."

"Why? What's happened?"

"There's been an earthquake. In Ecuador."

"A big one?"

"Yes."

"People died?"

"I don't know."

"Balor caused it," I whispered, not wanting it to be true.

"Yes," Simon confirmed.

"How do you know it was him?"

He hesitated. "He's very proud of what he's doing and tends to celebrate after a disaster."

"He's celebrating?" I asked, incredulous.

Simon nodded and took my hand in his.

When we got back to Ballecath, we went to one of the drawing rooms, the television already turned on and showing footage of the disaster. The announcer was saying that the death toll stood at over twenty-five thousand, but was expected to rise significantly over the next few days. Video showed a woman sitting on a curb at the side of the road, covered in dust and wailing mournfully as she cradled a small, lifeless child in her arms. Nobody tried to comfort the woman. People passing by her looked dazed and injured, and I knew they were dealing with their own losses. Balor had done this. He'd caused the deaths of so many people and the grief of so many more. The small child in that woman's arms hadn't died as a result of forces beyond control. The child had died because of Balor, and I became more determined than ever to stop him. I would risk my own life and I would fight him until I died. He had to be stopped, and the longer it took, the higher the death toll.

"We need to stop him," I said quietly to Simon. "Now."

Simon wrapped his arms around me and pulled me close to his chest, tucking my head under his chin. "I know, *cushla macree*."

🙰

"Does it bother you to have faeries with you all the time?" Simon asked as he held my hand on the plane ride home.

"No," I admitted. "I think I prefer it, actually." I was nervous about leaving the safety of Ireland. Granted, I was probably physically closer to Balor while I was there, but I was also surrounded by hundreds of faeries willing to risk their own lives to protect me. Some of those faeries were making the trip home with me, and their constant presence reminded me how important it was to deliver the sacrificial virgin to the mouth of the volcano unscathed at the appointed time. Unfortunately, nobody seemed to know when the appointed time might be.

Simon kissed my hand. "We'll keep you safe, Maggie," he whispered. "We have the network of Guardians more active than ever."

Our flight landed at four-thirty in the afternoon, and by the time we went through customs and drove to the southern suburbs, it was nearly seven-thirty when we pulled into the driveway at my house. My parents and Brandon ran outside to greet us, all of them throwing their arms around me.

Simon took my bags inside and turned to kiss me before he left with Finn and Erin. "I'll come back after everyone's asleep," he promised.

I ate some dinner while I told my parents and Brandon about the trip, carefully omitting the events of the first week. Brandon was already looking through the pictures on my digital camera, too anxious to wait for me to download them onto my computer. I pulled the gifts that I'd brought for them out of my bag—the Belleek candy dish for my mom and matching t-shirts for everyone that had a large shamrock on the front and the name "O'Neill" printed above it.

Brandon was the first to notice the ring.

"It looks really old," he commented when he saw it.

"It's like the ones Simon, Finn and Erin wear, so I thought I should have one too." Not one part of that explanation was a lie, but it was still so far from the whole story.

After talking with my family and catching up on the two weeks we'd been apart, I went to my room and called Lexie. I was hoping she could forgive me for the way I'd been acting before I left, but more than that, I hoped I could be a better friend to her than I had been.

"Hi!" she said enthusiastically when she picked up the phone. "Are you back?"

"Yes. I'm back. I can't wait to see you, Lex. I'm sorry I was being such a brat before I left."

"Happens to the best of us. Are you your old self now?"

"Getting there, I think. Can you come over tomorrow? I have a souvenir for you." I'd bought Lexie a necklace with a glass pendant from the Artisan's Village in Donegal.

"Presents? I'm there! See you tomorrow."

"Goodnight, Lex." I felt a warm glow knowing that Lexie could forgive me so easily.

True to his word, Simon came over after everyone was in bed. I didn't hear him come into my room, so I jumped a little when he materialized in front of me, and I wondered if having someone appear out of nowhere was something you could ever get used to.

He smiled as he put both of his hands on my hips and pulled me toward him. He nuzzled his nose against mine momentarily before moving his lips to kiss me gently. It wasn't long before I felt the aching need rise inside of me, and I moved my hands through his hair. He pulled away and smiled, his breath matching the speed of my own.

"We're not alone, *cushla macree*."

I sighed but didn't pull away from him. "Between knocks on doors and bodyguards, I'm convinced we're both destined to stay virgins for the rest of our lives," I said quietly, hoping the invisible faeries hadn't heard me.

"And I am determined that will not, in fact, be the case. *That* is a destiny I will fight very hard against. I don't think my self control is going to hold much longer."

"Good to know," I teased.

I got under the blankets, and he lay down beside me. It felt like this was the way it had always been—Simon cuddled next to me while I fell asleep. With Simon beside me I felt more protected and at peace.

☙❧

Once I was home, I fell into a routine of school, homework and Simon. I was determined to end my junior year with legitimate grades that were not a product of Finn's use of persuasion, and that meant I was going to have to work hard to catch up on everything I'd missed during the weeks preceding my trip to Ireland. Simon was a willing tutor and helped me to understand the material I'd missed during my funk, but he was also a distraction. It was hard to focus on the causes of WWII when I really just wanted to kiss him and run my hands through his hair.

Sadly, he didn't spend another night in my room after our first night back from Ireland. I think he was determined that I would live a normal life for as long as possible. I knew there were always invisible Guardians with me, but I generally didn't think about them, and beyond their presence and the ring that was always on my finger, my life did go back to normal, and I soaked up every single moment of that normalcy. I knew it could—and would— be taken away at any moment.

"Can you tell Simon I'll be out in a minute?" I asked Lexie as we walked out of the library one afternoon. "I forgot my book for World Lit."

I walked toward my locker quickly, not wanting to keep Simon waiting. I wasn't paying attention, my thoughts drifting to Simon and the prospect of some time alone together—well, as alone as we ever got with the Guardians always hanging around.

"You still dating Leprechaun Boy?" Luke was standing by my locker, a bemused look on his face. I panicked for a moment, thinking that Luke had somehow figured out that Simon was a faery, but I realized he was just making fun of the fact that Simon was from Ireland.

"What do you want, Luke?" We hadn't talked after Cameron and Connor's party, and I was a little concerned when I realized we were the only two people in the hallway, but then I remembered the faery guard and relaxed slightly. They wouldn't show themselves unless there was serious danger, but it was a comfort knowing they were there.

"Have you had sex with him?"

"That's really none of your business." I kept my tone firm but calm, trying not to escalate the situation.

Luke walked toward me, forcing me to step backwards against the lockers. He moved closer and caught my wrists before I could turn away.

"I know you want to be with me, Maggie. I got your message loud and clear at the party," he said seductively.

I turned my head away from him. "Luke, if you don't let me go right now I *will* hurt you. I may be small, but I pack a pretty mean punch. You should know that—remember Halloween?"

"I remember Halloween. I also remember the party and how you kissed me. You would've kept going if Brady hadn't shown up, and I think we should pick up where we left off." He leaned in to kiss me, trying to move his head around to reach my lips. My first thought was to kick him in the balls again, but I decided to try a warning kick to the shin first.

"What the hell?" He was angry, but it had worked. He let go of my wrists.

"Please leave, Luke."

"God! You are such a tease! You need to decide what you want, Maggie."

"I want Simon. I can't be more clear than that. What happened at the party was a mistake." I started to turn away, then hesitated. "And Luke, forcing yourself on someone is assault. You should keep that in mind the next time a girl tells you to stop."

He called me a few choice words and when he turned to go, we both saw Simon standing a few feet away from us.

"Luke," he said, his voice quiet, but angry, "if you ever touch Maggie again, you'll get much worse than a kick to the shins."

"Threatening me again, Brady?"

"Yes."

"You two freaks deserve each other." Luke started to walk away, but Simon put his hand on his shoulder and stopped him.

"Where I come from, a gentleman does not hurt a lady."

Luke shrugged him off and walked away. Simon walked over to where I was standing by my locker and lifted my face with his hands.

"You okay?"

"I'm fine." And I really was. It was hard to be afraid of Luke when I had the threat of Balor looming over me.

Simon held my wrists up and inspected them. "If there is even a hint of a bruise, I *will* kick his ass." He sounded a lot like Brandon, and I couldn't help but smile.

He pulled my bag from my shoulder while I got the book I needed from my locker.

"I'm proud of you," he said as we walked out of the building. "You're quite formidable. Not at all the same girl I happened upon last Halloween."

"My perspective has changed considerably since last Halloween. The things that made me afraid then seem like chump change compared with the things I have to worry about now."

He laughed. "Well put."

"Which reminds me, why were you really driving around last Halloween? You said you were checking on a friend."

"I was," he said simply. "I can't lie, remember?"

"Yes, I remember, but you were evasive with your explanation, so I figured there was more to it."

He laughed again. "The friend I was worried about was you," he explained. "I was keeping tabs on you because it was Halloween."

"Why should it matter that it was Halloween?"

"Well, Halloween is a potentially dangerous day because November—our strongest time—technically starts at midnight on Halloween. I was worried Balor might have something planned for that night. I was using my special ability to keep tabs on you and when I saw that you were on the highway that late at night, I decided to check it out."

"I'm glad you did."

"Yes, me too."

"So, how does that work exactly—your ability to find people and things?"

"I think about what I want to find, then I see where it is. So, if I want to find you, I think about you, then I get a mental picture of where you are."

"So, you can see me whenever you want to?"

"Wouldn't that be nice?" he said, smiling. "Sadly, however, I just see the place where you are. Not you in that place."

"Well, to be honest, that's a relief. I have enough faeries watching me already."

We were standing beside his car and he opened the passenger door for me.

"There was something else I was wondering about," I said.

"What's that?"

"The night of Cameron and Connor's party, you said something about talking to Luke before. When did you talk to him?"

Simon looked reluctant to answer. "After I saw the bruises on the your arm. I went to his house and we had a talk."

"A *talk*?" I couldn't imagine Luke and Simon hanging out and talking. "About what?"

"You. About what he'd done to you."

"What did you tell him?"

"I might have threatened to cause him harm if he ever hurt you again," Simon said slyly.

"And he listened to you? Was he in pain or something?"

"Discomfort," he admitted, "but not pain."

I smiled. I guess it made sense, though. Luke wasn't the kind of guy to slink away with his tail between his legs. I hadn't thought about it in the months since Luke and I had broken up, but I should have realized something was going on since Luke let me go so easily. There'd been no teasing or taunting, and he hadn't talked to me at all until the night of the party.

"Thank you."

ᏚᎧᏣᎡ

Simon and I went bowling with Lexie and Max that night. I was an absolutely horrible bowler and was lucky to get over fifty points on any game. Fortunately, everyone else was just as bad as I was, and we joked at one point that we should consider putting the bumpers in the gutters like they did when small children bowled. The four of us had more balls in the gutter than not, and bumpers would have been our only hope for getting scores that weren't completely humiliating.

I was happy as I watched Lexie and Max together at the bowling alley. I still felt bad for the way I'd treated Lexie before leaving for Ireland, and it was comforting to know that Max had been with her during that difficult time.

I was happy for Lexie, and I wouldn't take away even a tiny piece of her happiness, but I was also jealous. Lexie didn't have to worry about her boyfriend dying in the quest to defeat an evil faery. She didn't have to worry about faeries that had walked to the dark side and were intent on destroying the world. She didn't have to worry about not being strong enough to play her part in history. For all of that, I was jealous. I wanted more than anything to be able to go back to being normal.

I never took these moments for granted anymore. I appreciated the fun I was having with friends I loved, savoring every carefree second. I clung to the simplicity of life because I knew all of this was going to end for me at some point. Eventually I would trade carefree days for days spent stalking Balor and worrying about the future of my family and friends—the future of the world as we knew it. But not that day. That day, I was bowling.

"What are you thinking about?" Simon asked. He had come up from behind me and wrapped both of his arms around my waist, reaching around to kiss my neck.

"I was thinking about how lucky I am to have days like this," I told him.

He understood what I was really saying and pulled me closer, kissing the top of my head.

"I love you," he whispered against my ear.

"I love you, too."

"Hey, are you two going to bowl or make out?" Max called over to us. "Not that I have a problem with either one, but make a choice. You're up, Brady."

Simon nuzzled my neck before moving away to get his ball.

Chapter Twenty-Seven

I was sitting on my bed Saturday afternoon reading *Siddhartha* for World Lit when there was a knock on my door. "Maggie," my dad said when he poked his head in, "Simon's here to see you."

When he opened the door wider, I could see Simon standing in the hallway. I felt a jolt of worry. Simon never just dropped over unexpectedly or unannounced, at least not when he was visible.

"Hi," I said as he walked past my dad and into my room.

"Hi," he said. "I hope you don't mind that I didn't call. Can I ask you some questions about Western Civ class?"

"Sure," I said, guessing that this was all said for my dad's benefit since Simon's education over the past two hundred years far surpassed my own and he never needed my help with homework. My dad left us, but not before pushing my bedroom door open a few inches more.

Simon pulled his textbook out of his bag and opened it up randomly as he sat on the chair at my desk. "We got word today that Balor knows about you. He knows the ring fit," he said in a hushed voice. I concentrated on taking steady breaths, and Simon took my hands in his. "We're going to increase security to keep you and your family safe. We're going to do everything we can to keep him away from you." I knew he wanted to promise me that Balor wouldn't be able to reach me, but he had no choice but to be completely honest.

I nodded and tried not to freak out. It had been too easy since coming home from Ireland to pretend that everything was normal again. I almost never saw the faeries that were guarding me and generally only knew they were near me because Simon told me they were. Almost everything had gone back to normal in my life. I went to school. I did my homework. I hung out with Simon and Lexie and Max. I fought with Brandon. I was trying very hard to switch gears back to Margaret, defender of the universe, but I really just wanted to stay Maggie, high school junior. Balor knew where I was and knew I was the one mentioned in the prophecy. To ensure his own survival, he would make finding and killing me his number one goal.

I looked at Simon. He leaned toward me, his face filled with concern. "You okay?" he asked calmly.

I nodded again. I didn't trust myself to talk yet. I was worried that I'd really lose it if I tried to talk. The problem was that once I started to nod to Simon's question, I couldn't stop. I just kept nodding like a cheap dashboard ornament.

"Maggie," Simon said in a calm and soothing voice. "It's going to be okay."

"I'm a little freaked out," I admitted.

He leaned in further and kissed my forehead. "I'd be worried about you if you weren't, *cushla macree*."

"What do we do now?" I asked, not certain I really wanted to hear the answer.

"We've already started to mobilize the Guardians in the area," he said.

"Will they be willing to help?"

"Protecting you is the number one priority for every Guardian in the world right now," he assured me.

I was comforted by that, but worried. From what Simon had told me, I knew Balor didn't care if he killed a few faeries on his way toward world domination. I figured he'd happily kill any faery that stood in his way.

"We've increased your guard and the guard around your family," he continued. "There will always be someone in your room, even when you're not here, and there will always be someone with your parents and Brandon—invisible, of course." He rubbed his fingers along both of my arms, up and down from the wrists to the elbows. "We've also gone ahead and assigned someone to Lexie—just in case Balor tries to use her to get to you."

I started nodding again and I felt like I might start hyperventilating. These were all of the people I loved most in the world. My parents. Brandon. Lexie. Simon. They were all in serious danger.

"Maggie, I won't pretend this isn't serious, but we're doing everything possible to make sure no one gets hurt."

"And you guys?" I asked. "Who's protecting you? If he'll use Lexie to get to me, surely he would be willing to use you or Finn or Erin."

"We're being protected, as well," Simon said.

"Pretty soon," he joked, "it's going to be hard to walk the southern suburbs of Denver without bumping into an invisible faery."

Simon filled me in on some of the details. He told me there were a few faeries working with Balor who were actually sympathetic to our side of the fight. These faeries put themselves in considerable danger in order to feed information to Finn and the others. It was a certainty that Balor knew about me. What wasn't certain was what he'd do next. They were waiting to hear from the faeries close to him, but there'd been no word.

"How many fairies are involved in this?"

"It's hard to say. There are faeries all across the world not trained as Guardians, and it's hard to keep track of them. As word spreads, we seem to get more and more calling up to support us, but we have to be careful. We don't know if Balor will try to plant some of his people close to you, just as we've planted people close to him."

"What do you mean there are faeries across the world? I thought faeries were just an Irish thing."

"They're called something different in each language and each culture, but there are faeries in every part of the world."

"Are the faeries from other cultures involved in this, or is it just the Irish faeries?"

"All of us are involved. The fey are all one race, and it's hard to turn your back on something this powerful."

I tried to wrap my head around everything he was saying, but it was just so unreal. How many were out there? How many would fight for Balor? How many would fight for us? How many would die?

"I'd like to spend the night with you for a while," Simon said after a few minutes of silence. "I'll stay invisible the whole night if it'll make it easier for you, but I'd feel better if I were here to watch over you when you're sleeping. It's your most defenseless time."

"My *most* defenseless time?" I asked, laughing humorlessly. "When am I *not* defenseless, Simon? What time of day do I have *any* defenses against Balor?"

Simon turned and flourished his hand toward my door. I was pretty certain he'd just done some magic, but couldn't see anything different about my room.

"What did you do?" I asked.

He blushed before answering. "I put a spell on your door so your family won't hear us. You were starting to get a little loud."

He watched me silently. I suppose he was waiting to see if I'd start freaking out again, and I did, but not because he'd used magic in front of me. Balor was no longer an abstract threat I might have to face at some point in the future. He was real and he was coming after me, and that's why I was freaking out.

"I have no clue how to defend myself against Balor," I said, jumping up and pacing the room. "If you have some secret defense you're not telling me about, now would be a really good time to share it."

He looked at me with a pained expression, and I realized he had nothing. My only defense was to hope the faeries guarding me would be able to keep Balor away from me.

"You guys have known for hundreds of years that I was going to have to defeat the most powerful entity in the world. Did it not occur to you to spend those years figuring out how, exactly, I was going to do that?" I knew what I was saying was unfair. I knew they were all putting their own lives in danger to help me defeat Balor, but I needed to vent the frustration and the fear that had been building in me. Simon seemed to know and let me rant on uninterrupted.

"You've known for hundreds of years, Simon," I said, trying to keep my voice low, worried my family might hear me despite Simon's spell. "And still nobody has a clue! *Well, Maggie, you're the chosen one. Put on this ring so we'll know for sure, but after that, you're on your own. Good luck to you.* What am I supposed to do?" I asked, working really hard to keep my voice from rising. "How do I kill him? How do I save my parents and my friends? How do I save you?" I slumped to the floor, my body shaking violently with the fear that was overtaking me.

Simon came and sat next to me, putting his arms around me and kissing the top of my head. "You will *never* be on your own, Maggie—literally or figuratively. We don't have all of the answers yet, but we'll make sure you're protected until the very end. If you die, it will be after each and every one of us has laid down our own lives before you. Balor won't get to you unless he kills each of us first." I sat with my knees pulled to my chest, my face resting in my hands. Simon started rubbing my back. "I wish it weren't you," he said so quietly I could barely make out the words. "Oh, *cushla macree,* I wish it weren't you."

"But why *is* it me?" I asked for the millionth time. "Of all of the things I've learned about in the past few weeks, the one thing that is most baffling to me is why

I'm the one who has to kill Balor. I'm an ordinary girl in an ordinary family in an ordinary suburban town. I don't have special powers. I can't compete with him. You or Finn or Erin or any of the other faeries stand a much better chance of defeating him than I do. He's going to destroy me, then destroy every human on the planet. It just feels like this whole prophecy was doomed to failure long before I was even born."

"I don't have an answer to that question, Maggie. None of us do. You seem like a very unlikely candidate for taking down Balor, but please know that you are not, by any stretch, ordinary. I've seen you accept your strength in the past couple of months. I've seen you handle some very difficult situations with grace and courage. You can't make yourself invisible and you can't fly, but you are not now, nor have you ever been, ordinary."

Chapter Twenty-Eight

Simon went back to his house for a while to check in with Finn and Erin and to get any updates on Balor and his plans before coming back to spend the night with me.

"Go to sleep, *cushla macree*," he whispered when he was lying next to me on the bed. "I won't leave your side until you wake up, so no reason to have anything but very peaceful, very sweet dreams."

I was immensely grateful to have Simon beside me while I slept that night. It was comforting to know I didn't have to face the scary demons on my own. "What would I do without you?" I wondered aloud.

"You'll never have to find out," he assured me. Then he kissed me and whispered, "I love you."

"I love you," I whispered back.

☙❧

"Maggie," Simon said quietly while shaking me roughly. "Wake up!" My door flew open and both of my parents stood in the doorway, my mom switching on the light. I could feel Simon next to me, but he'd made himself invisible before they could open the door.

"What's wrong?" my dad asked, coming toward me.

I sat up quickly and moved to the edge of the bed, not wanting them to sit where Simon was lying down. "I don't understand," I said. I honestly didn't know why Simon was trying to wake me up, or why my parents had come rushing into my room.

"You were screaming," my mom explained.

"Oh," I said, still a little sleep-dazed. "I must have had a nightmare."

"Do you remember what it was about?" my dad asked.

"No," I admitted.

"You okay now?"

"Mm-hmm," I said. "I'm fine. Sorry I woke you."

"No problem." He leaned down to kiss my forehead. "Try to have better dreams this time," he teased.

Simon reappeared at my side as soon as they'd gone. "You really don't remember what the dream was about?" he asked.

I shook my head and yawned.

"I'm sure I gave very specific instructions for you to have *sweet* dreams."

"'K," I mumbled as I settled into his chest to go back to sleep.

"*Sweet* dreams, love," he reminded me once again before I drifted off.

৪০৫৪

I woke up again some time later and felt an invisible hand clamp down firmly on my mouth, another hand wrapped around my waist. The window in my room flew open, and I felt myself being carried through it and into the darkness. I had no idea who had me. Simon? Finn? One of the Guardians? One of *theirs?* *Please not one of theirs.*

I tried to fight against the hands holding me, pulling me higher and higher into the air. As I flailed my legs, hoping to make contact with solid flesh, I felt a set of strong legs wrap around mine, immobilizing them.

"Stop fighting me, Maggie," Simon whispered in my ear. "I need to get you away from here. If I take my hand off your mouth will you be quiet?" I nodded against his hand and he removed it, fastening it tight around my shoulders, holding my head close to him, my back to his chest. As he moved his arms, he made himself visible again, and I felt a little more secure once I was able to see his arms around me.

"What's happening?" I whispered.

"I'll explain when you're safe," he said quietly.

We were flying through the air surprisingly fast, and the distance between us and the ground was well beyond my comfort level. The wind was whipping around me, and I shivered with cold. He tried to hold me closer, wanting, I'm sure, to keep me warm, but I was wearing only my pajama bottoms and a t-shirt, and they were failing miserably at keeping out the frigid wind. It wasn't long before the discomfort of being cold gave way to downright pain. I was shivering uncontrollably, and my teeth chattered, and the distraction of being so cold kept me from thinking too much about why Simon had flown me out of my bedroom window in the middle of the night.

We started to move closer to the ground near the

high school, but before we could land, Simon spat out a choice four-letter word and started flying away quickly.

"What's wrong?" I asked.

"We had a car parked at a safe location in case we needed to get you away quickly, but there are faeries—Balor's—all around it. They know it's ours."

"Balor? He's here? He's found me?"

"I'm going to fly you someplace safe. I'm sorry. I know you're cold, but it's not safe to land right now."

"But what if someone sees us?"

"We don't have a choice. A non-faery seeing us fly is really the least of our problems right now."

I looked and saw that the lights of the city faded upwards toward our left. I knew that was where the mountains started, and since the mountains were on our left, that meant we were flying north. After flying long enough that I felt like I might be turning into a solid block of ice, we started to fly lower to the ground. We were in the foothills west of the city and as we got closer to the ground I saw that we were headed to Red Rocks Amphitheater. We landed in a small cave etched into the rock high above the ground on the north end of the stands, and I turned around as soon as my feet hit to face Simon.

"What's going on?" I asked, still shivering. The rock where I stood was ice cold and bit at my feet painfully.

Simon walked to the back of the cave and came back with a large backpack. "Here," he said after rummaging into the bag and finding a thick parka. I took it from him and put it on before taking the fleece pants he was handing me.

"We were attacked," he explained, giving me a pair

of socks. "The Fomorians found your house."

"Fomorians?"

"Balor's followers."

I felt the terror rise inside of me but fought to hold it off as long as I could. I sat down and pulled on the socks he'd given me. He handed me a pair of running shoes, and I put those on before he pulled me to sit between his legs. I drew my knees up to my chest, trying to chase away the cold, and collapsed into his warm body. He wrapped his long legs and arms around me, holding me tight against him. We sat together and looked out of the cave toward the stands and the stage below, the city lights glimmering in the distance.

"Is my family okay?" I asked, afraid of his answer.

"I don't know," Simon confessed. "Someone will call as soon as they can with news."

That certainly didn't make me feel better. I couldn't think about the possibility that my parents or Brandon or anyone else I cared for was hurt, or worse.

"Why did you bring me *here*?" I asked, thinking that surely there was someplace warm he could have taken me.

"I can see out over the city, so I'll know if any faeries are flying toward us," he explained. "We arranged several meeting spots in case we were attacked, and I got the idea to come here on Halloween when I came to get you."

We sat entwined for a very long time. Simon did his best to warm me up, and I did my best not to think about what was going on at my house. Simon's cell phone ringing in his jeans pocket made us both jump, and he reached for it quickly, looking at the number on his screen before answering it.

"Finn," he said with relief. He listened for quite a while but didn't seem to relax at all. "We'll wait for you here. See you in a bit."

He hung up and put the phone back in his pocket.

"They're gone. The Guardians were able to fight them off, and your family's safe. Finn said they slept through the whole thing." I felt the tension in my muscles ease a little, but my mind went immediately to the Guardians who were protecting my family.

"What about the others? The Guardians?" I asked him.

"Finn said they're trying to account for everyone now. He's sending a group up here to drive us back to your house. We're not sure where the Fomorians are or if they'll come back, and the trip back to your house will be safer if we have backup."

My family was safe. Balor's people were gone. I felt calm and suddenly tired after the burst of adrenaline. I leaned back into Simon's chest and started to fall asleep while we waited for the others.

I woke to the sound of Simon stringing together a long list of expletives, and for the second time in one night, I was woken out of my sleep to find myself flying through the air.

"Stay quiet," Simon whispered urgently. He flew us over the walkway at the top of the stands and over the patio of the restaurant at the back of the amphitheater. Behind the patio were some large bushes and boulders scattered in a small clearing on the side of the mountain. Simon landed beside one of the boulders and told me to hide underneath the bushes.

"Listen to me, Maggie," he said after I was sitting

on the ground with my back to the boulder. "Balor's people found us here. One of our faeries gave me some warning by shouting it in my head, but they'll be here any second. I need to go and help fight them, but you need to stay here." I started to protest, but he stopped me. "There's no time to discuss this. You're not equipped to fight with my kind and you'll only get in the way. They won't hesitate to kill you."

"Please don't go," I said so quietly I barely heard myself speak.

"I have to go, but I *will* come back. No matter what you see or what you hear, you're not to move from this spot until I come for you. If anyone comes who you don't know, I want you to kick and yell and scream. Do you understand?"

I nodded. He kissed me quickly, and then he was gone.

Chapter Twenty-Nine

I tried to stay as still as I possibly could, partly because I didn't want to bring attention to my hiding spot and partly because I was straining to hear something. Anything. I was pretty far from the fighting and separated by the visitor's center and walkway. I didn't hear any yelling, but I did hear a few loud pops. I thought, at first, that it was gunfire, but it didn't sound quite right to be gunfire. Admittedly, my only experience with guns came from movies and television, so maybe that *was* what they sounded like in person.

I also heard a couple of cars pull into the parking lot and the slamming of several doors. Had someone called the police? Had other faeries driven instead of flown?

I felt the boulder cutting into my back, but I didn't want to move. As I sat trying to hear what was going on with the fight, I heard the crinkling of twigs and grass and knew someone was walking toward me. I looked up quickly, hoping more than I'd ever hoped for anything that it was Simon, but I saw nothing. I held my breath and waited to hear another footstep, another crackle of the twigs and gravel, but I again saw nothing.

I felt hands grab me roughly and pull me from behind the rock. It wasn't Simon. I knew as soon as the hands touched me that it wasn't Simon. I started to scream as loud as I could and kicked at the air around me, hoping to make contact with my abductor. A hand clamped over my mouth quickly, and I felt the cold blade of a knife against my face. I bit at the hand holding me, and the knife cut into my temple as my assailant pulled back his hand in surprise. I was thrown to the ground and hit my cheek on the boulder before clambering to my feet.

I heard a struggle and knew another invisible faery had joined us. I watched as the two moved in and out of invisibility. One of the faeries was an older man, close to Liam's age. The other was a dark haired boy who looked like he could have been a student at our school. I hadn't seen whoever had abducted me from my hiding spot, so I had no idea which one was on our side and which was the enemy. They both had small daggers, and each time they threw one, it seemed to disappear after hitting the ground, or their opponent, only to end up back in the hand of the faery who had thrown it. One of them—the older man —threw fireballs from his opened palm. I watched as they flew through the air before dissolving as if they'd hit a wall before reaching the other faery. Then thousands of red sparks flew between them, but I didn't see where the sparks originated or what their purpose was. At one point, I couldn't see either faery, and it became eerily quiet in my little hideaway. I felt arms around me and I was once again being lifted into the air. I screamed and started to struggle. My kidnapper dropped me, and I fell about ten feet to the ground. I landed face down and felt pain in every part of my body. Unseen hands turned me over so that my back was on the ground, and I started to panic because I wasn't able to breathe. The dark haired faery I'd seen fighting was leaning over me, looking concerned.

"You got the wind knocked out of you. Try to relax and it'll pass quicker," he said with an unmistakable Irish accent. He smiled kindly, and I wanted more than anything for him to be on our side, but I knew bad guys could smile too. "Before you get your breath back and start screaming again, let me tell you that Simon's in the middle of a fight and sent me to get you and take you back to his house."

I shook my head vigorously, still not able to breathe or talk. Simon had said not to go with anyone I didn't recognize.

"He said to tell you he thinks knocks on doors will kill him before a fight with the Fomorians. He said you'd know that was something only he would know about."

I didn't want to trust this strange faery, but I couldn't think of how else he'd know about my joke with Simon about knocks on doors. I nodded to let the faery know I would go with him without a struggle.

He cradled me in his arms and lifted me into the air, not bothering to make himself invisible. We flew over the wall at the back of the visitor's center and headed in the direction of the parking lot.

"We're going to try to get to one of the cars so we can drive. If we can't, I'll fly you back to Simon's house."

"Okay," I said, finally able to breathe and talk, but before I could get the word completely out, I felt myself falling through the air. The faery carrying me had dropped me again, and I landed hard on a concrete patio. Fortunately, we were closer to the ground this time, and the pain wasn't nearly as intense as it had been before. I saw that two new faeries had appeared and were fighting with the one who'd taken me from my hiding spot. The faery that had been carrying me was being double teamed—or worse. It was possible there were invisible faeries also fighting against him, and there was nothing I could do to help him—I was worthless in a fight against faeries. I saw two knives flying through the air and scurried against the wall of the patio. After watching the fighting for a few minutes, I decided it was time to make a run for it. I thought my best option would be to run directly for the parking lot and hope one of the cars had keys in it. I looked around to plan my route. We'd landed on the patio at the back of the visitor's center, and the parking lot was to the north. Unfortunately, the fight I was watching stood between me and the parking lot. To the west there was a low wall with a thirty-foot drop that led to my original hiding place. To the east was the visitor's center with two sets of doors I assumed would be locked in the middle of the night. My only option was to run to the south. I watched intently, waiting for an opportunity to flee unobserved, but when I realized there was never going to be a good time, I decided to go ahead and run and hope for the best. I stood up from my spot by the wall and ran as fast as I could, my feet slipping on the ice that dotted the concrete, making it difficult for me to gain enough traction to go as fast as I wanted.

I ran around a large boulder that was on the patio

toward the south end of the visitor's center and came to a set of stairs that led to the walkway at the top of the stands. I crouched low at the top of the stairway, trying to keep myself hidden while I developed a plan. I could see the stands in front of me and, below that, the stage. Faeries faded in and out of invisibility everywhere I looked, and I guessed there were well over a hundred of them. Fire and sparks illuminated the night sky. I was terrified. I knew I wouldn't be able to get across the stands and to the other side of the walkway unnoticed, but I didn't know how else to get to the parking lot. I looked around and tried to assess my options.

And that's when I saw him. He was standing calmly under the lights along the walkway at the top of the stands and he looked so very ordinary, maybe even handsome. He was younger than I'd expected, and tall, with dark hair that flipped up slightly on the ends. His long legs were covered in a pair of jeans and a black graphic t-shirt was stretched across his torso. If it weren't for the look of pure evil in his eyes, I might have thought he was a Guardian. But he wasn't, and I knew instinctively who he was. Balor. Our eyes met, and he smiled, his face expressing pure malice. I was frozen in the spot where I crouched on the stairway, unable to tear my eyes away from his sadistic gaze.

"Well, if it isn't Margaret O'Neill—*the* Margaret O'Neill," he taunted.

I felt hands seizing me yet again. My snatcher wasn't invisible this time, and I felt overwhelming relief when I looked up and saw that it was Simon's hands gripping me. He flew north toward the parking lot, but we didn't get far before I was once again hitting the ground. I looked up to see Balor standing over us and, before Simon could pull me away, Balor grabbed him by the throat and pushed him against the hard brick wall. Balor's face twisted with pleasure and anger, and as his grip tightened, I could see that Simon was having trouble breathing. I could hear him making choking gasps, trying to push some air through to his lungs, his hands making a futile effort to pry Balor's fingers away from his throat. I didn't think about what I should do. Simon was in trouble, and I needed to help him, and in that moment, it didn't matter if the man hurting him could pulverize me with one swipe of his hand. I ran at Balor's knees, hoping to knock him over and give Simon time to get away. When my shoulder made contact with his legs, it did cause him to let go of Simon, but instead of falling to the ground, he took a step back and pulled me with him by the back of my jacket. The feel of him so close to me made the core of my bones turn to ice. I watched as Simon stood up quickly and threw a knife at Balor, hitting the arm that held me and forcing Balor to let go of my jacket, dropping me to the ground.

"Is that all you've got, m'boy?" Balor asked in a taunting voice. The red glow of a nearby "Exit" sign illuminated his face in a way that made him appear even more evil than he had a moment before. "I've heard you're considered to be something of a prodigy amongst the Guardians, but you're no match for me, son."

Without taking his eyes from Simon's, Balor raised his right hand casually in my direction. I thought maybe he had a gun and was going to shoot me, but instead he just pointed his index finger at me and smiled mockingly at Simon. As he pointed his finger in my direction, I felt as if the bones throughout my body were exploding, creating millions of little knives that pierced each and every nerve ending. I was certain that I was going to melt and turn to ash and I started to panic. I knew I was dying. I knew there was no way I could live through pain that horrible and I knew I should be spending my last moments alive thinking about my family and friends, but the only thing I was thinking was that dying really sucked. Really, really sucked.

Chapter Thirty

As I writhed in pain on the cold, hard concrete, I saw Simon raise his right hand and point his index finger at Balor. Balor's eyes widened as he fell to the ground, gasping for breath. My own pain started to subside.

"Don't you even *think* about harming her again, you pernicious bastard," Simon said. His voice was quiet and calm, but I could hear the contempt and anger in his tone.

Six fairies appeared between Balor and me, and Simon grabbed me up once again and flew toward the parking lot. As I looked back, I saw Balor struggling to get to his feet.

"I want you to go with Ian," Simon said as we neared the parking lot. I assumed he was talking about the faery he'd sent to get me before. "I need to stay here, but I'll come for you as soon as I can."

We made it to the parking lot without any more interference, and Simon set me down near the passenger door of his black SUV. Ian was already in the driver's seat, and I climbed into the passenger seat while Simon leaned in to talk to Ian.

"Keep your cell phone turned on," Simon said. Ian nodded and pulled out of the parking lot before I had closed my door, driving down the curving road at a dangerously fast speed. We hadn't gotten far before we heard two loud thumps on the hood of the car.

"Damn it!" Ian said loudly. "Hold on!"

I quickly grabbed at the seatbelt, trying to pull it around me as he swerved from left to right. I heard another thump on the roof of the car, then all was quiet, and he slowed down slightly.

"Finn and my father pulled them off," he explained. "We should be fine now."

I relaxed a bit but was still overcome with fear for Simon and the others.

When we got to the end of the road leading out of the park, Ian turned left.

"We should be going right," I told him. I'd been to Red Rocks many times in my life and I knew exactly how to get to Simon's house from Red Rocks.

"We're not going to Simon's house. We're going to the airport until we get the all-clear to take you home."

"Why the airport?"

"There'll be a lot of people there—even at this time of night—so the Fomorians will be less likely to attack there. We can also put you on a flight and get you out of here quicker than flying you ourselves." He glanced in my direction then asked, "How do you feel?"

I hadn't thought about it before he asked, but I suddenly started to feel all of the aches and pains from the fighting. "Like I've been beaten up by a bunch of bad-ass faeries," I said.

He laughed loudly. "Nicely put," he said.

"Who are you?" I asked. It probably sounded more accusatory than I'd intended, but I was really curious. I knew Simon wouldn't trust just anyone to be alone with me.

"Sorry," he said, his eyes glued to the freeway in front of us. "I'm Ian. Liam's son. Keelin's brother."

"Keelin has a brother?"

"A twin brother, actually."

"Why weren't you at Simon's house in Ireland when I was there?"

"I *was* there. The night you tried on the ring."

I thought about it and realized there had been so many people in the room that night that I couldn't say for certain if he'd been there. "You didn't come for dinner the night I met Liam and Keelin."

"I was in Germany when you first got to Ireland, then I had to leave again before you woke up. I travel a lot for the *greater good*." He'd said the last part with a hint of sarcasm. "I'm able to convince people to tell me things they may not be willing to tell other people."

"Faery power?" I guessed.

He smiled and nodded.

Once I was able to calm down enough to look properly, I noticed that he did, in fact look a lot like Keelin. Same wavy black hair. Same tall, slender build. Same long, straight nose. Same smirk when he smiled.

We were both quiet as we drove through the city, but as we made the turn from I-70 onto Peña Boulevard, I looked at him and saw a worried expression on his face. "Ian, is Keelin back there? Is she fighting?"

"Yes."

"Are you worried?"

"Yes," he answered.

We pulled into the parking garage on the east side of the airport. Once we were stopped, Ian reached behind his seat and pulled out a couple of water bottles, handing one to me. I drank it quickly and he handed me the second bottle.

We sat in silence for about twenty minutes. I was too exhausted to say much and I imagined Ian was on high alert, watching and listening for any signs of danger. When the phone he was holding in his hand started to ring, we both jumped.

"Okay," Ian said to the person on the other end of the line. "We're on our way." He hit the "End" button and put the phone away. "We got the all-clear to head to Simon's house."

⅚⅛

I stepped out of the car and crumpled to the ground, pain exploding through my ankle. I hadn't had any trouble running on it at Red Rocks but suspected adrenaline had masked the pain while I was there. Without a word, Ian scooped me up and took me quickly into the house, setting me down on the sofa in the living room.

"What hurts?" he asked.

"Everything," I said through gritted teeth, the pain overwhelming me.

"Okay," he said soothingly. "Let's break it down."

I nodded and slipped the shoe and sock Simon had given me off my right foot so that Ian could take a look at my ankle. He left to get some ice and when he walked back in the room, he looked a little overwhelmed.

"What?" I asked, wondering if he'd gotten some news by faery phone.

"We're going to need a lot more ice." He shook his head in disbelief. "I just got a good look at you." He walked over and put the ice he was carrying on my ankle and left again to get a washcloth to clean up the blood that was now dried to my face and the palms of my hands. While he was out of the room, the front door opened and Finn came in, followed by Sloane.

"Simon's on his way," Finn assured me. "He's not seriously hurt."

"But he's hurt?" I asked in alarm.

"Not as bad as you, I'd guess," he said as he took in my injuries.

Simon walked through the front door, and I was so happy to see him. He was okay and he was home and everything would be fine now. I expected him to come to me and hug me, but instead he turned to Ian and said, "Get her upstairs."

Chapter Thirty-One

Ian lifted me off the couch and started to carry me toward the stairs.

"What? No!" I fought against Ian's grip, managing to free myself so that I was standing on the floor. The pain in my ankle torpedoed through me again, but I pushed it aside so I could focus on what was happening.

Simon looked frantic. "For god's sake, Ian!" he shouted. "Get her up there now!"

"What's going on?" I continued to fight Ian, but he put his arms around my chest and lifted me off the ground, my feet dangling under me. I tried kicking him with my one good foot so that he would put me down, but I was too weak to kick with any sort of a punch, and he just tightened his grip on me. As we started up the stairs, I caught a glimpse of a faery being carried into the house. He appeared to be unconscious and he looked an awful lot like Max Levy, but of course that was ridiculous. Why would Max Levy have been involved in a fight with faeries?

Ian took me to Simon's room and put me down on the dark blue and red duvet that covered the bed before turning to close the door.

"What's going on?" I demanded.

Ian took a deep breath and appeared to be debating

whether or not to answer me. "They brought some people back who are hurt. A couple of them are hurt badly. Simon didn't want you to see them."

"Who?"

"I don't know."

"Why didn't Simon want me to see them?"

"I don't know," he admitted.

There was a knock on the door. Ian opened it and Keelin stepped into the room. The two of them hugged each other tight for a few moments, and when they let go of each other, she looked at me.

"Simon wanted me to tell you that he's very sorry he made you come up here and that he'll be up as soon as he can." Her tone was flat and emotionless.

"Who's hurt?" I asked.

"He told me not to tell you." There was no sympathy or regret in her voice.

I sat down on the bed and focused on not hyperventilating. Ian sat down next to me, and Keelin glared at me from her position by the door. I tried not to think about who was injured or how serious the injuries might be. I tried not to think about the fact that Balor, and every evil faery working for him, knew where I was—knew where my family was.

"Are there faeries still at my house?" I asked Ian.

"Yes. Only ours. Your family's safe."

Safe. For now.

When Simon finally came into the room ten minutes later, he looked grim. He came to me and knelt down in front of me, taking my face in his hands.

"I was so worried about you." His voice and hands both trembled.

I wrapped my arms around his neck and pulled him

close to me, ignoring the pain the movement caused in almost every millimeter of my body. Ian and Keelin quietly walked out of the room and closed the door behind them.

"You look awful," he said remorsefully when he pulled away from our embrace.

"So do you." His face was dirty and smeared with blood from a cut that ran along his left cheek. He also had blood on his clothes—a lot of it.

"Where are you hurt?" I asked him.

"I have a few scratches and a cut on my hand, but it's not deep. Most of this blood isn't mine," he said while gesturing to his jacket. "What about you?"

"I'm not sure. I hurt everywhere." I told him what had happened at Red Rocks—about the invisible faery that had tried to take me and how I'd fought against him, about the knife slicing into my temple. I told him about fighting against Ian because I didn't know who he was and how that had caused me to fall.

"I'm sorry about that. I saw Ian running from the parking lot and told him to get you. I forgot you'd never met him."

"Simon, who's hurt?"

"Erin lost a lot of blood. She was stabbed, but she seems to be doing better now. There's another healer here helping her. There are a lot of Guardians with injuries, but the healers are taking care of them." He hesitated, and I knew there was more. "And Max Levy."

"What?" So it *had* been Max Levy being carried through the door. "Max is a faery?"

"Yes."

"And he's hurt?"

"Yes," he said, his voice cracking.

"Is it bad?"

"Yes."

I felt sick. My stomach was flipping wildly, and I started to panic again.

"Blaine, the other healer here at the house, is looking after him," Simon explained. "If anyone can save him, he can."

"Save him? He might die?"

He hesitated. "Yes."

I couldn't wrap my mind around it. Why hadn't Max told me he was a faery? Was he a Guardian?

"Why didn't you tell me?" I demanded, angry now.

"He asked me not to."

"He didn't want me to know he was a faery?"

"He didn't want Lexie to know. I had to respect his wishes, Maggie." Simon looked defeated.

"Is he a Guardian?"

"Yes."

"But he's Jewish!"

"It's genetics. Nothing more. If you're born with the gene, there's nothing you can do to stop it. It's not something that's limited by religion or race or nationality."

Simon was still for a moment, and this time I could tell he was listening to the voice of another faery in his head.

"Max's parents are here," he explained. "Blaine may not be able to get up here for a while, so I'm going to do what I can for your injuries."

I nodded numbly while Simon got up and walked into the bathroom. He came back with a first aid kit in his hands and started cleaning all the cuts he could see.

He started with the gash to my temple and the abrasion on my cheek and moved to my palms. While he was busy cleaning me up, I noticed blood on the parka I was still wearing and on my pants. He helped me unzip the parka and slipped it off my shoulders. There were several tears in my pants and the pajama bottoms underneath. Blood was seeping through both layers. Simon pulled off the one shoe and sock I still wore and looked at both of my feet and ankles.

"I guess the ring didn't protect me after all," I said.

Simon looked uncomfortable as he responded. "Actually, Maggie, I think the spell Balor did on you was intended to kill you, so it may not have protected you from your injuries, but it protected you from death."

"Oh," I said, more than a little unsettled. I didn't like to think that the only thing between me being alive and me being dead was a very thin piece of metal.

"You bellowed?" Keelin asked dryly as she walked back into the room, saving me from thinking too much about this new piece of information. She had some clothes in her arms and handed them to Simon.

"Thank you," he said, turning his attention quickly back to me. Keelin rolled her eyes.

"I had Keelin get you some of Erin's things so you can change," he explained. Faery phone. It was really annoying to be out of the loop all the time. "Keelin, help Maggie change and clean up any cuts you see. I'm going to get some ice."

"Always at your service, m'lord," Keelin said, her tone dripping with derision.

Simon glanced at her with annoyance as he left the room.

I started to undress, a little embarrassed to have Keelin watch me. I slipped off the sweat pants and pajama bottoms and looked at my legs. There was a long cut that started at the back of my calf and snaked around to my shin. Keelin kneeled down and, with a gentleness that shocked me, cleaned the wound with an antiseptic wipe from the first aid kit. The cut wasn't deep, but it was still bleeding, and the antiseptic stung. Keelin found some gauze and wrapped it around my leg, then continued with her inspection. Both knees had deep areas of road rash, and she cleaned those, pulling off a few pebbles that had adhered to my skin and cuts, then she wrapped my knees in the gauze she'd used on my leg. After she'd made sure there were no more injuries on my legs, she let me put on the pants she'd brought with her. Next, she had me take off my top. I could see bruises on my arms and shoulders, but no deep cuts.

"I think the parka was thick enough to keep you from getting too much damage," she said, turning me around to look at my back.

I put on the t-shirt she handed me while she went to the door and opened it to a waiting Simon.

"She's bruised all over, but nothing too serious. There's a nasty cut on her leg, but not deep enough to need stitches or anything. I think there's going to be a pretty ugly bruise on her lower back. You might want to put some ice on that." She walked out the door without another word.

Simon came to me and lifted me in his arms, setting me down so that my back was against the headboard. He propped my injured foot on a couple of pillows and wrapped a thin blue ice pack around it. He wrapped the other ice pack in a towel.

"Can you lean forward so I can look at your back?" I did as he asked, and he lifted my shirt to look at the bruise. He put the ice pack against my back and helped me ease myself against the pillows.

"I'm going to get cleaned up and change," he said when I was settled.

"I should go home soon. My parents'll be waking up and wonder where I am." It wouldn't be long until the sun started to rise, and my parents would be awake soon after that.

"Finn will go over in a bit." He looked more exhausted than I felt, and I wondered when he had last slept. "He'll persuade them that you'd already arranged to go on a weekend trip to the mountains with us and that you won't be back until later tonight. We'll reevaluate the situation later today and see what we need to tell them."

"Why would we have to reevaluate?" I asked.

"Because you look like you offended a large group of Hell's Angels, love. You have a lot of cuts, and I don't think there's one square inch on your body that won't have a bruise—at least the parts I've seen. We need to decide how we're going to explain that."

"Oh." I hadn't thought too much about how I'd explain my appearance to everyone and was grateful that Simon and Finn were working to cover my butt.

Simon walked into the bathroom and closed the door. I tried to relax against the pillows behind me to wait for him, completely worn out from lack of sleep, emotional stress and the fall from the biggest adrenaline rush of my life. I was drifting off when the sound of the door startled me. Simon had come back into the room. He was wearing fresh jeans and a t-shirt and had cleaned off the blood that had been on his face. He lay down on the bed beside me and pulled me into his arms.

"I'm sorry this happened, Maggie. I thought we had everything under control."

I didn't respond. I didn't know what to say. I knew the fight at Red Rocks was just a small taste of what was coming. I wouldn't feel safe until Balor was dead, but lying with Simon holding me to him made me feel as close to safe as I could get. He kissed my forehead, and I tilted my head up so I could kiss him back. His lips touched mine very gently, and I could feel the cut on my lip. Kissing would be difficult for a couple of days.

I lay my head back on Simon's chest and tried to let the rhythm of his breathing soothe me. There were so many worries screaming for attention inside of my head. It was overwhelming. I forced myself to focus on Simon. Only Simon. Everything else would have to wait.

I felt Simon tense beside me and heard his breathing and his heart rate quicken. I sat up and looked at him, the tears in his eyes telling me what I didn't want to know.

"What's wrong?" I asked with dread, knowing his answer before he said it.

"Max is dead, love."

Chapter Thirty-Two

I shook my head in disbelief. Max couldn't be dead. He couldn't.

"His parents would like to talk to you before they leave," Simon said gently. "Do you feel up to speaking with them?"

Max was dead. That wasn't possible. It just wasn't possible. He was dead and it was because of me. He'd been there to protect me and now he was dead.

"Maggie?" Simon prompted when I didn't answer. I nodded, letting him know I wanted to see them, knowing I owed his parents at least that much.

We stood up, and I once again ignored the pain that started throbbing in my ankle. We walked down the stairs, Simon's hand in mine.

"I'm so sorry," Simon said, looking first at Max's mom and then at his dad. "I am so very sorry."

I didn't know what to say. Everything seemed too trite and trivial. What words could bridge the gap between the two people standing in front of me and their dead son? In the end, I didn't say anything. Tears fell down my cheeks. Max's mom came to me and wrapped her arms around me in a tight embrace. *She* was comforting *me*!

"Maggie," Max's dad said when his mom had let me go, "I want you to know that Max died doing what he knew was right—what we all know is right."

My tears flowed, but Max's parents were completely dry-eyed.

"He died because of me." I started to sob, tears wetting my face and my shirt. Simon pulled me to him, hugging me close.

"Shh. Shh." Simon tried to soothe me, but I couldn't calm down. Someone I cared about was dead, and it was my fault. When I continued to sob loudly, Simon lifted me in his arms and carried me back to his room. He placed me on the bed and lay down next to me. I cuddled into him and tried to bury my grief in his shoulder. I knew Simon was grieving, too. Max had been his best friend in Denver, and the loss was just as painful for him as it was for me.

"Oh, Simon," I moaned, unable to think of a single word that might offer him comfort in that moment. I desperately wanted to take away some of his grief but couldn't figure out a way to reach across my own.

He leaned toward me and kissed me, his tears mixing with mine as our faces met. "Max was my responsibility," he said roughly, leaning his forehead against mine. "I should have been there to protect him."

"Simon, you couldn't have been beside each Guardian as they fought tonight. There were too many. It's not your fault."

He moved away from me so that he could look into my eyes. "And it's not your fault either," he said slowly and sternly. "We both need to forgive ourselves for Max's death."

My brain understood the words he was telling me, but I wondered if they would ever make their way to my heart.

He pulled me to him to rest my head on his chest, and I listened to his heartbeat and his breath as it went in and out and I felt guilty that my boyfriend was alive and safe and Lexie's boyfriend was dead.

Simon patiently rubbed my back and tried to calm me, but too much had happened. I continued to sob, and the tears drenched the spot where I lay my head on Simon's shirt. Eventually, exhaustion overtook me and I slept a very fitful sleep.

When I woke up I thought of Lexie. Had anyone thought to tell her that Max was dead?

"What's wrong?" Simon asked.

"I need to go to Lexie," I told him.

"No, Maggie, you can't," he said firmly.

"She needs to know, Simon. I need to be with her."

"Maggie, no," he repeated. "Max's family is with Sloane and Liam now. They're trying to decide what story they're going to give to explain his death. If you go to Lexie and tell her, she'll know we aren't who we say we are."

"It's Lexie. I have to be with her."

"No. This is a part of who we are—of what we have to do. We have to keep up the act, even when it's painful and difficult. We'll wait until Max's parents announce his death, then we'll go over together."

I didn't like what he was saying but I knew he was right. I took a deep breath and nodded my head. Simon lowered his head to the pillow once more, pulling me with him.

"Are you okay?" I asked him, knowing he wouldn't

volunteer the information.

He took a deep breath. "I wish I could have done something to save him."

I raised my head and looked at him. His eyes were pooled with tears, but they weren't yet falling. "It's not your fault, Simon." I rubbed the side of his cheek before kissing it gently. "It's not your fault."

Chapter Thirty-Three

Later that day, I went downstairs with Simon to find Erin. She seemed completely recovered from her injuries, and Simon wanted her to look at the cuts and abrasions that covered me from head to toe. He'd been right when he said that every square inch of my body had some sort of mark—even the parts he hadn't seen. Erin held my hands and closed her eyes, and I saw the abrasions on my arm fade slightly, but they were still very obvious.

"It's the best I can do," she told me. "Balor's brand of magic tends to penetrate deeper. It's going to take a few weeks for all of this to fade."

"Sledding accident?" Finn asked.

"Sounds as good as any," Simon replied. "Out of control sled sent her careening down a ravine?" I knew they were talking about the story I was going to give everyone to explain my injuries. It was a good story and would certainly explain the cuts, abrasions and multiple bruises that were starting to form. If a wayward sled had sent me down a ravine, I would have bounced from tree to tree before I got to the bottom, thus causing widespread, yet superficial, injury. They both looked at me expectantly, and I nodded to let them know it was a story I could live with.

I called my parents later in the day to tell them

when we'd be home from our fictitious trip to the mountains and mentioned that I'd had a little incident with a sled, hoping to ease the shock when they saw me.

Sloane and Liam had worked out the details of Max's death with his parents and decided to tell everyone he'd drowned in a boating accident while fishing with his dad. Simon pulled Sloane aside to talk with her in hushed tones, and when I walked up to them, they both stopped talking. There was a time when I didn't really mind if the faeries stopped their conversations when they saw me because I really didn't want to hear what they were saying. A very large part of me wanted Simon and the others to protect me and to take away the nightmares and the prophecies and the new life that I'd been sucked into. The other part of me, however, knew that Simon couldn't protect me anymore—not in the way he wanted to. He wanted to keep me from knowing any more than I absolutely needed to know and seeing any more than I needed to see, but if I was going to be successful in what they were asking of me, I needed to know and see as much as I possibly could. I needed Simon to start acting less as a protector and more like a partner.

"You need to stop ending your conversations when I'm nearby. You all do," I said to everyone in the room. "I need to be a part of this. I need to learn all I can and prepare myself to face him."

"We can find ways to protect you," Simon protested.

"Can you find ways to protect everyone?" I asked. "And do you think Balor will stop with wiping out humanity? I don't know much about Balor, but I think he'll want to get rid of every living creature that opposes him or gets in his way. He won't stop until the only thing left on this planet is himself and a bunch of minions that follow him around like a litter of lovesick puppies ready to do his bidding. If you can come up with another plan, then great! Let's go with that plan. But if you can't, we need to go forward with the plan we're currently developing."

"We don't have a plan!" he said in a very loud and angry tone.

"We know the general direction we need to go," Sloane corrected him.

"We've made it to step three of our plan, Simon," Liam told him harshly. "I think that's saying something."

"What were the first two steps?" I asked.

Liam turned to me to answer. "Step one was finding you. Step two was verifying that you're the one we're looking for by having you try on the ring."

"And step three?" I asked.

"Step three is figuring out how you'll kill Balor."

"Oh, well, as long as it's not complicated or anything," I said a little louder than I'd intended, sarcasm pouring out of me. "Just three simple steps. I didn't realize it was going to be so easy."

I took a moment to calm myself before continuing.

"So, we're on step three of the plan," I told Simon, trying to stay as calm as possible, knowing he was voicing the same concerns I had. "We discovered one small piece to this puzzle the night I tried on the ring. We know it's me, and right now that's the best we've got. If you can come up with something else, let me know. In the meantime, however, we need to stay on the path we've started, and that path requires that I have to be the one to defeat Balor. I don't like it any more than you do, but I don't see any other options."

He was silent, and I took that as a sign that he knew he didn't have an argument against what I was telling him. I continued with what I wanted to say to him and to everyone there. I wasn't sure how I mustered the courage to confront them, but I knew I was going to have to get in touch with my courageous side in the days ahead, and confronting a group of faeries that supported me seemed much less daunting than killing Balor. "I need for you all to respect that I'm a big part of this. You need to stop ending your conversations when I come into the room and you need to stop talking to each other in your heads and you need to speak only in languages I can understand. I want to be included in all discussions and all decisions. I have to learn as much as I can about Balor and everything he's done and about the people who work with him. I need to start being a part of this and stop being a spectator on the sidelines."

It was quiet when I'd finished speaking, and I forced myself not to get nervous about their reaction. I needed to have the confidence to stick by my decision.

"You're right, Maggie," Sloane finally said. "We haven't been fair to you, but we're going to start. What do you want to know?"

"Well, first of all, I want to know why this happened. How did they find us?"

Sloane was the first person to speak up. "There could be a traitor among the Guardians," she speculated. "It would explain how the Fomorians would know where you live."

"They could have tracked her through Facebook or any number of other ways," Liam argued.

"Yes," Sloane agreed, "but that doesn't explain how they knew that our meeting place was Red Rocks."

"They also had the car I stashed surrounded. They knew too many details about our plans," Simon told everyone. I knew it was hard for him to include me in this conversation and loved him a little more for doing it anyway.

"They could have followed you," Liam reasoned.

"Nobody was following me. We were at Red Rocks for almost an hour before the Fomorians got there," Simon explained. "If someone had been following us, they would've attacked while Maggie and I were alone."

"Maybe someone followed you, then hid while they called the others," Alana suggested. "Maybe they wanted to wait for backup."

"It's possible," Sloane said reflectively. "But it just doesn't feel right. I think we've been compromised."

Compromised? If there were a traitor among us, who would it be? Keelin certainly would have reason to want me out of the way, but would she go to such extremes? Liam and Simon were often fighting. Maybe Liam was the traitor, but that didn't feel right either. His own children had fought the Fomorians, and they could have been killed just as easily as any of the other Guardians.

"I don't like how quickly they retreated," Simon speculated. "Both sides were holding their own, so why would they retreat?"

"They saw that Maggie left," Ian pointed out. "They attacked the car as we were leaving."

"But why didn't they go after me?" I asked. "Why didn't they go back to my house or follow us here?"

Nobody had any answers.

"I'm guessing Balor's still alive," I stated. I wanted to believe that someone had been able to kill him in the fight, but I also knew that if he'd been killed, it would have been the first thing Simon told me when he'd returned from the battle.

"Yes," Simon said. "He was able to get away soon after you did."

"So he might have been following me."

"Nobody saw what direction he went," Sloane said. "We've questioned all the faeries who were there."

"But now he knows where I live," I confirmed. "Where I go to school. He could be watching me now."

"Yes," Finn confirmed quietly.

I wondered if a person's brain could actually explode from too much scary information. It felt like mine was one scary story away from splattering itself against the walls of Simon's living room. The change in my life that I'd been dreading was here. I would never be a normal teenager again. From this moment on, I was in for the fight of my life, and nothing would ever be the same.

"We have a lot to figure out," Sloane admitted. "We're going to have to step up our efforts to keep Maggie and her family safe while we figure out our next move. Simon, can you organize an increased presence?"

He nodded. Liam rolled his eyes and shook his head, but said nothing.

Chapter Thirty-Four

With Finn's help, my parents had completely accepted that I'd been on a weekend trip to the mountains with Simon's family. They were both understandably alarmed when they first saw me and took in all of my injuries, but Erin assured them that I'd been checked out from head to toe and that none of my injuries were serious. Brandon had a great time making fun of my lack of coordination, and I knew I was in for several weeks of bad sledding jokes. I was surprised to find that the consistency of Brandon's teasing was actually a comfort.

"Hey, Maggie, does your face hurt?" he asked. "Because it's killing me." *And the fun begins.*

"Does your butt hurt?" Simon asked Brandon. "Because I'm about to kick it."

"That...that doesn't even make sense," Brandon said, shaking his head.

"It means that you are in no way obligated to tease your sister *all* of the time," Simon explained.

"Yeah," Brandon said sarcastically, "I heard about a kid once that didn't tease his sister all the time, but it turned out to be an urban myth."

I smiled, enjoying the very normal banter between my boyfriend and my little brother.

After Simon, Finn and Erin left, I went to my

bathroom to take a shower and change out of the clothes Erin had lent me for the trip over. I removed all of the bandages and gauze that Simon and Keelin had swaddled me in and stood in the shower, letting the hot water run down my body and wash away all of the new blood that had caked onto my skin. I felt so much better after I'd washed my hair and body—like I was reenergized. Then I felt guilty. Soap and shampoo would never bring Max back. He was gone forever.

When I'd changed into my pajamas I walked back into my room. Simon was sitting on my bed looking out my window, but when I opened the door from the bathroom, he turned around and opened his arms to me. I worked really hard to keep myself from sobbing, knowing I would have to make up some excuse for my tears if my parents were to hear me.

"I can't believe he's gone," I said quietly.

"Me too." He put his hand under my shirt, rubbing my back, and the touch of his skin on mine helped to calm me down. Then I felt guilty again because I knew Max wouldn't be there for Lexie when she needed him most—when she found out he was gone. Simon held me close, but it didn't feel close enough. We held each other for a very long time, and while it did help to ease the pain, it didn't take it away, leading me to wonder if we would always feel the sharp sting of Max's death.

"I love you, Maggie," Simon whispered.

"I love you, too." I put my hand on the side of his face and kissed him, trying to fuse myself to him with a kiss in an attempt to block out the rest of the world—to block out the pain. I felt the sting in the cut on my lip, but the physical pain helped me to block out the emotional pain.

"I want more," I said, hoping he would too. I needed to be closer to him—a lot closer to him.

"Maggie," he moaned softly. He moved me to my back in one very swift motion, shifting his body so that he was lying on top of me. I moved my hands under his shirt to rub his back while we kissed. There was almost a frantic quality to our kisses. We were hungry for each other. We both wanted to forget about Max and the fight and everything that had happened and everything that might still happen. We wanted to lose ourselves in each other and fill the void created in our lives by Max's death.

He continued to kiss me deeply, one hand behind my neck, one hand on my back, while he pulled me to him and rolled over so that we were lying side by side, facing each other. His lips moved to my neck, kissing below my jaw and up toward my ear. I reached my hands to the bottom of his shirt and pulled up. He grabbed at it and pulled it over his head, throwing it to the floor beside my bed. He pulled roughly at the bottom of my own shirt and lifted it over my head. When he looked at me, I could see so much love and I felt a burn flow across my skin, the overwhelming emotion causing me to shiver. We came together again and started kissing, his hands exploring the newly exposed areas of my body.

Then—of course—there was a knock on the door. Simon gave me a look of complete incredulity, summoned my shirt from the floor, handed it to me and made himself invisible in one very brief moment. I pulled the shirt quickly over my head just as my mom opened my door and walked into the room. Too late, I realized that Simon's t-shirt was crumpled at the side of the bed. I prayed that my mom would think it was one of my own.

"I just wanted to check to see how you're doing," my mom said as she sat down on my bed next to me. "You looked pretty banged up from that sledding accident."

"I'm okay. Just sore." I worked to slow my breathing and pulse rate. Not seeing Simon shirtless definitely helped with that.

My mom grabbed a tissue from the box on the nightstand beside my bed. "Your lip's bleeding, sweetie." She dabbed my lip with the tissue, and when she pulled it away, I saw that there was quite a bit of blood on it.

"I've heard that cuts on the mouth tend to bleed more than cuts elsewhere. It might take this one a while to stop completely," I explained. *It might stop bleeding sooner if I stopped kissing Simon like he was a drug and I was an addict.*

"Let me know if you need anything."

"Thanks, Mom."

She handed me the tissue so I could continue to dab at my lip and kissed me on the forehead before leaving the room. Simon made himself visible next to me, a look of concern on his face when he saw the blood.

"I'm sorry for that," he said. "I can't believe I didn't notice."

I laughed softly. "I can. Your attention was elsewhere."

"Yes. It certainly was." He smiled lightly before turning serious again.

"Simon, I don't want to do—what we were about

to do—not tonight. I don't want the memory of our first time to be mixed together with everything that happened last night."

He smiled and nodded. "When we're ready," he assured me.

"Thank you." I was very happy when he didn't make a move to put his shirt back on.

"I still think that knocks on doors are going to kill me long before Balor's people get a chance," he teased.

I knew he was joking, but death had been too close that night.

"I can't help but think about losing you. What if it'd been you instead of Max? Then I feel guilty because I'm grateful it wasn't you."

"I know. I feel guilty it wasn't me, too. Max was a good guy. A truly amazing person."

I nodded. "When will Max's parents tell everyone?"

"They're starting the process now. Max's dad will call the school and tell them. He's going to call Lexie's parents before he calls the school so they can get her home before everyone else finds out. We want to spare her from the craziness."

"So, I'll have to act normal tomorrow morning when I see her," I confirmed.

"Yes, but you'll have an excuse to not feel quite yourself. You really do look like hell warmed over."

"Thanks," I said sardonically.

"You're still beautiful. And I still love you—always have and always will." He took the tissue from my hand and started to dab at the cut on my lip. When the bleeding stopped, he got a washcloth from my bathroom and gently wiped away the dried blood before returning to lie next to me on the bed. I rested my head on his bare chest, and he once again started rubbing my back.

❧❧

Everything happened exactly as Simon said it would the following day. He left my house while I got ready for school, then came back to pick me up at the usual time. Lexie was at my locker when I got there. Her jaw dropped when she saw me, and she asked what had happened. I gave her the story about the sledding accident, and before she could question me too much about it, the first bell rang and we had to go our separate ways.

I got through my first two classes in a daze. I couldn't focus on anything the teachers were saying or what my fellow students were doing. My attention was completely taken up with my efforts to keep from crying. I had to wait for the official announcement before I could break down at school.

When Simon came into our third period history class, he leaned over and kissed me on the top of my head. Before he stood up, he moved his lips to my ear and whispered, "Mr. Warner just told me that Lexie was pulled out of class ten minutes ago. They're going to pull you and me as soon as Lexie and her parents leave."

I was relieved and anxious at the same time. I was a really horrible actress, and the tension was difficult to experience for longer than a few minutes. I was anxious because it meant I'd have to start the process of comforting Lexie. Her grief was going to remind me of everything that had happened and my role in Max's death.

"Simon. Maggie."

I jumped when Mr. Warner announced our names in class a few minutes later. I hadn't noticed when a student walked in with the note that Mr. Warner now held in his hands. "You're wanted in the office." His announcement was met with catcalls and crude remarks from the rest of the students in class.

Simon and I gathered our things and walked toward the main office. He took my hand in his and squeezed gently. "I'm right here. You're not alone."

One of the guidance counselors, Mr. Johnson, was waiting for us in the main office when we walked in. He led us to his own office and shut the door before he sat down at his desk and motioned for us to sit down in the chairs opposite.

"I'm afraid I have some really bad news." He looked appropriately bereaved as he began. "The worst possible sort of news, really. Max Levy's parents called the school this morning. They said there was an accident this weekend. A boating accident. Max fell overboard and he wasn't wearing a life jacket." He paused to let this all sink in before delivering the final blow. "I'm very sorry. Max died. He didn't make it out of the water."

I let the tears I'd been fighting all morning flow freely.

"We thought it best to tell the two of you before we tell the rest of the school. I know you were both friends of his. Lexie has already left the school, and your dad's on his way to pick you up, Maggie. Your brother and sister-in-law are coming to get you, Simon. We thought it best if you not drive under the circumstances."

Simon nodded in agreement. He looked genuinely stunned, and I knew he wasn't acting. He was simply letting the emotions he'd been bottling up express themselves.

"Classes will be cancelled tomorrow, and grief counselors will be available all day. I strongly encourage both of you to meet with one of them. Losing a good friend is one of the worst things to experience." Simon and I both nodded.

There was a knock on Mr. Johnson's door, and my dad walked into the room.

"Mags," he said dolefully, opening up his arms to me. I went to him and let him wrap me in his arms— the arms that had made me feel safe for so long. My dad. My protector. My first knight in shining armor. I wanted him to save me from all of this. To make everything okay. To put everything back to the way it was.

Finn and Erin walked in soon after my dad, and the five of us walked to the parking lot, Erin taking Simon's keys so she could drive his car home.

"Mr. O'Neill, can I have a moment with Maggie before you leave?" Simon asked.

"Yes, of course."

Simon pulled me aside and hugged me, whispering quietly in my ear, "Are you going to Lexie's?"

I nodded.

"I'll meet you there. I won't make myself visible, though."

I nodded again.

"I'll stay with you until you tell me to go away."

"I'll never tell you to go away."

He hugged me tight, and when he let go, I felt like I was freefalling without a net or a safety harness.

"Are you okay?" my dad asked when I was in the car.

"No," I told him honestly. "I want to go to Lexie's, Dad. I need to be with her."

"I know. I already called her mom and talked to her."

I was overwhelmed with gratitude. He definitely made my life easier, even now, when it was so impossibly difficult. "I love you, Dad," I said.

He smiled and took my hand in his. "I love you too, kiddo."

Lexie's mom opened the door when I rang the bell, and I made a point of turning slowly to wave to my dad before going inside. I knew Simon would be going in and I wanted him to have plenty of time to get through the open door.

I went straight to Lexie's room and found her lying on her side on her bed, facing the window. I stretched out next to her and put my arm around her, finding one of her hands and holding it in my own. We held each other most of the day, just as Simon and I had earlier that morning. Sometimes she would cry. Sometimes I would cry. Sometimes we would both cry. I felt Simon sitting beside me, his hand rubbing my back and shoulders the whole time. Simon had told me once that staying invisible took a tremendous amount of concentration, and I knew he'd be exhausted with the effort of staying invisible for so long.

Eventually, Lexie and I both fell asleep, completely depleted from carrying the prohibitively heavy weight of Max's death.

8003

"He was a strong swimmer," Lexie's voice jolted me from my sleep. I wasn't sure if she was talking to me, or if someone else had walked into the room. I felt Simon's hand on my back, but nobody else was with us. I wondered if maybe she was talking in her sleep.

"Lex?" I said quietly, testing to see if she was awake.

"I've seen him swim, Maggie," Lexie said softly, obviously awake. She was staring out the window, not moving to look at me. "He's on the swim team at school. He's *really* good."

"But it was a lake, Lex. It's harder to swim in a lake, and I imagine the water was really cold." I hated lying to my friend.

"And he didn't tell me he was going fishing yesterday. He never goes fishing. Why would he go fishing in the middle of March? He called to cancel our date on Saturday, and he said he wanted to go to the library with me yesterday. But he didn't even call to cancel. If he was going to go fishing instead of going to the library, he would have called."

I was starting to wonder if Finn was going to have to use his special ability on Lexie. She was smart, and it would be harder to convince her that Max's death happened the way everyone was saying it had.

"It doesn't make sense, Maggie." Her tone was flat and emotionless. "Something's not right. And didn't tell me you were going to the mountains. You tell me stuff like that. Something's not right."

Chapter Thirty-Five

Max's funeral was, without question, the hardest thing I've ever had to sit through, and I wondered how many more funerals I'd have to attend before all of this was over.

The people closest to Max didn't cry at his funeral. We were cried out. We sat in the first row, stoic, resigned and dry-eyed. I knew Max's little brother and sister were technically older than I was, but they looked so young, and the fact that they were able to be so brave caused the waves of sorrow to swell inside of me. They'd lost their big brother, and I couldn't even begin to fathom the grief they must be experiencing.

The synagogue was overflowing with people, mostly students and staff from school. Max was one of those rare people who couldn't make an enemy if he tried, and everyone from school was feeling the loss to some degree. It made me angry when I saw how many people were affected by Max's death. We lost a great guy that night at Red Rocks, and an evil man had walked away. It should have been the other way around. I wished so much that it could have been the other way around.

After Max's funeral, Lexie told me she wanted to be

alone, so I went home with my parents. Simon had offered to take me home, but it had been an arduous few days, and I decided we could all use some time alone.

I went to my room with the intention of spending some time by myself. I knew a few invisible faeries would follow me, but I'd been doing a better job of forgetting they were always there. I changed out of the clothes I'd worn to the funeral and into a pair of jeans and a T-shirt before sitting on my bed, unsure of what to do with myself. I had homework to do, but I didn't think I had the mental focus it would require. I thought about calling Lexie, but decided against it, wanting to give her the space she needed to grieve Max in a way that was comfortable for her.

Being alone gave me too much time to think about ugly and depressing things, but being with people felt even worse. I decided to go for a bike ride. It seemed like a nice compromise. I'd be out in the open with lots of people, but I wouldn't have to actually talk with any of them. I also thought that keeping my body moving might help release some of my pent up anxiety, so I grabbed a fleece jacket and headed outside.

I got my old bike out of the garage and rode to the park, not concerned whether the Guardians following me were able to keep up. My injuries from the battle at Red Rocks screamed out with the unfamiliar movement, and I had to ride at a slow pace to keep my body from actively resisting each time I pressed down on one of the pedals. When I got to the park, I sat on a bench, letting my bike slide to the ground beside me, and watched everyone having fun, enjoying a carefree spring day. There were small children with their parents, older children playing alone and teens playing basketball and hanging out on park benches, talking. I envied them their innocence. I wanted so desperately to go back to a time when the worst I had to worry about was a stranger wanting to lure me away from my friends with candy. I wanted my innocence back. I wanted Max back. I didn't want to fight Balor. I didn't even want to know that Balor, or faeries, existed. I wanted to go back to a time when I didn't believe in faery tales or monsters. Max's death, and the ripples of pain it sent out to the people I loved, made me question more than ever whether I was strong enough, or willing enough, to face my implausible fate.

I felt tears starting to well up in my eyes. I was grieving and I wanted to cry and rant and yell and throw myself on the ground and kick and scream like a child, but it wouldn't do any good and I knew that. I would still have to fight Balor. I would still have to grieve the loss of the people I loved that would give up their lives to help with that fight.

"Hi." I looked over to see Simon sitting next to me on the park bench. I wasn't surprised that he'd been able to find me. Hiding from Simon was impossible.

I glanced at him briefly but said nothing. I was too busy wallowing in my own self-pity. He seemed to sense that and said nothing more. He just sat next to me, the two of us quietly watching all the happy people around us.

The quiet that lay between us didn't accurately reflect the screaming that was going on in my head. I wanted to tell Simon how horrible I felt. I wanted to tell him I hated the life I'd been given and that little pieces of who I was died every single day and that I knew those pieces of me could never come back. But he knew. He'd always known.

And he understood my guilt over Max's death. He'd explained his own guilt in a way that I related to completely. In my head, I knew Max's death was Balor's fault, but in my heart, I still blamed myself. So many times in the past few days I'd been grateful that Lexie didn't know the truth about Max's death because I was certain she too would blame me if she knew the truth. But there were also times when I wished she did know. I wished she would rage against me for taking something so wonderful away from her. I wanted someone to hate me as much as I hated myself.

I couldn't talk with Simon about that part. He wouldn't understand.

I'm responsible for my best friend's misery! I wanted to yell at him, but I kept silent. He'd just argue with me, and I wasn't in the mood to hear how blameless I was in Max's death.

Simon's head snapped up to look at me sharply. He sat completely still, a look of profound shock on his face.

"Simon?" I prompted. I was starting to worry that maybe he'd had a brain aneurism or something.

"Did you just direct a thought at me?" he finally asked.

"I don't understand," I said.

"Did you just think something in your head that was directed to me? Did you just yell at me in your mind?"

"I guess I did," I admitted.

"Did you yell that you're responsible for your best

friend's misery?"

It was my turn to look shocked. "You...you heard that?"

"Yes," he said, still looking stunned.

"You heard what I thought? What does that mean?"

He hesitated. "I think it means that you're not only getting in touch with your Irish side, you're also getting in touch with your faery side."

"What? No. That's not possible. I'm not a faery. I can't be a faery. I don't want to be a faery."

"I don't think you have a choice, *cushla macree*."

"No, Simon. Please, no."

"Maggie, it's okay," he said moving toward me and taking my hand in his. "It's actually really good news. It means you have a faery power, and if you have that one faery power, then it's possible you could develop other faery powers. It'll help tremendously in the fight against Balor."

"Maybe *you're* just developing a new faery power and you can read the minds of humans now," I reasoned. Being a faery didn't seem like a good thing to me. It seemed like one more thing to worry about on top of a very long list of things to worry about.

"Let's go try it on Finn and Erin," he suggested, unable to contain his enthusiasm.

I didn't want to leave the park and face another hurdle in my life. I was fighting to hold onto any piece of normality that I could manage and being able to communicate telepathically was definitely *not* normal.

Simon encouraged me to try saying something to him again. "It has to be directed at me, and if you think something that has a strong emotional connection, it'll come through clearer."

NO! I shouted in my head at him, wanting this new development to go away.

"Well, that was pretty obvious, love. I would've known that was your thought even if I hadn't heard it."

I rolled my eyes and looked away from him, angry that he was so excited about something that was making me so unhappy.

He sighed and put one arm around me, resting his hand on my shoulder. "I'm sorry. This is obviously upsetting you. No more mind reading." He pulled me closer, and I started to relax.

"I've been wanting to ask you about something," I said after a few minutes of calm silence.

"What's that?"

"I was wondering what happened at Red Rocks— with you and Balor. He pointed his finger at me, and I was in so much pain that I thought I would die, then you pointed your finger at him and he fell to the ground. What did you guys do?"

He waited a full minute before answering. "Magic."

I twisted around so I could look at his face. "What sort of magic?"

"Faery magic."

"All faeries can do that? Point their fingers and cause excruciating pain?"

"No. Not all faeries." He hesitated again. "What we did is a very advanced level of magic that only a few faeries can do."

"But you can."

"Yes."

"And Balor can."

"Yes."

"Seriously. Tell me why *I'm* the one who has to defeat this guy. You're obviously more qualified for the job than I am."

He stroked my jaw, a melancholy expression falling over him. "I know, love. I know."

"You don't do stuff like that in front of me," I said. "You don't even make yourself invisible or use any of your other powers unless you absolutely have to."

"I know it makes you uncomfortable to know what I am, so I try not to remind you."

"Do you use it when I'm not around?"

"Sometimes. If it's useful."

"You should be able to be yourself," I said. "Maybe we could ease into it. You could start small, then build up to doing more of it."

He smiled. "I think that's a good plan."

When we left the park, we decided to go to Simon's house for a while. He put my bike in the back of his SUV, and I called my parents on the way to let them know where I was going. Finn and Erin were sitting on the back patio when we got there. Sloane, Liam, Keelin and Ian were with them, and they were all enjoying the nice weather and having a beer. I was surprised to see Keelin and Ian each with a beer in their hands, but then I remembered they were both over two hundred years old—definitely over the legal drinking age in Colorado.

We sat down to join them, and everyone became silent for a few minutes. The meaningful looks passing between all of them told me they were having a telepathic conversation, and it wasn't hard to jump to the next conclusion. They were having a silent conversation about me.

"At the risk of sounding totally paranoid, I know you're talking about me and I can guess what you're talking about. Just say it out loud."

"I didn't want to upset you," Simon said sheepishly, his face turning red.

"So Simon heard something I said in my head. Big deal. It doesn't mean anything." I *hoped* it didn't mean anything.

"Maggie, this would actually be good news," Sloane said.

"No," I mumbled, "it wouldn't."

Everyone was silent again, and the silence was starting to get awkward. I rolled my eyes dramatically and said, "Fine. Fine. Who do you want me to test it on?"

Everyone laughed uncomfortably.

"How about me?" Sloane suggested. "I'm as good as any."

I remembered what Simon had said in the park and tried to decide what I felt most emotional about and easily came up with one very intrusive thought. *I don't want to be a faery!*

The shocked look that I'd seen on Simon's face earlier was now spreading across Sloane's face. "I'm not sure you have a choice," she said bluntly.

"What did you say?" Simon asked.

"I said I don't want to be a faery," I told him, the tears welling up in my eyes. Could I not go more than an hour without crying any more? Was that a part of my new life too?

Simon pulled me to him, wrapping his arms around my shoulders. "Oh, *cushla macree.* Being a faery isn't such a bad thing. It actually has quite a few advantages."

"So now you guys can read my mind?" I asked, pulling away from Simon. I was still angry that this was making him so happy.

"No," Simon said. "We can only hear thoughts that you intentionally direct toward us. None of us could hear what you were directing toward Sloane because you intended it only for her."

"Have you tried hearing a thought directed at *you?*" Erin asked me.

I shook my head.

"Try picking up what I'm telling you," Simon suggested. He was silent for a moment before asking, "Did you hear that?"

"No. I didn't hear anything. What did you say?"

He blushed. "I said that I love you. It's the strongest emotion I have."

I caught a glance of Keelin as she rolled her eyes, looking thoroughly disgusted. "You two should really hand out barf bags before you say stuff like that out loud."

Simon gave her a look of warning, and everyone else ignored her.

"Do you think she's developing faery powers then?" Liam asked Sloane.

"It's possible, I suppose," Sloane answered. "Being a faery is genetic. Maggie could have inherited that gene as easily as she inherited any other, or it could be the ring. It might be giving her some special abilities to help her with everything ahead of her."

"She obviously has faery ancestors," Finn said.

"But even if she does have faery ancestors, that doesn't guarantee she'd inherit that trait," Erin reasoned. "The faery gene is just like any other gene. You might get it. You might not."

The seven faeries on the deck became very involved in the debate about the source of my newly discovered faery power, and I took advantage of their distraction to slip away from the group and go into the house. I went to Simon's room, knowing it was out of the way enough that I'd be alone for a while. I sat on his bed and pulled my knees to my chest, wrapping my arms around them. I wanted to be small and insignificant and inconspicuous.

"Are you hiding?" Simon asked, opening the door to his room.

I shook my head.

"Are you mad at me for telling them?"

I shook my head again.

"Are you mad at me for something else?"

"I'm mad that you're so happy about something that makes *me* so *unhappy*."

He nodded and sat next to me, taking a deep breath as he did. "I'm sorry. You're right. I should have been more sensitive to your feelings about this."

"Well, don't start being nice about it," I teased. "That'll just make me even more angry."

He smiled and took my hand in his.

"Explain faery genetics. How does it work?"

He shrugged. "It's just like brown hair or green eyes or freckles—it's something you can inherit from a parent, but the faery gene isn't a dominate gene, and if a non-faery and a faery conceive a child, that child may or may not inherit the faery gene."

"But at least one of my parents would have to be a faery for me to be one," I reasoned.

"It's like your red hair," he explained. "Neither of your parents have red hair, but one of them must have had the gene and passed it on to you."

I really wished I'd paid better attention in biology class. I was having a tough time wrapping my mind around all of that.

"Well, even if I did get the gene, I would have known it before now. I'd be able to do the things that you can do."

"Not necessarily," he continued, his logical tone inexplicably annoying me. "People tend to rearrange themselves and the world around them to fit into a sometimes rigid world view. If you didn't believe that faeries were real, you would behave as if they weren't."

I crossed my arms against my chest, blocking my soul from what Simon was telling me.

"Why are you so opposed to being a faery?" he asked softly.

I had to think about my answer because I wasn't even sure myself why it bugged me so much. I wanted to go back to my normal life, and that was certainly part of it, but there was also something more that I couldn't quite put my finger on.

Finally, I told him the best explanation I could come up with. "Right now, I have a lot of faeries protecting me because I don't have faery powers and I can't do the things faeries can do. I'm more helpless and I need more protection and I guess I've gotten used to knowing that there are always invisible faeries around me, making sure nothing bad happens to me. If I start developing faery powers, they won't need to protect me any more and I don't want them to stop protecting me. I'm already afraid every second of every day. I'd be even more afraid if my faery guard stopped following me everywhere."

"Maggie," he said, "we'll never stop protecting you. Even if you become the most powerful faery in the world, we'll always be there, protecting you. You're putting your life at risk for this cause, and there's not a single Guardian out there who's going to let you fight this fight alone. Nothing's going to change. There will always be faeries with you, guarding you."

"I'm just so afraid all the time, Simon. How can I be brave if I'm always afraid?"

"Maggie, love, courage is not the absence of fear." He ran his hand along my jaw tenderly. "Courage is choosing to put aside your fear in order to do what's right. You've already done that. You move closer to your destiny every day, even though you're afraid."

"I'm not moving closer," I scoffed. "I'm no better equipped to take on Balor today than I was when you first told me about the prophecy."

"Do you not see the changes that have happened inside of you in just a few short weeks?"

I looked at him with confusion, completely baffled about any changes he might be talking about.

"You stood up to a room full of faeries the day after the fight," he said. "You demanded that we include you and keep you informed. Do you think you would have done that last fall?"

I looked at him and thought about what he was saying.

"And you attacked Balor at Red Rocks," he continued.

"I didn't even think about it," I admitted. "If I'd stopped to think about it, I probably wouldn't have done it."

"That tells me courage is at the core of who you are. When you stop to think, you lose that courage, but when you stop thinking and give in to who you are, the courage is there. You've developed the ability to communicate telepathically, but you've also found the courage that was hiding deep inside of you. Of all the tools you'll need to get you through the days to come, that one is the most important."

He was right. I *had* changed. I could stand up to people now and tell them what I thought and argue with them when I thought I was right. The old me, the me Simon had known when we first met, wouldn't have done that, but would courage alone be enough to get me through?

He took my hand in his. "So, it's not because you think faeries are monsters. That's not why you're upset about this new faery power?"

I shook my head. "I know I was really afraid of what you are when you first told me, but I don't think you're a monster. I think you're wonderful, and if you don't know that by now, I must be doing something wrong."

"Hmmm," he said reflectively, humor in his eyes. "Maybe you should show me how wonderful you really think I am."

His kisses started out as little whispers against my cheeks and lips. I thought about the cut on my lip, then realized I didn't really care if it started to bleed again. With one hand behind my neck, he leaned me against the pillows at the end of his bed. I put my hands around his neck and pulled him down to me, reaching up to meet him, pressing my lips roughly to his, letting every bit of the passion I had for him flow through me and into him, showing him, I hoped, just how wonderful I really thought he was. He responded quickly, running his hand along my hip and thigh, kissing me in a way that was so passionate I lost myself. When he moved his hand to rub my bare arm, I shivered visibly, goose bumps rising on every inch of my body, making me feel so alive and so connected to Simon. I moaned softly, which made Simon breathe faster.

He shifted his weight until he was lying on top of me, our hips meeting. The heaviness of Simon on top of me felt solid and real. His curves and crevices melted into my curves and crevices and pushed away the sadness and fear and hate. Yes, hate was there, and sometimes it felt like the hate in me was going to scare away all of the other emotions. It felt like it would always be with me, but with Simon on top of me, it went away for a moment. Just a moment.

I was starting to wonder if one of us should get up and lock the door before our clothes started to fly, when—predictably—there was a knock on the door.

"Oh, for the love of Pete!" he muttered, rolling off me.

"Can I come in, Simon?" Erin asked from the other side.

"Of course. Why not?" Simon said ruefully.

Erin opened the door and walked in. "I just wanted to let you know that we're ordering pizza. Any requests?"

"Hawaiian," Simon said. It was what we always ordered at my house.

"Got it. Should be here in about an hour, I

imagine."

"Thanks, Erin," Simon said.

"Knocks on doors," he muttered when she'd gone. "There is *always* a knock on a door." I laughed with him, appreciating the ridiculousness of our constant interruptions. "It's a conspiracy. I know it must be." He shook his head. "Every person we know is in on it."

"We could always lock the door and ignore them," I suggested.

He shook his head again. "Keelin and Liam can both open locked doors. Extra faery power."

"Then I suppose we'll have to accept that we'll be virgins forever," I teased.

He pushed me down on the bed and rolled back on top of me, kissing me gently, the passion having receded in both of us. "Not forever, but maybe for now."

I pulled him closer to me, wishing we could stay entwined on his bed together forever.

₧₨

After we had pizza with the rest of the faeries at the house, Simon helped Erin and Finn clean the kitchen while I walked up to get my jacket from Simon's room. As I started to head back down the stairs, I heard voices coming from an open door in the hallway and realized it was Sloane and Liam, arguing quietly. I moved closer to try and hear what they were saying.

"I don't trust him, Sloane," Liam said.

"We have no reason *not* to trust him," Sloane argued.

"You continue to turn a blind eye to who he is. He's capable of doing as much damage as Balor— maybe more. How do we know that we can trust him? How do we know he isn't working with Balor? It would make sense. And if he *is* working with Balor, we're giving him complete access to Maggie."

"Liam!" Sloane snapped. "You need to stop this. Simon is *nothing* like Balor."

It really bothered me that Liam didn't trust Simon, and I wondered what had caused him to believe that Simon was capable of doing anything to hurt me.

"Eavesdropping?" I jumped, not noticing that Ian had walked up behind me.

"Yes," I admitted, blushing.

"Your secret's safe with me," he promised.

"Thank you," I said, feeling like a naughty kid caught with a hand in the cookie jar.

"Ian, why doesn't your dad trust Simon?" I asked as we started to walk downstairs.

Ian looked uncomfortable. "I think that's a question best asked of Simon."

I didn't like his answer, but understood why he wouldn't want to be the one to tell me something private about Simon. I respected him for it. "Do *you* trust Simon?"

"Yes," he said emphatically.

SOCR

Simon drove me home later in the evening and promised to return after everyone was in bed. I was glad he was going to spend the night with me again, but I was also feeling a lot better about my situation. I was still struggling with what I'd have to do, but I'd talked with Sloane about getting some training that might help me, and that made me feel a lot braver about the situation than I had before.

When I walked in the house, my mom told me someone had sent me flowers and that they were in my room. I thought that was odd. Simon never sent me flowers—he just handed them to me—and I couldn't think of anyone else who would give me flowers.

I went to my room and closed the door. On my desk was a large vase filled with lavender, the fragrance filling the room. Stuck amidst the flowers was a card with "Margaret O'Neill" printed on the front. I opened it and found a small piece of paper folded over three times. I unfolded it and read the message:

Dearest Margaret,

And so it begins. I had rather hoped my challenger would be someone more formidable than a seventeen-year-old human girl, but I still look forward to killing you and everyone you love. I know your grandfather told you that your Grandma Margaret died in her sleep, and while that is true, she did not die without assistance. I killed her, and I will kill you. Simon can't protect you. The Guardians can't protect you. This can be as easy or as difficult as you'd like it to be. The harder you fight me, the more difficult it will be for you and for every human and faery you love. The pain you felt at Red Rocks is only a small taste of the damage I'm capable of inflicting. I assure you, you do not want to fight me. You will *lose.* Coimhead fearg fhear na foighde.

   -B.

So much information, so little space in my brain.

He'd killed my great-grandmother? He'd read my email? He'd read my email! What other invasions of privacy had he committed? I crumpled the note and threw it on my desk. The anger in me had reached its boiling point. Balor had threatened me and threatened the people I loved. He'd kill my grandmother and Max, and I knew I couldn't stand by and let him kill anyone else. I saw my place in this world differently. I was no longer a victim of a prophecy that was made hundreds of years ago. I was the master of my own destiny and I *wanted* to bring Balor down. I wanted him to pay for killing Max and my grandmother. I wanted him to pay for putting the lives of everyone I loved in danger. I wanted him to pay for being so mean and sadistic. I knew I would probably die in the process. I knew the chances of me being able to kill him were miniscule, but I had to try. The fight was on. There was no way I was backing down.

"Bring it on, old man," I said fiercely to myself. "Bring it on."

The folktale "Simon and Margaret" is adapted from a story in the book "West Irish Folk-Tales and Romances" by William Larminie, first published in 1893 by Elliot Stock, London.

Acknowledgements

There are so many people I want to thank, but in the interest of letting a few trees live to see another day, I'll limit the list to the ones who had the biggest impact on the completion of this book.

First, my mom, Bonnie Grable—without her constant support and encouragement, you'd be reading another book right now, and you probably wouldn't have liked it nearly as much as this one. If you enjoyed this book, you might want to consider sending her a thank you note.

I also want to thank my editor, Robbi Makely. I could have saved myself a lot of time and head pounding if I'd realized sooner that the world's best editor had been in my address book all along. (She owes me a margarita for every error, so please let me know if you find any.)

I had an amazing group of beta testers who read the book several times and offered so many invaluable suggestions: Maggie Brooke Grable (my absolute favorite non-fictional Maggie), Breya Grable, Abbey Daugherty, Morgan Farmer, Elly Makely, Amber Derrera and Jaycien Derrera. You guys are so awesome! And to Bradon Grable—just because.

To the real life Jake the Dog: you provided such wonderful inspiration for one of my favorite characters.

And last, but not least, you, the reader. Thank you for taking this adventure with an unknown writer!